STA

Please return / renew by date shown.
You can renew it at:
norlink.norfolk.gov.uk
or by telephone: 0344 800 8006
Please have your library card & PIN ready

withdrawn from stock

NORFOLK LIBRARY
AND INFORMATION SERVICE

301

D1334125

OUT OF THE SHADOWS

Mary Jane Staples

CORGI BOOKS

OUT OF THE SHADOWS
A CORGI BOOK : 0 552 15266 8

First publication in Great Britain

PRINTING HISTORY
Corgi edition published 2005

3 5 7 9 10 8 6 4 2

Set in 11/13pt New Baskerville by
Kestrel Data, Exeter, Devon.

Corgi Books are published by Transworld Publishers,
61–63 Uxbridge Road, London W5 5SA,
a division of The Random House Group Ltd,
in Australia by Random House Australia (Pty) Ltd,
20 Alfred Street, Milsons Point, Sydney, NSW 2061, Australia,
in New Zealand by Random House New Zealand Ltd,
18 Poland Road, Glenfield, Auckland 10, New Zealand
and in South Africa by Random House (Pty) Ltd, Isle of Houghton,
Corner Boundary Road & Carse O'Gowrie, Houghton, 2198, South Africa.

The Random House Group Limited supports The Forest Stewardship
Council® (FSC®), the leading international forest-certification organisation.
Our books carrying the FSC label are printed on FSC®-certified paper.
FSC is the only forest-certification scheme supported by the leading
environmental organisations, including Greenpeace. Our
paper procurement policy can be found at
www.randomhouse.co.uk/environment

MIX
Paper from
responsible sources
FSC® C016897

Printed and bound in Great Britain by Clays Ltd, St Ives PLC

To Katherine, a bright sprite
who will, I hope, be a writer
herself one day.

THE ADAMS FAMILY

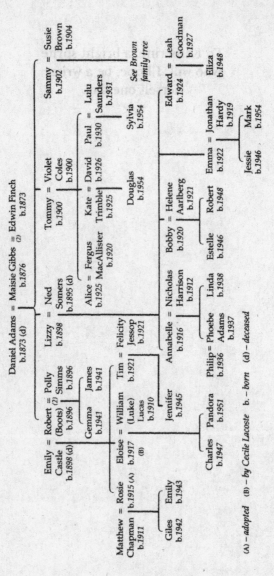

Daniel Adams = Maisie Gibbs = Edwin Finch
b.1873 (d)   b.1876   (2) b.1873

Emily = Robert = Polly   Lizzy = Ned   Tommy = Violet   Sammy = Susie
Castle (Boots) Simms   b.1898 Somers   b.1900 Coles   b.1902 Brown
b.1898 (d) b.1896 (2) b.1896   b.1895 (d)   b.1900   b.1904

                                                                    See Brown
                                                                    family tree

Gemma James   Alice = Fergus   Kate = David   Paul = Lulu
b.1941 b.1941   b.1925 MacAllister Trimble b.1926 b.1930 Saunders
                            b.1920   b.1925   b.1931

Eloise = William   Tim = Felicity   Douglas   Sylvia   Edward = Leah
b.1917 (Luke)   b.1921 Jessop   b.1954   b.1954   b.1924 Goodman
(B)   Lucas   b.1921   b.1927
        b.1910

Matthew = Rosie   Annabelle = Nicholas   Bobby = Helene   Emma = Jonathan   Eliza
Chapman b.1915 (A)   b.1916   Harrison   b.1920 Aarlberg   b.1922 Hardy   b.1948
b.1911   b.1912   b.1921   b.1919

          Jennifer   Philip = Phoebe   Linda   Estelle Robert   Jessie Mark
          b.1945   b.1936 Adams   b.1938   b.1946   b.1948   b.1946 b.1954
                                            b.1937

Giles Emily   Charles Pandora
b.1942 b.1943   b.1947   b.1951

(A) – adopted   (B) – by Cecile Lacoste   b. – born   (d) – deceased

THE BROWN FAMILY

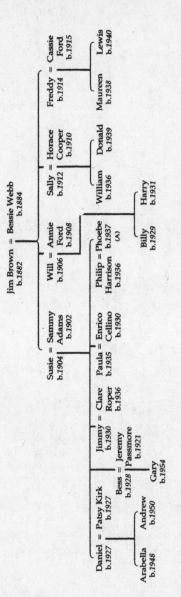

Chapter One

A man who had been known to his SS comrades as 'The Wolf' was released from a prison in Bavaria in May 1958. In 1948 he had been tried and convicted as a war criminal for his part in the inhuman elimination of untold numbers of Jewish men, women and children in the Auschwitz concentration camp of infamous memory. For the appalling nature of his crimes, he had been sentenced to a prison term of twenty years. His release came after he had served ten.

As a sergeant in the wartime SS, Ernst Thurber earned his nickname by reason of his mouthful of large white teeth that seemed to gleam with animal-like pleasure whenever he was torturing or brutalizing an inmate. However, in April 1944, following a bout of severe influenza, he began to have nightmares, as if the horrors of his own deeds were catching up with him. Before he could disgrace himself, and the SS itself, by having a breakdown merely on account of eliminating Jews, his commanding officer sent him on home leave.

His arrival coincided with that of his younger brother, Hans, a German army corporal on leave from the fighting in Italy. Although they were very different in character, they had a mutual empathy that made each the other's greatest friend, the more so after their parents were killed in an early bombing raid on Berlin. It was to Hans that 'The Wolf', temporarily ravaged by nightmares, disclosed what he had officially sworn not to, all the grisly details of the events taking place in Auschwitz. His brother, a disciplined soldier rather than a fanatical Nazi, was appalled, so much so that the night-mares were transferred from the guilty to the innocent.

The guilty, refreshed, returned to Auschwitz to carry on as before. The innocent, suffering, returned to his unit in Italy, was captured by the British following the German defeat at Cassino and, still traumatized by what he now knew about Auschwitz, unburdened himself to a British staff officer, one Colonel Robert Adams. He was taken to London for interrogation. There, he hanged himself.

The release of ex-SS Sergeant Ernst Thurber from prison in 1958 did not attract any great attention, although it was noted among other reports in the Polish press by a minor official who worked for a government department in Warsaw.

But the Polish press was noted for reporting on German war criminals who had acquired their murderous reputations in occupied Poland. That being of no consequence to 'The Wolf', still a Nazi at heart and contemptuous of Poles, he used his freedom to set about tracing the only person he cared about, his brother Hans, from whom he had not heard since their reunion on that fateful day in 1944.

His first request for help was made to the regular Army Records Office. He was advised after some while that because the wartime records of many regiments were still in a state of flux, no details of his brother were presently available. He thought this a piece of bureaucratic unhelpfulness, so he contacted an ex-SS war veterans' association, an underground organization. In a Germany committed to rebuilding itself after the war under a democratic government, ex-SS officers and men could still wield some power and influence, provided they remained invisible. More time elapsed, and then 'The Wolf' was told to get in touch with one of the senior officials at the Army Records Office. He was given the name of this official. He made contact and asked again if anything was known of his brother, whose unit had been the 114th Bavarian Regiment.

The answer took time to reach him, but it did come, and to the effect that Corporal Hans Thurber of the 114th Bavarian Regiment had been taken prisoner by the British in May 1944. The details of the capture were given.

When was it, he asked, that his brother was released from the prisoner-of-war camp and returned to Germany?

The answer was that Corporal Hans Thurber had never returned, since he died as a prisoner of war in England.

Died?

Yes, according to details supplied by the Red Cross, he had committed suicide.

That seriously disturbed the Wolf, and since no other information was forthcoming, he made further contact with old comrades of the SS. They ferreted around on his behalf, and eventually provided him with an answer. His brother had hanged himself while under British interrogation in London. Ex-SS Sergeant Ernst Thurber no more believed that than any other kind of fairy story. He smelled a cover-up by the British. He knew about methods of interrogation. He had used them himself on more than one concentration-camp inmate, bringing death to the victims.

Quite sure that British methods were no different, he was easily able to believe his beloved brother's death had come about through torture, not suicide. The belief incensed him, although he did not examine his conscience about his own record as an interrogator. The temporary nightmares he had once suffered were long gone, and, like many of his kind, he still believed that his actions had been undertaken for the good of Hitler and Germany. He decided, after being given further details by old comrades of the SS, that he had a score to settle on behalf of Hans.

In August, a woman said goodbye and thank you to her surgeon and emerged from a London clinic into the brightness of a sunny day. She made her exit a little tentatively, her eyes blinking in the light. As escorts, her husband was on her left, her daughter on her right. There was also a nurse in attendance, and a waiting car at the kerbside.

'Now how do we feel?' asked the nurse with a smile.

'Personally,' said Mrs Felicity Adams, treading more firmly, 'I feel reborn. How about everyone else?'

'Everyone else, Puss, feels great, and all on your account,' said her husband, Tim Adams.

'Super-duper,' said her daughter, thirteen-year-old Jennifer, thrilled to bits. After what the surgeon called a quite simple operation, her mother's eyesight, lost when she was caught in a bomb blast during the blitz on London, was now fully restored.

Optimism about the outcome had been high. It was a fact that during the last two years and more, there had been signs of a natural healing process taking place. Felicity had experienced many moments of blurred vision and, at times, even flashes of clear sight. Clarity had become more frequent and for longer periods, and finally her consultant, Sir Charles Morgan, said it was time to complete the process. Now, on this August day, with the operation well behind her, she was alive with the bliss of knowing unblighted vision was hers again. No more darkness, no more clouds, no more hazy pictures, just the natural clarity that one took for granted until an accident or a devil's happening brought down the shutters.

The nurse said a smiling goodbye to her. Felicity thanked her with all the effusion of a grateful patient.

'Mrs Adams, we're all delighted for you. Good luck now.'

Sunshine enhanced the apricot hue of Felicity's pencil-skirted Tricel dress, and flooded her face with light as Tim and Jennifer brought her to the waiting car. The driver was standing beside it, smiling.

'Happy days, Felicity,' he said.

'Happy days, Boots,' said Felicity. Her father-in-law, Robert Adams, known as Boots, was among her very favourite people.

'Ready to go home?' asked Boots, opening the door to the back of the car. 'Or do you have a delayed urge to see the sights?'

'I've seen them,' said Felicity, slipping into the

back seat. 'In my girlish days. Right now, dear man, I'd prefer the sights of home.'

'Home it is, Pa,' said Tim to his father.

'Home is where the birds are singing,' said Boots, sliding into the driving seat.

'Golly, yes, they'll be singing today,' said Jennifer. She and her dad joined her mother in the back. From the front passenger seat, Boots's wife Polly, head turned, was paying glad tributes to the radiant look of reborn Felicity.

And when the car moved off, slipping into the London traffic to head for Waterloo Bridge and the south-east, everybody was talking at once, and with unchecked animation. That included Boots, as he drove the happy family home.

Tim thought no-one deserved the successful outcome more than his wife. She had borne the unbearable, sudden blindness at the age of twenty, the age when life, especially in wartime, was at its most active and precious. She had known years of groping in the dark, and she had lived through times when, out of sheer frustration, she had resorted to some of the ear-pinging words she had picked up from the husky, bruising commandos of Troon. But never once could Tim remember her breaking down. No wonder everyone was so delighted for her today.

Felicity really was radiant. She was going home, to a home and garden that would be clearly visible to her every day for the rest of her life, as would her husband and daughter and all the other people who meant so much to her.

She found Tim's hand. She squeezed it. The pressure was returned amid the sound of cheerful voices.

Jennifer summed up the situation.

'Think of it, Mummy, when Elvis Presley comes on the telly news, you'll be able to see just how great he is. Before, you've only been able to see him in – well, sort of in bits and pieces.'

In September, a visitor from Germany arrived in Harwich from the Hook of Holland. His passport and visitor's visa showed him to be Rolf Seidler, West Berlin businessman. Both passport and visa were excellent forgeries, and passed inspection without question. He had been advised not to use his own name, for although he had served his time and no UK authorities were looking for him, it would be as well not to risk discovery by some inquisitive journalist, the kind who would make a meal of his erstwhile notoriety.

From Harwich, the German made his way to London.

The date was 12 September.

Chapter Two

September 12 was a momentous day for Sir
Winston Churchill, Britain's renowned wartime
leader. It was the day he and Clementine, his
wife, celebrated their golden wedding anniver-
sary. The old boy, now out of the political arena,
was happily retired, spending much time with his
paintbrush and easel in the South of France.
People wondered if he and Clementine had celebrated with champagne. Wags said they didn't
know what Clementine had treated herself to,
but ten to one old Winnie had enjoyed an extra
cigar and a double Scotch.

Later that month, there was another eventful
day. Not for Winston and Clementine, but for
Polly Adams. It was the day of her sixty-second
birthday, celebrated by the Adams family, if
not by herself. To reach the age of sixty had been
bad enough, but sixty-two, well, ye gods, she
told herself, being as old as that was absolutely
ghastly. One could almost hear the deep tolling
of the bell heralding the arrival of one's coffin.

She said so to Boots and their children, Gemma and James, at breakfast in the dining room on the morning after the day before. Once upon a time they had breakfasted in the kitchen, but that had become the domain of their daily maid, Flossie Cuthbert of Peckham, as soon as she arrived at eight o'clock. That had been the case from the first day of her employment. And since she was a treasure, the family willingly ceded the kitchen to her.

Boots received Polly's comment halfway through his enjoyment of toast and marmalade. Gemma and James received it when they were girding themselves for their dash to school. Gemma, in fact, was gulping down her last mouthful of tea prior to jumping up, and James was already on his feet.

However, husband and children all managed a sympathetic response.

'It's a curse, I know,' said Boots, 'but nothing that a shopping trip to Bond Street won't cure.'

'Yes, and anyway, Mother dear,' said Gemma, 'I bet you can still ride a bicycle better than Auntie Vi's mum.'

'Sweet child,' said Polly, 'Auntie Vi's mum is almost eighty.'

'Well, you're not,' said James. 'In fact, from where I'm standing you don't look a day over – well – ' He went for the jackpot. 'Well, say, thirty-odd.'

'Thank you, darling,' said Polly, 'even if thirty-odd is very odd and won't stand up to an examination. James – Gemma – do you realize your mama will soon be on a par with those old bits and pieces you find mouldering away in a shed?'

'Sounds pretty grim,' said James, 'but can't talk about it now, must dash.'

'Me too,' said Gemma, and away she and her twin brother went. Schools and colleges had recently reopened after the summer recess, and Gemma and James were both veterans of school life. Their own birthday would occur in December, when they'd be seventeen, but neither would regard the event as worrying. When one's mother saw the curse of old age creeping up every time she looked over her shoulder, though, you just had to feel for her.

Actually, Polly had acquired the equanimity of a woman who felt life had been exceptionally good to her, since there was nothing she wanted that she did not have. Even so, equanimity sometimes took a bit of a hiding, particularly on the occasions when she and Boots attended parents' gatherings at the twins' respective schools. Horrors, she saw herself then as almost decrepit compared with the mothers of her children's contemporaries, some of whom were no older than their late thirties. That kind of thing made a sixty-second birthday a definitely unwelcome event. However.

'Boots, old dearie,' she said, as the front door

closed with a rattle behind Gemma and James, 'I'm not complaining, of course.'

'Merely commenting?' said Boots, whose own sixty-second had happened in July.

'On what Old Father Time gets up to?' said Polly. 'Yes, the blighter never stops hanging around, even though he knows he's unwanted. I think women of the Wild West would call him pesky. Or ornery. Some Americanisms are very apt, don't you think?'

'Well, I certainly think "Howdy, Sheriff" is more picturesque verbally than "Hello, Copper",' said Boots. 'As for Old Father Time, he treats you as one of his favourite chicks.'

'Chicks?' said Polly. 'Chicks?'

'Yes,' said Boots, 'every year he makes sure you still look far younger than an old hen.'

Polly laughed.

'That's my lover,' she said. 'I say, old thing, exactly how old is Felicity?'

'Thirty-six?' said Boots.

'No, she's thirty-seven,' said Polly, thereby showing she was only testing the man in her life. 'I mention it because I thought she outdid all the young ones last night. What do they call all that body movement and elbow-jerking?'

'Jiving?' said Boots. 'And in Felicity's case, an outpouring of all the energy she had to bottle up all these years?'

'Not half, old dear, and with knobs on,' said Polly. 'I really am so happy for her. And isn't it wonderful news about Linda?'

'Yes, Lizzy is so pleased about her engagement. Alec is a fine young man. A lucky day when the Gibsons moved in next door to us,' said Boots.

Polly smiled in agreement. She saw Linda as a charming and modest girl, Alec Gibson as a happy-go-lucky young man. They'd met fourteen months ago. Everyone at the party last night had received the announcement with enthusiasm. Mere acquaintances, however, would have wondered why a feller and his fancy took as long as a year and two months to make up their minds to get spliced. That amount of time was how long the dodos took to mate. These days guys and dolls made up their minds after only a couple of dates. Everyone knew life was moving faster day by day, and only a dozy lump wanted to get left behind. The Adams family, however, felt it appropriate that a girl should wear an engagement ring for quite a bit longer than a week.

As far as Boots was concerned, he went along with some things that were new and challenging without giving up on everything that was old and tried. He considered the time Linda and Alec had taken to arrive at an engagement meant they had come to know each other very well as prospective bride and groom. Nothing wrong with that.

'A pretty sound way of going about getting

married,' he murmured, and drank the last of his second cup of breakfast tea.

'What was that?' asked Polly.

'I was thinking of Linda and Alec, and the fact that Alec took time to pop the question,' said Boots. 'I believe the modern fashion for some young people is to dash up the aisle as soon as they're on first-name terms.'

'Most young people, old dear, are on first-name terms as soon as they meet,' said Polly. 'Wasn't it ever thus among the young?'

'Not if Queen Victoria was listening,' said Boots.

'What a swine,' murmured Polly.

'Pardon?' said Boots.

'No, not you, old scout, or Queen Victoria,' said Polly. 'I meant that when we were born she was still alive, which has to make us sound a hundred years old. That's the swine of it. But concerning our young people, I hope this wretched Cold War isn't a threat to their future. They're an unlovely lot, those old men of Moscow.' She thought that Khrushchev, Russia's present premier, lacked manners. His visit to Britain earlier in the year hadn't been a great success.

'Nothing will happen while both sides have the bomb,' said Boots, rising from his chair, 'so worry not.'

'Where are you going?' asked Polly.

'As usual, to the office,' said Boots.

'Wouldn't you like to stay home and entertain me, on this my day of regret for my lost youth?' asked Polly.

'Love to, of course,' said Boots, 'but I'm fixed to have one of my pub lunches with Edwin.'

He was referring to his stepfather, Sir Edwin Finch, with whom he was always on the easiest of terms, as with his mother, Lady Maisie Finch, even if she frequently informed him he was still too airy-fairy for his own good or hers. She was the family matriarch, still known to her sons and daughter as Chinese Lady. This appellation she owed to her almond eyes and to the fact that when Boots was a young man, she had been friendly with Mr Wong Fu of the Chinese laundry off the Old Kent Road.

'Well, enjoy a happy lunch with Edwin, old love,' said Polly, 'but before you go, be frank.'

'Sincerely frank?' said Boots, who guessed what she was after.

'Sincerely,' said Polly. 'So tell me, do I look my age or not?'

Boots smiled. Polly was not so much afraid of old age as of looking the part. There she was, at the breakfast table, her dark brown hair with its coppery tints well styled, her grey eyes showing a hint of amusement. Much as she went on about the curse of old age, he knew that at this moment she was laughing at herself. She could afford to, for there wasn't a single strand of grey in her

23

hair, nor any deep lines of age on her face. True, there were a few crow's feet at the corners of her eyes, but even so, she still owned traces of the piquant look of the Twenties flapper. Her looks, in fact, were a frequent reminder to Boots of her wild and giddy days.

'Well, sincerely, Polly,' he said, 'I rate you capable of rocking around the clock with any of our teenagers.'

'I've love to believe you,' smiled Polly. 'Incidentally, have we said goodbye for ever to the foxtrot and the Charleston?'

'I think we said goodbye to the Charleston long ago,' said Boots. He bent and kissed her. 'I like it that you're always you. You'll still be a Bright Young Thing when you're ninety.'

'Tell me more.'

'You're a sweet woman, Polly.' Boots kissed her again, and went on his way.

Polly, touched, watched him leaving the dining room. He no more looked over sixty than their postman, who was forty-seven and a stalwart. What frequently concerned her was the frightful possibility that one day she really would look ancient while Boots remained impervious to the effect of his years, probably due to his ability not to take life or people too seriously. Heavens, suppose one day someone mistook her for his mother? That'll be the day when I collapse and die, she thought.

In came Flossie, now over thirty but still too

addicted to the family to worry about starting one of her own.

'Can I clear the table now, mum? And did you have a lovely birthday party?'

'My birthday party, Flossie, was memorable,' said Polly, and simply forgot about old age in her love of life.

Chapter Three

On arrival at the Camberwell Green offices of Adams Enterprises Ltd, Boots looked in on Sammy, acknowledged by the family as the foundation stone of the business. Not that anyone considered him a mute lump of granite. No, far from it. He always seemed charged with energy.

'Morning, Sammy.'

'Same to you, old mate,' said Sammy from his commodious desk. 'Great birthday party last night. Tell Polly she's a living marvel, considering. She could still model our winter designs and look like Queen of the Ritz. You ever been to the Ritz for afternoon tea and cream cakes?'

'No, not for that, just to Lyons Corner House in Leicester Square for morning coffee and a doughnut,' said Boots.

'Blind O'Reilly, on a date with Polly?' said Sammy.

'No, on a pre-war bus with Emily,' said Boots. 'Listen, Sammy, you were late back from your trip to Southend yesterday, and I didn't get a chance to talk to you about it at the party. How did it go?'

'Just the job,' said Sammy. He had spent most of yesterday in Southend, in company with his personal assistant, Mrs Rachel Goodman, and Rosie, Boots's assistant and adopted daughter. Last year, the Adams property company had acquired a dress shop in Southend, a resort still popular with London's cockneys, and a money-spinner for shop-owners in the summer. Unfortunately, the Adams shop had been destroyed by fire last year, and the cause had to be officially investigated. Not until months later did the result come through. It was to the effect that the fire had developed after a burning cigarette was carelessly dropped by a customer. Accordingly, the insurance company paid up, and Sammy, together with son Daniel and nephew Tim, directors of the property company, had set about the business of having the shop redesigned and rebuilt. Everything had finally been finished last week. It was an inspection of the new shop that had taken Sammy, Rachel and Rosie to Southend yesterday. He now declared to Boots that the rebuilding had restored his faith in the British workman.

'Come again, Sammy?' said Boots.

'Well,' said Sammy, 'you know as well as I do that when you start a new business and take on your first worker, along comes a trade union official to ask about what wages you're paying, what amenities are available, where's the place where the worker can eat his lunchtime sandwiches, will he get time off for his afternoon cup of tea, who's looking after his mother's chilblains and is he being insured for injury. I tell you, chum, it all gives the worker the impression that he only has to turn up, that any actual work is kind of incidental, not – um – um – '

'Obligatory?' suggested Boots.

'Meaning obliged to? That's the word,' said Sammy. 'Not that it's too popular with some trade union leaders. It makes 'em think bosses are coming it a bit.'

'They'd like it better if work was optional?' said Boots.

'You bet,' said Sammy, 'and let me admit I admire your wordage, as always. Anyway, the blokes who rebuilt the Southend shop did us proud, believe me.' He went on to say Rachel and Rosie had been delighted and inspired to offer highly valuable suggestions regarding a layout for shop and window that would be halfway classy.

'Halfway?' said Boots.

'Just right for Southend, where they don't go in for window displays that frighten the customers,' said Sammy. 'Well, you know what I mean, like one of those Bond Street hat shops with a window display of just one hat with a feather in it. Everyone knows what that means, a hundred smackers at least, and that might not

28

even include the feather. So Rachel and Rosie came up with something halfway classy for layout and window display.'

'I'm with you, Sammy,' said Boots, amused as well as interested. Sammy had his own way of recounting events, developments and everything else.

Halfway classy, said Sammy, would look highly inviting to Southend customers, even if the fashions on offer weren't of the expensive and exclusive kind. Exclusive and expensive fashions, he said, were only for Mayfair birds and film stars, of which only a few had ever been seen in Southend. The opening of the shop would take place next Easter and business would carry through to the last day of September. Tim and Daniel, with Rachel's help, would be responsible for employing staff on a seasonal basis.

Boots smiled.

'Well, providing you keep your usual eye on everything, Sammy,' he said, 'there'll be one more source of profit in Adams Enterprises.'

'Decent of you to say so,' said Sammy, 'and as for profit, well, what's the point if there ain't any?'

'Exit the enterprise,' said Boots.

Sammy said the year had been a good one for the firm so far, even allowing for their Bethnal Green factory having to cope with regular inter- ference from Barney Burridge, the local trade union convenor. According to Sammy, blokes like

Barney Burridge believed profit was achieved at the expense of the sweating workers, and that the Government ought to make it illegal. He did, however, agree with Boots that effective trade unionism had come about because of exploitative old-time employers giving employees a bad time all round by paying them starvation wages in factory hellholes. He considered such employers pig-ignorant and short of common sense as well. Treat workers fair and square, and they responded in kind, and sometimes also asked if you'd like to accept a bagful of ripe rhubarb grown on their allotment. Incidentally, what did Boots think about the ugly punch-ups going on in Notting Hill?

Notting Hill, in west London, was the scene of ongoing race riots, brought about by resentful young thugs complaining that black immigrants were always ten too many. Some of the incidents were violently ugly, and the police were having daily trouble in clearing the streets. Parliament was talking about an official Commission of Inquiry.

Boots answered Sammy's question much as Sammy had expected.

Live and let live. That had always been his way. The problem, anyway, he said, was one for the politicians to sort out. If they could. Boots was no great admirer of the general run of politicians, very few of whom he believed to be capable of running a shop, let alone a country.

'Got you, Boots,' said Sammy. 'By the way, I'm taking Rachel and Rosie out again tomorrow. Up to town to see the winter fashions show at the Mayfair Gallery. We're in the show ourselves.' Adams Fashions had their own designer, Elizabeth Ames, whose talents had been fostered and nurtured by Sammy's original designer, one Lilian Hyams, now retired. Sammy thought Elizabeth, called Betsy by the Bethnal Green factory staff, was showing a fair amount of Lilian's flair. British designers, once either non-existent or little thought of, were beginning to make a name for themselves, although not yet spoken of in the same breath as Christian Dior or young Yves St Laurent of Paris. Sammy kept a keen eye on what these French maestros came up with. In the past, he and Lilian, heads together, had been known to draw the germ of an idea of their own from some aspect of what originated in Paris. But not on any account had they ever brazenly copied a new fashion – such an act could lead to professional suicide.

Boots, general manager of the whole of the Adams business, and noted for holding everything together, said, 'Well, fashion shows are for you, Rachel and Rosie, but would you care to take Polly along too?'

'Polly,' said Sammy, 'still looks like a fashion plate herself. Tell her to be here at the offices by half nine tomorrow morning, and I'll drive her to town along with Rachel and Rosie. By the way, you lunching in the canteen today?'

'Today?' said Boots. The canteen for the office workers was another venture that had been completed. It provided morning coffee, midday lunch and afternoon tea, and was already prized by the staff. Boots and Sammy often lunched there themselves, although Boots still frequently favoured a light meal at the pub opposite the offices, and Sammy sometimes enjoyed a business lunch with a client or supplier. 'No, not today, Sammy. Today I'll be at the pub with Edwin.'

'Fair do's,' said Sammy. Now fifty-six, he was like Boots in that his years sat lightly on him. He was still a man of very agreeable looks, his dark brown hair still thick and healthy, his blue eyes as lively as always, projecting inner energy. 'Give our stepdad my respectful regards.'

'Will do,' said Boots, and left Sammy to his morning's work. In his own office he spent time sifting through the pile of morning correspondence. Some letters he would hand to Rosie to deal with. The rest would require the assistance of his shorthand typist. At twenty to ten, as usual, Rosie came into his office to collect her share of the correspondence.

'Good morning, sir,' she said, tongue in cheek. 'How are we today, might I ask?'

'Still with the living,' said Boots, looking up at her. She smiled. Nothing ever diminished the affection and regard Boots and his adopted daughter felt for each other. At forty-three, Rosie dressed as well as Polly and owned the same kind of elegance. Elegance, Boots always thought, was something that women like Polly and Rosie were born with. Others acquired it.

'How's the garage?' he asked.

'I'm utterly blissed to inform you that Matt's already in profit,' said Rosie. After several years running a poultry farm, Rosie and her husband, Matthew Chapman, had opted for a change. Matthew, long a qualified motor engineer, had gone back to his first love by having a garage built on a site in Peckham, and Rosie had accepted the offer of a job from Sammy and Boots. They had moved to be nearer the family, and actually ended up close to the home of Grandma and Grandpa Finch. 'Matt's now living with overalls, engines and oil again. I'm like you, I'm living with civilization.'

'It's a little better than digging for coal,' said Boots. 'By the way, I understand you enjoyed your trip to Southend yesterday.'

'Oh, not half, chum,' said Rosie, 'and that included a plate of cockles and mussels. The shop's empty, of course, but it's in the heart of the shopping area and I rate it a very promising prospect as a new retail outlet.'

'Does very promising mean halfway classy?' asked Boots, and Rosie laughed.

'You've been listening to Sammy,' she said.

'So I have, for most of my life,' said Boots, 'and

it's taught me that never mind his Sunday-school attendance average, he always knew how to use ideas and initiative. Adams Enterprises Limited is Sammy's own grown-up baby.'

'Well, if he's its daddy, you're its uncle,' said Rosie. 'You're the one who keeps the ship steady all through rough waters, and I'm told no-one has ever had to complain about being seasick. Any letters for my attention, old chum?'

'Here,' said Boots, and handed her several. Rosie took them to the office she shared with Rachel. Boots then called for his shorthand typist, Miss Queenie Richards, to take dictation in respect of the correspondence he'd retained.

Miss Queenie Richards, born of working-class parents, had bettered her prospects of finding a job outside a factory by going to night school and studying shorthand typing as soon as she finished her primary State education. She was now the latest in Adams Enterprises' long line of shorthand typists. Most of her predecessors had left to get married. At twenty, Queenie was plump, perky and pretty, and accordingly an eligible prospect for any feller who wasn't keen on the slender kind of girl who photographed well but slipped through one's fingers when being treated to a goodnight necking session on her doorstep.

Incidentally, in respect of fellers, Queenie had recently seen off a prime example. He'd actually tried to take liberties with her behind a tree on Wimbledon Common. Perky she might be, and outgoing as well, but although girls today were becoming much more unconventional than those of their parents' generation, Queenie wasn't going to let any bloke undo her buttons behind a tree on any common, which was what Charley Baxter had tried to do. Queenie poked him in the eye as notice of goodbye, and went back home by herself.

The reason why she worked for Adams Enterprises was because her previous firm had filed for bankruptcy a year ago. She counted herself lucky to have secured a new job as short-hand typist to Adams Enterprises' general manager, Mr Robert Adams, since he turned out to be just about the most good-tempered boss ever. It didn't take her long to realize that some of the girls had a bit of a crush either on him or his brother, Mr Sammy Adams, the managing director. Which was a kind of knockout, con-sidering both men were – well, sort of mature. Mind, she had to admit they still had their share of man appeal, one being very humorous and civilized, while the other sort of gave off sparks of electricity. The undercurrents among some of the general office girls were a bit of a lark, really, and anyway, neither Mr Robert nor Mr Sammy took any notice. Queenie found it a giggle to be an onlooker. She liked both men, of course, and supposed some girls might see them as sugar daddies. Mind, sugar daddies were only for frizzy blondes who couldn't manage to live without being given a diamond bracelet once a week in a helping of apple pie and custard. Well, you could always clean off the custard.

What Queenie herself fancied was a decent bloke with a decent job, all leading to a semi-detached nest somewhere in airy suburbia where you could see trees from your bedroom window, which you couldn't if you lived in the Elephant and Castle area, as she did. There it was all new post-war concrete. So she really did fancy a decent bloke and airy suburbia.

What she didn't fancy was something creepy, and something creepy was on her mind when she answered the call from her boss, the man she knew was called Boots by his family and friends. With her shorthand notebook, she entered his office in less sprightly fashion than usual.

'Good morning, sir,' she said in a subdued tone.

'Good morning, Queenie.' Boots recognized her Christian name as one quite popular among cockneys. He also recognized that she was not her usual self. 'Something bothering you?' he asked.

'Well, yes.'

'Sit down and tell me about it, if you'd like to.'

Happy to have someone to confide in, someone civilized and mature, Queenie went into detail. She was, she said, being followed home almost every evening after work, by a man in a grey raincoat and a blue peaked cap. The collar of the raincoat was always turned up and the peak of the cap pulled down, so that he looked like Humphrey Bogart in a gangster movie. She couldn't say exactly how long he'd been following her, only that she'd begun to notice him about two weeks ago. He kind of appeared out of nowhere whenever she boarded her home-going bus.

'Out of nowhere?' said Boots.

Queenie said well, she never noticed him in the queue, only at the moment when she was on the bus and edging towards a seat. Then he'd board the bus himself, and climb to the upper deck. He couldn't see her from there, but somehow, at her home stop near the Elephant and Castle in Walworth, he always stepped off the bus a few moments after she herself had alighted. How he knew her movements she had no idea, considering he hadn't been able to see her from upstairs. Boots intervened here to suggest that when the man first took a fancy to her, as he obviously had, he'd occupied a lower-deck seat on her bus, and noted where she got off. Since then, he'd kept out of her immediate way by riding on the top deck. Such people were like that.

'Oh, the crafty beast,' said Queenie. Anyway, she said, he followed her after she got off the bus, but always kept at a distance. She'd recently begun to stop and look back, as a sort of challenge. He'd stop too, and interest himself in a shop window while people walked past him. The area, of course, was always busy with shops and passers-by, but she was sure she was the only person he was interested in. He'd follow her to her home in Hampton Street, and walk straight past her without looking while she was opening the door with her key. After that, he'd return the way he had come. She'd been checking on that these last three days by going into the front room and watching from behind the window's lace curtain. Yes, he'd appear, passing by on his way back to the main road.

Boots decided that any interested party would consider her worth following. She was a pretty brunette with a pretty kind of plumpness. And she had no inferiority complex about her rounded shape. No, not a bit of it, for she was extremely fond of wearing sweaters, both colourful and form-fitting. Boots posed a question.

'This man walks straight past your house on his way back?'

'Yes, not half he don't, and without looking, as if he knows I'm watching him,' said Queenie. 'It's creepy, Mr Adams, and it's getting on me nerves.'

'Have you mentioned him to your father?' asked Boots.

'Well, no, I ain't,' said Queenie. While in cockney fashion she made a bit of a mess of her spoken English, once she was typing out what she'd taken down in shorthand, every word was perfect, and her spelling was excellent. She was well worth her wages. 'Me dad's a petty officer in the navy, and he's at sea somewhere just now. Of course, I've spoken to me mum in confidence, and she says to go to the police about this bloke, but I don't know they'd do anything, would they?'

'Not unless he attacked you,' said Boots. 'Have you thought about the possibility that he does fancy you, but is too shy to tell you so?'

'Here, half a mo, Mr Adams,' said Queenie. 'I don't want any bloke like him to fancy me. I want someone decent. Well, Mum says it's time I found meself a suitable feller if I don't want to turn into an old maid, which I don't. But like I said to her, what's decent or suitable about some creep that follows me home every day? I'll start having bad dreams in a minute, dreams about what'll happen if one day he makes up his mind to catch me up. I mean, what's he after?'

'I think this chap must have developed an obsession with you,' said Boots.

'Oh, I think I've read about that sort of thing,' said Queenie, looking very put out. 'I've thought about bringing me umbrella to work one day, and going up to the creep and bashing him with it. Only I pride meself I'm me mum's daughter and she's never done anything like bashing anyone all her life. Mind, I did—' She stopped, deciding not to tell Mr Adams she'd poked Charley Baxter in the eye. She didn't want him to think her unladylike. 'Yes, I did think I ought to stand up for meself. Am I taking up your time with me problem, Mr Adams? I don't want to, not when the firm's always so busy.'

'Leave it with me, and I'll see what I can do,' said Boots. 'First off, you need a man.'

'Beg pardon?' said Queenie, blushing a bit, which she hardly ever did, being a down-to-earth girl of Walworth, modern enough to know a lot more about life and people than her granny ever did. 'Beg pardon, Mr Adams?'

'I'm speaking of someone who'll follow the follower,' said Boots.

'Oh, crikey, then what?' said Queenie.

'Your creep will be taught a lesson,' said Boots.

'Mr Adams—'

'Cheer up, Queenie, I'll see to it, I'll find someone, but there'll be no blood spilt. Better that way. Now, let's do today's letters, shall we?'

Crikey, thought Queenie, he's me hero.

Chapter Four

Mr George Porter, costing clerk for Adams Enterprises and highly thought of by Sammy, received a call from Boots twenty minutes before the lunch break. Down he went, hoping he hadn't dropped a clanger somewhere, sometime. George Porter at thirty was conscientious, good-natured, large of frame and rounded of stomach. But he didn't lack muscle. Some people might have called him fat, but no-one could have called him flabby. In fact, some kids called him Big George, not Fatty. He lived in lodgings in Wansey Street, Walworth, and was judged by neighbours to be a confirmed bachelor. Secretly, however, he dreamt of the day when he would have the courage to sweep a real live cutie off her feet – as in a Frank Sinatra film – and live happily ever after with her. Yes, George Porter was a romantic, but, alas, a shy and retiring one for all his big frame. He felt self-conscious about the fact that his girth verged on the outsize, and he knew most women favoured a lean look in a man. Well, he wasn't lean, he was just large.

'You wanted me, Mr Adams?' he enquired when he arrived in Boots's office.

'Yes, I've got an outside job for you, George old lad,' said Boots, who liked the man and his unwavering application to his work.

'Outside?' said George, and Boots took an analytical look at the firm's excellent cost clerk, noting his size. Big, yes, and healthy in his appearance, even if he was a bit circular around the waist. 'What's outside mean, Mr Adams, if I might ask?'

'Well, sit down for a few minutes, George, and I'll tell you,' said Boots.

George sat down and listened. His ears began to twitch. What he was hearing was the last thing he'd expected. Poor Queenie Richards.

'She's being followed home from work every evening, Mr Adams?'

'It seems so,' said Boots. 'She isn't the kind of young lady who'd imagine it, would you say?'

'Well, of course, I only know her as one of the office girls,' said George. 'I'm not intimate with her – I mean – ' He coughed. He'd dropped a clanger, after all, although not about his work. He turned a little red, and Boots thought of what other staff members said about him, that he was a very shy sort of bloke, even at thirty.

'So, you don't take her to dance halls,' said Boots in light fashion, thus helping George's blush to recede. 'Still, at this time in her life, she needs a bit of a champion, and here's what I'd like you to do.'

George listened again, and this time his jaw began to fall open.

'Mr Adams, you want me to follow the character who's been following her?' he said.

'Yes, I'd like you to,' said Boots, 'but voluntarily. It's not an order. Once you finish work for the day, your life is your own, not ours. I'm really thinking of Queenie getting a helping hand from a willing workmate.'

'Well – er – ' George had been brought to the point where he had to consider whether or not he'd be able to master his inferiority complex, this shyness that pervaded him whenever he was in close company with women and needed to shine with wit, or at least to be passably entertaining, as were the characters in the American gangster novels he enjoyed reading. 'Well, I think I see what you mean, that I need Queenie to have confidence in me.'

'That shouldn't be a problem, since I'm sure you'd be the best bet for the job,' said Boots. Having considered George's retiring nature, he felt that here was a chance to chuck him in at the deep end, often a cure for the problem of self-doubt. So he went on to suggest that George followed Queenie to her bus stop, and stayed back to look out for the shifty character. Once the bloke was on the bus himself, George was to board it too, and follow him up to the top deck.

'I'm with you, Mr Adams.'

'All the way?' smiled Boots.

'Well, I think you want me to keep tabs on the blighter, all the way to Queenie's home, and then have a few words with him. Is that it?'

Boots, who liked the fact that George at least had no qualms about standing up physically four-square to the enemy, said he couldn't think of anything more effective than collaring the bloke right outside Queenie's front door and delivering some weighty warnings into his ear, weighty being the operative word.

'You still with me, George?'

'Still with you, Mr Adams,' said George, stirred by the fact that the much-respected general manager had this kind of faith in him. 'But I suppose I ought to point out there's a chance he'll turn nasty.'

'He might,' said Boots, 'but you're a fine figure of a bloke, and we did just agree on a weighty approach, didn't we? It'll be in a good cause. Queenie's cause.'

'He could sue me for assault,' said George.

'Oh, you won't need to rough him up unless he strikes the first blow, and even then try to avoid the messy business of drawing blood,' said Boots. 'Not that I think he'll want to complain to the police. And we ourselves don't want them butting in. We've nothing to offer them except Queenie's headache, and like my brother Sammy, I always prefer to let bobbies get on with looking after the traffic. I'll talk to Queenie about all this after lunch.'

George fumbled with his tie while thinking about Mike Finnegan, a Chicago private eye well known in American gangster fiction for the way he could down hoodlums.

'Mr Adams,' he said, 'would you let Miss Richards know I'll do my best to get this character off her back?'

'Of course,' said Boots.

'I must say it's damned decent of you to concern yourself with this aggravating little problem she's got,' said George. 'Very decent.'

'One can't ignore her distress,' said Boots, 'and among the things I very much dislike are men who creep about in the footsteps of innocent women.'

'Well,' said George, deciding that courage was of the essence, 'I like your idea of hunting the hunted. I call it good psychology. It'll shake him. Yes, I like it a lot.'

'And I like the way you've volunteered,' said Boots, and the lunch break began then.

Sir Edwin Finch was already in the pub when Boots arrived. His stepfather, seated at a corner table, lifted a hand, and Boots, acknowledging the welcoming gesture, joined him.

'Edwin, am I late or are you early?'

'I'm a little early,' smiled Sir Edwin, at eighty-five silver-haired and slender. If he was no longer sprightly, he was still distinguished in his appearance. Not that his health gave any concern. No, he was remarkably healthy, as was his wife, Boots's redoubtable mother, Chinese Lady.

'Happy to see you,' said Boots, himself still able to attract the wandering eyes of women on the lookout for a wild weekend in Brighton or Torquay. However, it must be said that Boots was his mother's son and accordingly not given to wild weekends with wanton wenches. Indeed, had he been of that kind, Chinese Lady would have long ago wondered why she gave birth to him.

Up came Joe, the veteran barman. Casual customers were served at the bar. Regulars were given table service.

'Morning, Mr Adams, what can I get you gentlemen?'

Boots and Sir Edwin both ordered ham salads, plus beer on the side. The pub's menu was simple, either sandwiches or salads. It was an old-fashioned house, unaltered since Victorian times, its saloon bar fitted with padded wall seats and its bar topped with grey-veined marble. On the bar were white china stands containing cold roast joints for carving. Concerned fusspots said there ought to be a law prohibiting the sale of uncovered cooked food, on the grounds that bacteria might find root and be responsible for poisoning people. Joe said anyone who'd been

46

eating uncovered cooked food for years had an armour-plated stomach, and that he'd never heard of any of his customers being poisoned.

The place catered mainly for Camberwell businessmen aiming for plain food and beers like old ale, bitter and stout. Elsewhere, lunchtime snack menus were changing, becoming more varied. Some cafes, especially in places like Soho, were offering a very new item, toasted sandwiches, with a choice of white or brown bread. Sammy's opinion of such was that the caterers responsible were mucking up perfectly good food.

While waiting for their order, Boots and Sir Edwin chatted. There was no special purpose for their meeting. It was simply that from time to time they enjoyed sharing a simple lunch in this old pub, one of Camberwell Green's landmarks. However, after Joe had brought them their food and their beers, Sir Edwin in low tones introduced a subject entirely confidential.

'Boots,' he said, 'my personal history is a complicated one.'

'True,' said Boots, 'but don't worry about it.'

'I often ask myself if, together with my will, I should leave a letter for your mother,' said Sir Edwin.

'Should you talk about that here?' murmured Boots, forking crisp lettuce into his mouth, and washing it down with a mouthful of old ale.

'I shan't mention anything you don't already

know,' said Sir Edwin, and Boots looked him in the eye. His stepfather smiled, and Boots thought, not for the first time, that although he was German-born he bore little resemblance to any German stereotype, such as a square-headed Prussian or a paunchy Munich beer-drinker. He looked like a retired English stockbroker whose manners were likely to be impeccable, and whose suits were as quietly impressive as any that had originated in Savile Row.

'The point is, Boots, that although I can resist telling your mother of my true origins while I'm still alive, do I owe it to her and my conscience to leave her a letter after I'm gone?' pondered Sir Edwin.

'D'you want a straight answer?' asked Boots.

'It were better thus,' said Sir Edwin, quoting from somewhere.

'Then it's no, full stop,' said Boots.

'You don't feel I owe a confession to your mother?'

'Only if you want to upset the proverbial apple-cart,' said Boots. The conversation was still being carried on in murmurs. The fact that his step-father had operated in Britain as an espionage agent for Kaiser Wilhelm's Imperial Germany was surely old hat now, and old hats could be dumped in the dustbin. What mattered was the invaluable service he had given to the UK since the day he defected in 1918. It had not been a matter of opportunism, but of acute dislike for

48

German militarism and an acquired affection for the people of Britain. 'Edwin, let sleeping dogs lie, that's sound philosophy in most circumstances, and certainly in your case. What made you begin to think about it?'

'Old age, Boots.'

'Well, old age should be able to treat you better than that.'

'Also,' said Sir Edwin, 'I feel that after I do go, someone or something might produce the truth about me. I'm certain your mother would then feel I should have confessed to her.'

'Not a bit of it,' said Boots. 'My mother simply wouldn't believe it.'

'Would she believe it if I told her myself?'

'If you told her yourself, I'd have to convince her you were out of your mind,' said Boots. 'She'd then make sure you said nothing more in case some men in white coats arrived to take you away. If I couldn't convince her, then the apple-cart would hit a bus and fall apart. That would do no-one any good. Edwin, forget it. Stay the course. You've earned everything you have.'

'Do you say so, Boots?'

'I do,' said Boots, 'and you can consider it underlined.'

'Then I'll take your advice,' said Sir Edwin.

'Without worrying?' said Boots.

'Without worrying,' said Sir Edwin, and they proceeded to enjoy the rest of their lunch.

*   *   *

49

At home, Chinese Lady was enjoying her own light lunch in company with her daily help, Mrs Harriet Plumstead, a widow and, to Chinese Lady, a godsend. It was much more sociable to eat lunch with one's invaluable daily than to eat alone.

'My,' said Mrs Plumstead, a homely body, 'I never knew any gentleman like the master. I mean, the way he gets about at his age.'

'Oh, he doesn't consider himself old,' said Chinese Lady, now eighty-two. She truly didn't consider either Edwin or herself old. Old to her meant being white-haired, toothless and bedridden. And she never thought about leaving this earth to enter St Peter's domain. That was for other people. True, she sometimes did feel concern if Edwin wasn't his usual ailment-free self, but even then she always assured herself that he wasn't really old, just getting on a bit. 'He wouldn't be going all the way to Camberwell Green to meet my only oldest son if he wasn't up to it.'

'Well, mum, I must say he's a good man, I never met no gentleman more distinguished or with such nice manners,' said Mrs Plumstead, 'and you can't say that about every man. Mind, me own hubby couldn't have had nicer ways or nicer manners, and I've always felt the Lord took him a lot before his time. Shall I do the master's study while he's still out, and wash up the lunch dishes after, like?'

'Yes, do that, Mrs Plumstead,' said Chinese Lady.

'All right, I will,' said Mrs Plumstead.

'Thank you,' said Chinese Lady. 'By the way, don't tidy up my husband's study too much.' She was always telling her daily that, since Edwin was always pointing out that he couldn't find anything after the good lady had tidied him up. That was how he put it.

'No, I'll just dust and straighten things a bit, that's all,' said Mrs Plumstead. Neither Chinese Lady nor Sir Edwin himself could deter her from attending to the study twice a week.

She always felt Sir Edwin kept it in a real pickle, with books all over the place and bits of notepaper littering his desk. She set about the task of dusting and tidying. My, he did have a lot of books. They filled shelves that occupied the whole of one wall. One book was actually on the floor, at the foot of the shelves. That wasn't unusual. This one looked as if it belonged to a lower shelf, where a number of books had been disturbed and needed straightening. She picked it up and began to tidy up the shelf. She handled the disturbed books in her quick efficient way, remembering that Sir Edwin was a bit fussy about not having his study tidied up too much. She put that peculiarity down to his age. A book fell from her busy hand, and it opened up as it hit the floor.

'Bother,' she said. She stooped and gathered it

up. A piece of paper came loose from its position between the flyleaf and the inside of the front cover. The book itself was old, a body could tell that, and blowed if it wasn't one of Charles Dickens's stories. *The Old Curiosity Shop*. The piece of paper was even older. It was dry and yellow from age, and the faded writing on it, well, she'd never seen that kind before. It wasn't English, nor was the printed title. It could have been double Dutch as far as she was concerned. Whatever it was, she supposed Sir Edwin had forgotten it was there. She decided to put it on his desk, and did so, then finished the work.

The German businessman, returning to the hotel in Bloomsbury after lunch, asked at reception for his room key.

'Certainly, sir,' said the receptionist, a polite and agreeable young woman. 'How did you find Wheelers?' she asked, taking the key from its hook. The new guest, having expressed a liking for seafood while enquiring about suitable eating places, had been recommended by the receptionist to Wheelers Restaurant in Old Compton Street, Soho. 'Was it to your liking?'

'*Ja*, good,' said the German gentleman, making the word sound like 'goot'.

'I meant to tell you, it's famous for oysters swallowed with Guinness,' said the receptionist, Miss Janice Browning, handing over the key.

'*Ja*? Oysters?'

'Oh, yes, very famous.'

'Oysters I don't like.' Spoken with feeling.

'Oh, sorry, sir.'

'Lobsters I do like.' Spoken with appreciation and a gleam of handsome white teeth.

'Lobsters, yes, sir, so do most of us.'

'*Ja?* Good.' And the new guest, whose passport identified him as Rolf Seidler of West Berlin, repaired to his first-floor room, his tall, muscular figure impressively athletic as he mounted the stairs two at a time.

What an interesting man, even if he is German, thought Miss Browning.

Chapter Five

Sir Edwin arrived home from his lunch date with Boots in the early afternoon. He found Chinese Lady in the living room, comfortably seated in an armchair knitting. Knitting for her many great-grandchildren was her productive recreation. He greeted her with a very affectionate kiss on her cheek. Chinese Lady blinked.

'Well I never, you're very loving, Edwin,' she said. 'Boots didn't make you drink a bit reckless, did he?'

'Maisie my dear, I don't need the stimulation of drink to demonstrate my affection for you,' smiled Sir Edwin, his confidential talk with Boots still fresh in his mind. 'It's there all the time, even if it rarely shouts out loud.'

Chinese Lady regarded him with an affection of her own. If she had deeply loved her first husband, Corporal Daniel Adams of the West Kent Regiment, her love for Sir Edwin had never been less than sincere. She had always considered him a gentleman of kindness and courtesy, and liking and respect had long been a forerunner of eventual love.

'Well, at least you always enjoy having lunch with Boots,' she said, 'and I daresay the two of you told each other the kind of jokes I never understand. Oh, by the way, while you were still out, Mrs Plumstead tidied up your study.'

'Mrs Plumstead is devoted twice a week to tidying me up,' said Sir Edwin, 'and twice a week I can't find anything. Not that I'm critical of the lady. Neither of us could do without her, and I hope she remains a fixture. However, in five minutes or so, I'll go and see if any damage has been done to my bookshelves. I spent part of the morning looking up one or two old volumes.'

'That reminds me, she found an old letter or something,' said Chinese Lady. 'It—'

'What old letter?' Sir Edwin was quick to interrupt.

'I'm sure I don't know,' said Chinese Lady. 'It fell out of a book when she was tidying up your shelves, and she—'

'She passed it to you?' Sir Edwin's second interruption was prompted by a dreadful suspicion that one of his chickens had come home to roost.

'No, she put it on your desk,' she said.

'You haven't seen it?'

'Edwin, you know I don't interfere with your private letters or anything else,' said Chinese Lady. Indeed, during all the years he worked for

55

the Government following their marriage, she had never asked questions or made his business her own business. She was not to know how thankful he was for that. 'Mrs Plumstead just thought you ought to know about it, so she didn't put it back in the book. She put it on your desk, like I've just said.'

Sir Edwin made an attempt at lightness.

'I'm sure no daily help could tidy up more thoughtfully than ours, Maisie. I'll take a look.'

'When you come back, would you like a nice cup of tea, Edwin?'

That homely question had been asked of him countless times, and his answer was the same as it had always been.

'I would, Maisie, yes.'

One never said no, in any case. Not to Maisie, who, like many women of her era, probably thought a pot of tea was the kind of blessing that originated from Above.

He heard Mrs Plumstead using the vacuum cleaner upstairs as he made his way to his study. He did not rush, although he had a sense of urgency. Maisie might not have thought the letter of any consequence, and, certainly, it seemed she hadn't bothered to inspect it, but had Mrs Plumstead read it, and if so what had it revealed to her of the past? It would have been natural to see what it was all about when she picked it up, or at least to read the first line or two. He could fault deliberate snooping, he couldn't fault a moment of curiosity.

There it was, on his desk, and even from the door he could see it was yellow with age. And as soon as he reached his desk and stared down at it, the years rolled away and he knew what it was, a letter from his Aunt Karina, written when he was at university. The inked words were faded, as was the printed address, but everything was still readable, including the date, 18 October 1892. He had been nineteen, and he clearly remembered what was in the letter after taking in the first sentence. His aunt had written to say she hoped very much he would enter the diplomatic service, since that buffoon, Kaiser Wilhelm, who'd only been Emperor for four years so far, was already boasting so loudly about Germany and the power of its army that the country needed a corps of outstanding diplomats to ease the sensitivities and suspicions of its neighbours and of Great Britain.

Yes, this was the letter. Why had he kept it? As a typical example of the kind of plain advice she liked to give him? Yes, he thought that might have been the reason. But why was it still extant when, along with so many other things appertaining to his German origins, it should have been destroyed? He had forgotten about it, of course, especially as it had been out of sight inside a book. What had Mrs Plumstead made of it? First and foremost, had she recognized the writing as German? He thought then about his conversation with Boots, and Boots's conviction that it was wise to let sleeping dogs lie. If Mrs Plumstead had been able to read German, his own sleeping dog would have awakened with more than a bark or two.

Hearing the good lady coming down the stairs, he called her. She entered his study, looking as busy as ever.

'You wanted me, sir?' she said.

'Yes, I wanted to thank you for finding this old letter.'

'Well, speaking truthful, sir, I didn't actually find it. It fell out of one of your books.'

'Thank you, anyway.'

'Is it sort of important, sir?'

'Not in the least. It's a letter I received when at university. From a foreigner.'

'Oh, a foreigner,' said Mrs Plumstead, and nodded her head, as if that explained everything about the queer writing.

Sir Edwin smiled.

'And at a time when Queen Victoria was still our queen,' he said.

'Oh, that was a bit before me time,' said Mrs Plumstead chattily, 'but we all know she made a bit of a name for herself, don't we? Me hubby, bless his resting soul, once said that Queen Victoria was the only person that could have shut Hitler up when he was bawling his head off. Queen Victoria, he said, wasn't afraid of the devil himself, and would soon have put Hitler in his place, and it's a pity someone didn't. Look what happened when . . .'

Mrs Plumstead carried on in the amiable fashion of a woman who liked a listener as receptive as Sir Edwin or his lady wife. Sir Edwin had once expressed to Boots his opinion that women, with a few exceptions, were all born to communicate and inform, as against the taciturn nature of most men. Boots had said well, thank God for women, who wants to live in a world silent except for the chatter of magpies?

Giving his ear to the daily help, Sir Edwin began to tear the ancient letter into little pieces, doing so at intervals while nodding and smiling at her. This made his action seem entirely casual. Just as casually, as she came to the end of her chat, he lightly dropped the pieces into the dustpan she was holding.

'More waste paper for disposal,' he murmured.

'Oh, you're welcome, sir,' said Mrs Plumstead, giving no further thought to a piece of old yellowed paper with funny writing on it.

But Sir Edwin regarded it in the nature of a sleeping dog that had almost awakened. Fortunately, Mrs Plumstead's reactions had been so innocuous that the dog had merely whimpered in its sleep. If someone else had disturbed it, someone with a knowledge of German, he could imagine Maisie being alerted and wanting to know what exactly was going on. Her endearing trait of minding her own business in regard to his private papers would have been set aside for once.

Was it the wisest course at this stage of his life to go along with Boots's advice and say nothing to Maisie? If she discovered the secrets of his past accidentally, might she not feel she had been deceived from the day they first met, when he became her lodger and she his landlady in that old Victorian terraced house in Walworth? A confession might bring about a more forgiving reaction. It might. But since the beginning of the First World War she had regarded Germany and the Germans as the devil's own. Hitler and the Second World War confirmed her opinion in the most extreme way.

Sir Edwin dwelt silently on the problem before rejoining his wife, when she then went about the homely task of putting the kettle on. Was there ever a woman more addicted to the comforting aspects of life?

Not for the first time, Sir Edwin kept his peace.

'Crikey,' breathed Queenie. It was mid-afternoon and Mr Adams had called her into his office to talk to her again about the creep who kept following her home. It had raised her spirits to confide in him, especially as he'd been so kind and understanding, and promised to help. But what help was he talking about now, actually? 'George Porter, Mr Adams? Him from upstairs, he's going to do something about this bloke?'

'Something effective, we hope,' said Boots, and explained that George would follow the bloke all the way to Queenie's house, where a man-to-geezer confrontation would take place.

'Man-to-geezer?' said Queenie, blinking dark sexy eyelashes.

'As Mr Sammy will tell you, a dubious piece of work like this is known as a geezer,' said Boots.

'Oh, go on, Mr Adams,' said Queenie, and did a bit of thinking. 'Mr Porter, he's going to follow the creep?'

'I think he'll be up to the job,' said Boots. 'He's built for it.'

'But he's – well, a bit fat,' said Queenie.

'Not fat, Queenie, no,' smiled Boots. 'It's all muscle. George is just large. And certainly large enough to confront your geezer. That kind of person likes to remain anonymous. Coming face to face with George will make anonymity fly off somewhere and leave him feeling undressed.'

'Well, I bet he won't look too pretty,' said Queenie.

'I don't suppose he will,' said Boots. 'And with luck and a few well-chosen words, George will at least get him down to his shirt and braces.'

'Shirt and braces?' queried Queenie.

'Figuratively,' said Boots, 'which means in a manner of speaking.'

'Oh, I'm up with that,' said Queenie. 'Listen, Mr Adams, is Mr Porter going to give him a bit of a bashing? I mean, Mr Porter?' She was still dubious, although she was prepared to be charitable. Only George Porter from upstairs wasn't the kind of man a girl saw as heroic. He read books, was a bit shy, a bit backward in coming forward, and a bit clerkish. And he wasn't at all like Mr Adams. A girl could easily fit Mr Adams into the role of a hero, even if he wasn't a young man any more. But he looked as if he still had a good body, whereas George Porter looked a bit fat, really. Queenie made a point. 'Well, I mean, I don't know if he really has got muscle, like. I know you said he has, but if you don't mind me saying so, he's sort of outsize round the middle, ain't he?'

Boots had his own ideas about George. George stuck with a problem in his costing work until he solved it, to his own satisfaction and to Sammy's. Boots felt George had the tenacity to stick with a problem outside costing, and that his avoirdupois was deceptive.

'He's large, Queenie, not paunchy,' he said. 'I think he's your man.'

'Well, if you say so, Mr Adams,' said Queenie, and looked thoughtfully at her boss. 'D'you really think he can sort out this creep?'

'Well, we'll let him give it a go, shall we, Queenie?' said Boots amiably.

'Yes, all right, Mr Adams,' said Queenie.

Naturally, she thought she'd be better off with a helpmate like John Wayne. However, despite her doubts, she knew it was only right to go along with Mr Adams and his choice of George Porter.

The gent himself spoke to her ten minutes before the end of the working day. That is, he put his head into the general office, coughed and said, 'Er – could I have a word, Miss Richards? In my office?'

'I'll come up right away,' said Queenie.

'Thanks,' said George, and his head disappeared.

'What's he after?' asked the switchboard girl.

'Probably wants to know if Queenie's read any good books lately,' said another girl.

'Never you mind,' said Queenie, who hadn't broadcast her problem to all and sundry. Up to George's office she went, George preceding her. In the office he turned to her, coughed again and addressed her from the back of his tonsils.

'Um, Miss Richards, Mr Adams has had a word with you, hasn't he?'

'Several,' said Queenie. 'Mr Porter, have you got a sore throat?'

'Er, no, just a frog.'

'Well, anyway, I can tell you Mr Adams did speak to me. He told me you're going to follow the man that's following me. He's a bad dream, that bloke is.' Queenie warmed to her exposition. 'He's behind me every evening, every time I leave work, haunting me like a shadow. Mr

Porter, you sure you can cope with a creep like him? I mean, suppose he turns on you for following him all the way to me home? You could get wounded.'

George, looking over the top of her head in case meeting her eyes brought on his shy rash, said, 'Oh, Mr Adams and I touched on that point, but it'll be no problem. Well, if he uses his fists, you see, they'll bounce off me.'

'What?' said Queenie.

'Oh, it's the way I'm built,' said George, at which Queenie emitted an involuntary giggle.

'Crikey, you made a funny,' she said.

'Did I?' said George, honest face expressive of earnestness rather than comedy. 'Well, anyway, I told Mr Adams I'd have a word with you before we left, to confirm I'd be keeping you and this bloke in sight all the way. And I'll do my best to warn him off you for good.' George glanced at the ceiling, eyeing it critically. 'It's not right.'

'The ceiling?' said Queenie. 'What's wrong with it? It's not going to fall on us, is it?'

'No,' said George. 'Well, I hope not. What I meant was that it's a shame that a – er – well, a nice girl like you is having to put up with a man like him. I'll do my very best to boot him out of your life.'

'Well, I wish you luck,' said Queenie, 'I need someone to help me get rid of him somehow, so thanks for offering. You're sure you'll be able to cope?' The dubious factor was still present.

George Porter might be willing, but he just didn't look – well, aggressive enough, even if he was a bit large.

'Leave it to me,' said George, and finally met her eyes. Queenie gave him an encouraging smile.

George turned faintly pink, which wasn't what happened to the tough cops and robbers he read about in American novels.

'Eh?' said Sammy. There were twenty minutes to go before the working day came to an end, and he was in Boots's office. They'd been discussing the firm's retail shops and the advisability of refurbishing them, in keeping with the improving economy. Then Boots had mentioned something concerning Queenie Richards and George Porter. 'Eh?'

'I don't think Queenie wants too many people to know about it,' said Boots, 'but I thought I'd put you in the picture, Sammy.'

'What, in case our one and only high-class costing genius gets his legs broken?' said Sammy. 'Frankly, I ain't in favour of him ending up in hospital, but if he does you'd better find out what kind of flowers he likes, and if the visiting hours suit you.'

'It won't be like that, Sammy.'

'You can say that with feeling, can you?' said Sammy. 'Wouldn't it be better to hire Joe Applegate for the job?' Joe Applegate,

Camberwell-born, was an up-and-coming heavy-weight boxer. 'George Porter's not the right type. He reads books and does crosswords. What makes you think he can see off the kind of bloke Queenie's getting stuck with?'

'Just my instinct,' said Boots.

Sammy groaned.

'Here, give over,' he said, 'that's the first time I've ever heard you talk like a woman. You're not telling me you've got their complaint, are you?'

'Intuition, you mean?' said Boots. 'No, no intuition, Sammy, just a feeling that George could surprise you, me and himself. And Queenie.'

'Well, if George gets damaged and needs to sue somebody, it won't be me,' said Sammy. He used a pencil in his hand to comb his hair. 'Still,' he said, 'something's got to be done to help Queenie get rid of her problem.'

66

Chapter Six

He emerged from nowhere, the lean, lanky man in the peaked cap and grey raincoat. One moment he wasn't there, or so it seemed to George, and the next second he was boarding the bus in the wake of four other people, the first of whom was Queenie. With the peak of his cap turned down, and the collar of his raincoat turned up, he had a shifty appearance, and George decided to file him in his mind as Shifty Stan.

The time was twenty to six, the evening mild and light, and George, noting everything, advanced towards the bus stop on the north side of Camberwell Green junction. Not so long ago, the junction would have been busy with trams as well as buses, but successive Ministers of Transport had overseen the elimination of the former and of tramlines too. The idea was to clear the way for increasing motorized traffic.

Tram drivers and conductors had had only one collective comment to make.

'They'll be sorry, you'll see.'

Reaching the bus, George boarded. Shifty Stan had gone upstairs. George glimpsed Queenie in a seat on the lower deck, her back to him. He climbed to the upper deck, and there he was, the creep, sitting next to a window, chin buried in his raincoat, peak of his cap hiding his eyes. It didn't take a Sherlock Holmes to conclude he was obviously opposed to being recognized by any-one except his own mother. And perhaps not even her, thought George, as he sat down behind him.

After a while, the conductor came up to collect fares. George asked for a ticket to the Elephant and Castle. Shifty Stan asked for the same, in flat middle-class tones. From the look of him when he boarded the bus, he was a six-footer. But he was also shabby-looking.

George, five feet eleven himself, reflected.

It was no wonder, he thought, that with a shifty character like this tailing her, Queenie Richards was having bad dreams. Damn shame. She's a nice girl, and pretty. Pity I can't bring myself to ask her for a date. Not that I'd get any joy, I know she thinks I'm what's called a stout party. Girls don't fancy stout parties. They don't see them as romantic. Now if I were built more like Mike Finnegan, Chicago cop, I'd be a lot more eligible. I suppose I ought to be thankful that I don't have a fat face or a double chin. Oh, well, there's always a good book from the Walworth public library or snooker at the working men's club.

But he inwardly sighed as the bus entered Walworth Road. Library books and snooker represented entertainment, but had nothing to do with real life.

The bus travelled on. Shifty Stan didn't move. He kept his gaze on the passing scene.

Downstairs, Queenie fidgeted a bit, wondering what was going to happen when she alighted at her stop.

After making one of his frequent brotherly calls on his widowed sister, Lizzy, Boots had just arrived home in his car. Gemma and James were doing their school homework in their respective rooms. As always, they had enjoyed a lively debate about the benefits of completing the chore either before or after supper. Before was best. It got rid of it and gave them the whole evening free. But leaving it until after was always tempting. This evening they had decided to knuckle down before the meal, so in the relative quietness of the living room Boots poured Polly a gin and tonic, and a whisky for himself. It was their evening reunion drinks time. Polly received hers as graciously as well-brought-up royalty in an amiable mood.

'Thanks, old lad.'

'You're welcome,' said Boots, and acquainted her with the story of Queenie and her unhealthy specimen, and how he had recommended George Porter as the right kind of candidate for seeing the bloke off.

'George Porter?' said Polly, knees curled up on the living-room settee. 'Isn't he that rather portly chap who looks into the costs of contracts? I think I met him on the day everyone celebrated the opening of your staff canteen.'

'That's the bloke,' said Boots, 'but he's large, not portly. Portly suggests a fat stomach.'

'Well, isn't that what the dear old lad has?' said Polly.

'It's all muscle,' said Boots.

'Does Queenie know that?'

'She's pretty sure he's simply fat,' said Boots. 'But she needs a man to help her get rid of her follower and I'm betting on George. He'll be all the better for adventuring himself instead of reading one more book.'

'You old fraud, you're throwing him at Queenie,' said Polly, eyes bright with amusement.

'Not intentionally,' said Boots. 'First and foremost I'm putting him on the heels of a nasty piece of male decrepitude in the hope that he'll flatten him.'

'Well,' said Polly, 'let's hope you're right and that George Porter will prove to be Queenie's Galahad. Isn't Queenie an imaginative name? It always makes me think of happy Hampstead, funfair rides and gypsy caravans on August Bank

Holiday. Now if my name could put you in mind of something equally exhilarating, I'd feel my baptism would have been well worthwhile.'

'Try to settle for putting me in mind of the wild and woolly Twenties,' said Boots. 'And the Charleston.'

'The Charleston?' said Polly. 'I'll settle for that, old soldier.'

'By the way,' said Boots, 'if you can manage to be at the offices by nine thirty tomorrow morning, Sammy will drive you, Rosie and Rachel to the winter fashion show somewhere in the wilds of Mayfair. You did want to go, I believe?'

'Quite right,' said Polly. 'Consider yourself an asset for arranging it.'

The bus was at the Elephant and Castle stop, and Queenie was following other passengers off the vehicle. On the upper deck, George was dawdling in his seat, waiting for Shifty Stan to stand up. The man did so, his turned-up coat collar and his turned-down peaked cap making him look like the caricature of a gangster on his way to tommy-gun a rival, while having already paid for a funeral wreath to show there were no real hard feelings. Well, that was the image George conjured up in his enjoyment of American gangster novels. He'd very much liked the one called *No Orchids for Miss Blandish*, although it left him feeling sorry for the lady. But right now it also strengthened his resolve to help

Queenie Richards escape any eventuality that was on a par with a fate worse than death.

Shifty Stan was descending. George came up out of his seat and followed. He wondered what was happening to himself. He felt unusually energized. Of course, yes, his adrenalin was high. He waited a moment while Shifty Stan alighted, then followed him off the bus. Shifty Stan peered from under his cap. Queenie, at a distance, was heading for Hampton Street and home. Shifty Stan began to follow. And George, after hanging back for a few seconds, began to tread in his footsteps.

Queenie, looking attractive in a light raincoat, stopped and turned. Shifty Stan at once halted and put himself close to a shop window. He studied the display like a man deeply interested in what was on offer, which on his part looked a bit odd to say the least, since they were mostly items of ladies' maternity wear.

George, pulling up amid a bustle of pedestrians, permitted himself a little grin, then took note of the challenging stare Queenie was directing at the geezer. He, affecting unawareness of her, continued, apparently, to admire a smock designed for a very expectant mother. What is he besides being a curse, thought George, an expectant father window-shopping on behalf of his wife? Not much he is, I bet.

Queenie, spotting George in the background, showed a brief smile of recognition, then turned about and continued on her way to Hampton Street. Shifty Stan, ceasing to interest himself in garments for pregnant ladies, resumed the pursuit. In a while, Queenie turned into Hampton Street. Shifty Stan followed, at a distance. George kept going, also at a distance. Queenie quickened her pace a little. Shifty Stan followed suit, his long and lean-shanked figure moving noiselessly. Rubber soles, thought George. Probably more psychologically frightening to the object of his pursuit than noisy hobnails.

Suddenly, the man took a look over his shoulder, and George wondered how he liked having someone at his back while he himself was at Queenie's back. Sauce for the goose.

Queenie turned towards her front door. She cast a look back as she fumbled in her handbag for her doorkey. The unpleasant character, peaked cap pulled further down and chin sunk deeper into raincoat collar, came straight on, at which point George, having accelerated, was right on his tail. Queenie, buoyed up by this, found enough courage to fling words at the approaching nightmare.

'You're sick, d'you know that? You ought to be locked up!'

There was no response. The man kept moving, and would have walked straight past her had it not been for a sudden obstacle in the shape of a large fellow who had cut in front of him. He had to stop, and did so, then made to sidestep

George. George went with the sidestep to prevent being passed, moving with an agility that surprised the watching Queenie. He planted himself as obstructively as an armour-plated tank in the way of Shifty Stan. Dark eyes, dark-rimmed, glared from under the peaked cap, and a shadowed mouth issued words.

'You're in my way.'

'Never mind that,' said George, 'just give me your name and address. I need to report you. You're a danger to this young lady.'

Queenie looked on with wide eyes. There was her nightmare in his peaked cap and high-collared raincoat, looking like George Raft having a bad day. And there was the other George, George Porter from the upstairs offices, in a very respectable grey suit and no titfer at all. Well, he did have a good head of hair. She listened to more words from the horrid fellow, words underlined by little vibrations, and by a good education.

'If you don't move yourself at once, Archibald, I'll punch a bloody great hole in your fat belly.'

Athough he regretted the demeaning reference to his stomach in Queenie's hearing, George wasn't worried by the threat. While the bloke was an inch taller, he didn't have any real weight to speak of. Still, best to be ready for action. George poised himself on the balls of his feet.

'I want your name and address, and your

reason for following this young lady home every evening,' he said.

The dark-rimmed eyes glared some more, and the shadowed mouth moved again.

'I really have no idea what you're talking about, so kindly stop standing on my feet, will you? Anyway, who the devil are you?'

'Her brother.'

'Really?' Shifty Stan, now mentally renamed Shifty Cecil by George, looked around, as if hoping assistance was somewhere in the offing in the form of a twin brother. But Hampton Street was quiet at the moment. 'I'm losing patience with you.'

'Listen, deadhead, if you don't give me your name and address, with proof that they're genuine, I'm going to have to take you through the house to my sister's back yard and change the shape of your face,' said George, and Queenie, still looking on, could hardly believe her ears. She had no idea that the kind of books George read were those that combined action with gangster-style dialogue. 'You hear me, you punk?'

Crikey, thought Queenie, talk about looks deceiving a girl. Who'd have thought George Porter could stand up to a creep and talk to him like that?

The creep suddenly lashed out. His balled fist landed smack in the middle of George's stomach.

'How d'you like your hot chestnuts, mmm?' he

hissed, and landed another one. 'How d'you like a second helping?'

'Not much,' said George, tough stomach hardly quivering, and he yanked the bloke's coat collar down, exposing his mouth and chin. Then he bashed him an all-time thump in the jaw. In front of Queenie's astonished eyes, the bloke staggered and fell. From the ground he coughed up obscene swear words. 'Shut up,' said George, kicking him in the ribs, 'there's a lady present.'

'Lor', you're not going to kill him, are you?' gasped Queenie.

'I'm going to have a go at that while it's all quiet and he's floored,' said George. 'If you could run indoors and fetch me a mallet, it'll only take me a couple of secs to make sure he never bothers you again.'

Shifty Cecil stopped groaning and swearing.

'You interfering swine, I'll kill you,' he hissed and was up on his feet in one bound, just like Tarzan. He flung himself at George. George simply used his large frame as a buffer, and then as a weapon. His body heaved and Shifty Cecil bounced off it and landed on his back again. He emitted obscenity and spittle.

'Now listen, punk,' said George, 'you're a dead 'un. Say a prayer and tell your mother goodbye before I dump you in the trash can.'

But the man, despite pain, was up again, and away he went, careering like a long bundle of straw before the wind.

'I don't believe it,' gasped Queenie.

'No problem,' said George.

'Crikey, you're a surprise packet, you are,' said Queenie, and looked up at him out of bright, admiring eyes. George coughed and turned slightly pink.

'Um, I don't think you'll see him again, Miss Richards,' he said.

'Well, thanks a million and more,' breathed Queenie.

'Well, er – it's been a crying shame having a man like that, a sick Shifty Cecil, dogging a – well, a nice girl like you,' said George, looking over the top of her head. 'I mean, well – you're – '

'Queenie?' The front door of the house had opened, and Queenie's mother was there. 'What's going on?'

'Oh, I'll tell you in a bit, Mum,' said Queenie, 'except you'll never believe it. I'll just speak to me office friend, George Porter, first. Thanks ever so,' she said to him, 'it just shows how right Mr Adams was when he said he thought you'd cope easy.' Queenie realized her boss had also been right when he'd said George was large, not fat. 'Yes, thanks ever so.'

'Only too pleased,' said George, and off he went before his shyness made him fall over his feet. Queenie called after him.

'See you at the offices tomorrow.'

Once she'd given her mother details of the amazing incident, her mother asked her why she hadn't invited Mr Porter in, so that she could thank him herself and offer him a cup of tea.

'I expect he'd of liked a nice cup of hot tea.'

'Well, he just went before I could ask him,' said Queenie, 'and, anyway, he's sort of quiet and retiring, and a bit shy as well.'

'A bit shy and quiet? After what he did to that horrible man?'

'I mean he doesn't socialize,' said Queenie, 'he reads books.'

'Well, you could read a few more yourself instead of all that gallivanting you get up to in Brixton on Saturday evenings,' said Mrs Richards.

'Crikey, Mum, a girl's got to do a bit of living while she's young,' said Queenie, 'or she'd never find the right kind of feller. I bet Mrs Adams didn't sit around reading books when she was young, or she'd never have met Mr Adams.'

'Mrs Adams? Who's she?'

'Me boss's wife, of course,' said Queenie. She reflected. 'D'you know, Mum, I'm never going to believe the way George Porter set about that creep. Crikey, you should've seen the wallop he landed.'

'Well, I'm only glad there weren't no neighbours about,' said Mrs Richards. 'I don't like punch-ups going on outside our front door. It's not respectable.'

* * *

As soon as Boots arrived for work the following morning, Queenie knocked on his door.

'Come in,' said Boots, and Queenie almost catapulted her pretty plumpness into his office.

'Oh, good morning, Mr Adams, what d'you think, you'll never believe it and I still don't know if I believe it meself, only yesterday evening when Mr Porter from upstairs—'

'Calm down, Queenie, I'm not going anywhere,' said Boots.

Queenie drew a breath and then, as evenly as she could, she described in detail what had happened yesterday evening. The telling flowed along, but of course, every now and again she couldn't help interrupting herself with interjections such as, 'Crikey, I couldn't believe me eyes,' or, 'Honest, I couldn't believe me ears, either.'

At the end, when she still sounded as if she had dreamt it all, Boots congratulated her on now being free of the obnoxious fellow, and said that he'd let George know he was much obliged to him. Queenie said she was the one who was much obliged.

'Well, so am I, Queenie,' smiled Boots, 'I don't favour losing my shorthand typist to a character with a sick mind.'

Queenie said George called the bloke Shifty Cecil because he was quite well spoken. Boots said that men who followed women about weren't confined to one class, and Queenie said well,

George Porter did for this one good and proper.

'D'you think I ought to show me gratitude in some way?' she enquired.

'I should think that if you've thanked George, he's happy with that,' said Boots. 'Or, of course, you could invite him round to Sunday tea.'

'Oh, go on with you, Mr Adams,' giggled Queenie, and went back to the general office, where for the first time she told the girls about the creep, and then about how George Porter had more or less done him in. Great was the astonishment.

'George Porter?'

'Him from upstairs?'

'The one that reads books?'

'Yes, him,' said Queenie.

'Well, you just can't tell, can you?'

'Mr Adams suggested I might like to invite him round to Sunday tea,' said Queenie.

Shrieks.

Rachel Goodman put her head in.

'Can we have some work out of you girls and not so much chat?' she said.

'Yes, Mrs Goodman.'

Boots, having gone up to George's office, was having a word with him, mostly to the effect that he'd come up trumps and that Queenie Richards was now a highly relieved and thankful young lady.

'Oh, no problem, Mr Adams,' said George, 'it all worked out as you and I thought it might.'

'I understand the man was quite well spoken,' said Boots.

'He was, yes, a real Shifty Cecil,' said George.

'And no less of a menace to young women,' said Boots. 'Anyway, I'm much obliged to you, and so is Queenie.'

'Well – er – she's a nice girl,' said George.

'Yes, very nice,' said Boots.

Chapter Seven

Sammy left his office at twenty to ten to drive up to Mayfair. With him were Polly, Rachel and Rosie, all of whom were looking forward to the viewing of what fashion designers had in mind for winter wear. London shows were not as internationally acclaimed as those in Paris, Milan or New York. Paris and Milan were where the cream of designers worked. And New York was favoured because that was where the real lolly existed: in the big stores and in the bank accounts of millionaires' wives, the kind who admitted to and indulged an incurable love for new fashions. Exclusive new fashions. London, however, was at least beginning to make a mark.

Adams Fashions had a place in today's show, and that was Sammy's major interest. His designer would be there. And he was sure Polly, Rachel and Rosie would enjoy the event and the atmosphere. He looked forward to the resultant publicity, and the possibility that Adams Fashions might get a mention.

'Out again, sir?' smiled the hotel receptionist, Miss Janice Browning, as she accepted the room key from Mr Rolf Seidler at eleven thirty. Mr Seidler, smartly suited and carrying a briefcase, offered her a smile, and his handsome teeth gleamed moistly, as if freshly minted with toothpaste.

'*Ja*, out again, fräulein – that is, Miss – ah?'

'Miss Browning, sir.'

'Browning? Good. I am out now for a few hours.'

'Very good, sir.' And Miss Browning put the key on its hook and watched the German gentleman as he strode towards the hotel's revolving door.

What a fine body he had for a man of forty-one. She had noted his date of birth in his passport. Forty-one was a good age for a man. A man was nicely mature by then, a woman worried about being on her way to fifty.

Oh, dear – look at that. In the athletic quickness of his movements as he exited from the revolving door, Mr Seidler had bumped into a sturdy passer-by and bowled him over. In obvious concern and apology, he at once bent over the unfortunate gentleman and brought him back on his feet as easily as if he had been no more than a small boy. He dusted him down, talking to him and obviously saying how sorry he was. The offended gentleman went on his way mollified.

Miss Browning thought that if Mr Seidler had served in the German army, he would have been a much more honourable and considerate soldier than any of those SS thugs who had turned concentration camps into murder depots. The sadistic brutality of such men had sickened the whole world. Mr Seidler looked far too wholesome to be of that kind. He'd said he was in the engineering business, and had come to London to secure contracts.

In fact, Rolf Seidler, otherwise Ernst Thurber, otherwise the Wolf, was *en route* to an address in Clapham, where a contact was of more importance to him than any contract.

At the Mayfair Gallery, the display of fashion collections was in full swing, the salon packed with international writers, journalists, friends of the designers, social celebrities and specially invited guests. Polly, Rachel and Rosie had all been enjoying the show given by hip-swaying models on the catwalk. Polly, of course, could remember the times when these were known as mannequins, and were somewhat haughty and remote.

Sammy was behind the scenes, along with his hired models, his designer and dresser. What had aroused the main interest so far had been the winter party wear, mostly based on improved versions of what had taken the eye in the spring fashion shows, the Trapeze and Sack looks, both originating in Paris. France, however, had sent none of its designers to attend in person. The French were a bit toffee-nosed about London as a fashion centre. And besides, General de Gaulle, the French Prime Minister, wasn't on very friendly terms with the British. He was still carrying the wounds of imagined wartime slights, although Churchill had backed him all through his tetchy relationship with Roosevelt and the Americans.

However, the British designers had come up with their own ideas for winter party wear. Polly and Rachel both thought these outfits attractive, although theirs was the approval of women who had a natural interest in fashion, while recognizing that very little was ever designed for the over-forties. It was Rachel's complaint that the Sack and the Trapeze, like the earlier New Look, only suited tall and slim young women. Though of reasonable height, even as a young woman she had never been slim. On the other hand, nor had she ever been fat. The Scots would have found the right word for her. Bonny.

Adams Fashions received a murmur of appreciation for a party frock based on a shirt-waisted style, the skirt crisply flared by means of a sewn-in, stiffened petticoat. The murmur was not unanimous, but it was enough to make the day for Sammy and Elizabeth Ames, his designer. In any case, loud applause was rarely heard at any fashion show.

The whole event imploded, however, ten minutes into the eagerly anticipated display of outdoor winter wear. A model glided onto the catwalk wearing a gloriously lush coat of sable fur, with matching hat. Both coat and hat represented a triumph of sleek dark brown that gleamed under the lights. It was then that a young woman in a back row stood up, reached into her capacious shoulder bag, brought out a tomato and flung it at the model. And she followed that with an egg, and another tomato, accompanying each missile with a shouted war cry.

'Criminals! How would you like to be skinned and turned into overcoats?'

Both tomatoes and the egg hit their target. The sable coat, splashed with raw tomato and raw egg, looked ruined. The model herself was cowering, hands over her face in frightened defence of her make-up.

Hysteria broke out, lady journalists and fashion connoisseurs jumping up and immediately getting in each other's way amid the MC's pleas for order. Nothing like this had ever happened before. True, at one show a few years ago, a tipsy cockney woman had somehow invaded the proceedings to loudly offer the sum of fourpence-'apenny for a mink stole she fancied for her cat's basket. But eggs and tomatoes? And war cries? One more tomato, aimed at random, struck a prominent lady journalist. It made a shocking mess of her bodice, and just where she was mainly

86

prominent. The sight of the bright red stain, spreading, induced panic in other ladies, all of whom were naturally dressed in their most fashionable outfits.

Yet another flung tomato, another war cry.

'Criminals! Go on, run! Do you ever think of innocent animals trying to escape fur trappers?'

Polly, Rachel and Rosie had retreated to the far side of the salon, while Sammy, appearing from behind stage, eyed the spectacle like a man seeing his richly endowed wallet disappearing down a drainhole. Amid scrambling, pushing bedlam, the MC was begging the warlike young woman to give up her struggle, but she kept chucking tomatoes. Sammy uttered a characteristic one-liner.

'Oh, me Gawd, who let her out of her loony bin?'

It had never been known, a public protest against the wearing of fur. Certainly, no-one present knew of any active anti-fur organization. This shambles was the work of one dotty female, as far as Sammy was concerned. And some clever photographer was capturing the scenes for the press. He was momentarily put off by a tomato that struck him in the mouth. He ate what was necessary to get the best part of it out of the way, then resumed his camerawork.

One more war cry.

'Criminals! Animal torturers! You'll all—'

Crash. She was bowled over by a swarm of people rushing for exits. Trodden on, run over and suffering similar torments, she nevertheless refused to be silenced, even if she sounded a bit hoarse and breathless.

'That's it, run.' Gasp. 'Run for your lives.' Gasp. 'I'm after you.' Gasp. 'And one day—' Gasp. 'One day I'll bring a whole army to fight the cause.' Gasp. 'One day.'

'Try putting a sock in it,' bawled a young man of otherwise good breeding, and he ran over her on his way out. What missiles were left in her shoulder bag were rendered unflingable.

'Idiots! Call the police!' shouted the representative of a well-known fashion house.

Someone did, but by the time two uniformed men arrived, the warlike young woman had long disappeared. The show, totally ruined, was about to make the kind of headlines not normally associated with fashion. A sad clearing-up process was taking place, and Sammy was among a number of people conducting a garbled inquest on the unfortunate events. The main point centred around the absurdity of anyone objecting to the wearing of furs. Furs had kept people warm since the days of cavemen. That loud and interfering young woman was a case for a psychiatrist, and the sooner her doctor took her to one, the better for her state of mind. Et cetera, et cetera.

Sammy pulled out of the noisy group after a while. He had never been keen on any kind of get-together in which everyone talked at once. Family gatherings, well, they were different, but business people ought to know better, even allowing for the fact that in the fashion world some people were a bit temperamental.

So, accepting that the day was a ruined one, he left the gallery in company with Polly, Rosie and Rachel. All three were free of egg or tomato stains. Wisely, they had kept well out of the way.

Outside the gallery was a mob of people, all of whom wanted to know more about how the fashion show had been sabotaged. Mayfair wasn't used to mobs – they were uncivilized and kept wealthy visitors away, beside making the place look untidy. A uniformed policeman was trying to clear the pavement without getting much co-operation. Neither Sammy nor any of his ladies were prepared to stop and hand out information. Resolutely, they pushed their way through, ignoring shouted questions.

'Here, did she have a bomb ready to throw?'

'It wasn't just rotten cabbages, was it?'

'Any hospital cases?'

'Who put her knickers in a twist?'

'Was she a Chinese commie?'

'Now, come along, sir, come along, madam, move aside – clear the pavement – it's against the law to cause an obstruction.' This from the constable.

Sammy and the other three got clear and went walking in the direction of their transport, Sammy's car.

'Extraordinary,' said Polly.

'The young Boadicea, you mean?' said Rosie.

'Her behaviour,' said Polly.

'She loves brown bears, I suppose,' said Rachel.

'I wouldn't advise her to cuddle one,' said Sammy, his mood on a par with the grey, cloudy day. He knew there'd be nothing in the news about the fashions. The press, radio and television would all concentrate on the potty female and her eggs and tomatoes. That would almost certainly mean the Adams party frock sinking without trace. 'Brown bears don't—'

'Hi! You, you criminal!' Springing out of a shop doorway, she was there, in front of him. Her hair was a mess, her sweater loose and baggy, her shoulder bag swinging in her hand by its strap. 'You were in there, I know it!' The light in her eyes was as fiery as her battlecry of 'Gotcha!' Vibrating with rage, she did her best to clout Sammy with her shoulder bag, swinging it full circle. Sammy ducked it first time round, and caught it with his hand on its next flight.

Passers-by stopped to stare disbelievingly. In Mayfair, no-one, simply no-one, ever tried to bash anyone outside a shop. Or alighting from a Rolls. It just didn't happen.

'Go home,' said Sammy.

'Let go!' The young woman tugged at the bag.

'Go home,' repeated Sammy. The tugging became frenzied. So he let go. The anti-fur female and her bag fell back into a collection of startled shoppers, some of whom uttered plaintive cries of upper-class embarrassment.

'Oh, I say. Really.'

This was followed by a collective withdrawal, and the young woman, flailing helplessly as she lost the support of bodies, sank to the ground. From there she might have been overcome by discomfiture, but no, not a bit of it. After yelling abuse, she spotted that one of the retreating shoppers was a woman who had elected on this cool day to wear a russet-coloured autumn coat with a black fur collar. A very misguided choice, because it brought the saboteur scrambling to her feet to launch a fresh assault, unaware of an approaching constable.

'Let's beat it,' said Sammy, 'Loopy Lou's heading for trouble.' And off he went, with Polly, Rachel and Rosie keeping him company. They didn't stop until they reached the car, when Rosie made a comment.

'That was no Loopy Lou, Sammy, that was Hannibal Alsop,' she said.

'Who?' they all asked simultaneously.

'Hannibal Alsop,' said Rosie. 'I had a feeling about her, and the penny dropped, Sammy, when she was trying to knock your head off with her bag. I recognized her then from having seen her in newspaper photographs.'

'Tell me more,' said Sammy. The four of them were gathered around his parked car in Grosvenor Square.

'Tell us all more,' said Polly, amused by everything rather than shocked. She was quite sure Sammy and his designer would quickly recover from the shambolic event. 'Exactly who is Hannibal Alsop?'

'She made the front pages of newspapers about three months ago,' said Rosie. 'Don't any of you remember? Her real name is Marjorie Alsop, but some newspaper sub-editor called her Hannibal Alsop because she tried to ride an elephant out of the Zoo and into battle.'

'Into battle?' said Sammy.

'Yes,' said Rosie. 'After Zoo staff had managed to get her off the animal, she explained that she intended to help it battle for its right to be free, if only she could get someone to ship it back to Africa. Any volunteers were to get in touch with her, Marjorie Alsop of Twickenham. So up popped the witty sub-editor and nicknamed her Hannibal Alsop.'

'I should remember that?' said Rachel. 'Well, now you mention it, Rosie, so I do. But I can't remember what she looked like in those newspaper photographs.'

'Myself,' said Polly, 'I can remember what the elephant looked like. Big.'

'I don't remember anything except flying tomatoes,' said Sammy. 'And as I've never had much to do with elephants, and I'm up to me eyebrows with Hannibal Alsop, let's go home.'

The window of the study on the first floor of a house in The Avenue overlooked Clapham Common from the south-west. Accordingly, the view was one of green and open space, very much to be coveted in an area of London as heavily populated as Clapham. Clapham, however, did have more than its well-known common to make it distinctive. Along with its swarm of working-class streets, it boasted handsome residential thoroughfares for middle-class families. The Avenue itself was one such.

In the study, the houseowner, a political commentator for a radio service broadcasting to overseas listeners, shook hands with his visitor.

'I've been expecting you,' he said.

'So? Well, I'm here now.'

'How have you been?'

'I've survived ten years of revenge inflicted by the Allies, the revenge of the victors over the losers. Another Versailles, but of a different kind. Along with many other comrades, I was made an imprisoned victim.'

'You don't look like a victim, you look remarkably fit and healthy.'

'I never gave in to depression, always I exercised, always I refused to hang my head. And since my release, I have eaten good food and drunk good German beer.'

The dialogue was in German. The visitor spoke with the broad accent of a Berliner, the houseowner with the acquired perfection of an excellent linguist.

'Isn't good food, good German beer, and your freedom, enough for you?'

'It might be enough for some SS men after ten years, but not for all, not for me. I lost my brother to torture inflicted by the English. Someone will pay for that. You're lucky, you escaped with Romanian documents.'

'I am Romanian, and the documents confirmed my story that I was one of the leaders of Romanian resistance to Hitler.'

'Some documents, I believe, were very useful. I was unable to get hold of any of that kind myself, but then in doing my duty, in obeying my officers, why should I have thought I needed any? It's a very peculiar world when a man can be imprisoned for doing his duty. However – ' The Wolf made a dismissive gesture. 'However, that's in the past. I'm only concerned now with avenging my brother's death. Do you have the information I want? I was told you had ways and means of getting hold of it.'

'It hasn't been easy,' said the man who was useful to the World Radio Service, due to his expertise on those nations of Central Europe now under the control of the Soviet Union. 'I have friends, of course, but have to be careful about what favours I might ask for. I don't wish to give any cause to be investigated.'

'Well, I believe you're still helpful to my excomrades' organization. Are you now going to be helpful to me?'

'I have the man's name—'

'I have that myself. I had it before I came here. What I need from you is any place where I can find him.'

'Don't rush me.'

'Rush you?' The Wolf smiled. It was not the same kind of smile with which Miss Janice Browning had been favoured. No, directed towards the Romanian, it featured teeth that implied ravening hunger. 'Consider yourself lucky I'm not in a position to hurry you up by breaking your leg.'

The Romanian was not intimidated.

'Come out of the old world, my friend,' he said. 'Forget your imprisonment, avenge your brother if you must, and then go back to West Berlin and the existing world. For you and for me, and for others like us, the swastika is dead, along with the Führer. Don't be silly enough to threaten me. Now, before you interrupted me I was about to say that as well as having the man's name, I expect within a week to be able to supply you with his home address. We have someone who, given time, will have access to British army regimental records. He's now manoeuvring to do just that.'

'So. Good. But don't lecture me.'

'Don't ask for it. And don't call again. Wait to hear from me.'

Chapter Eight

Only five minutes after Sammy and the other
three returned to the offices, everyone in the
building knew that the Adams winter fashion
collection, along with others, had been sent
up the spout by some loopy female who liked
elephants as well as teddy bears. It was rumoured
that Mr Sammy was so upset he might well
require a drop of what old Mother Riley always
fancied.

'Old Mother Riley, who's she?' asked a naive
girl in the invoice department. 'I mean, what did
she always fancy?'

'Gin or whisky,' said an informative colleague.

'Ugh, didn't she know about Coca-Cola?'

Boots commiserated with Sammy and the
ladies. But things could have been worse, of
course, he said. Sammy asked how much worse?

'She could have thrown fried tomatoes,' said
Boots. 'They're even messier than fresh ones.'

'Boo to you, that's out of order,' said Rosie.

'Yes, now is definitely not the time for painful

funnies,' said Polly. 'I've a personal suspicion there'll come a winter day when Hannibal Alsop will catch me wearing my fur coat. Ye gods, girls, if I don't duck in time, I'll get a faceful of something like a dog's dinner or cold rice pudding.'

'Look on the bright side,' said Boots, 'some specialists in white coats may have her locked up by then.'

Gloomily, Sammy said, 'Too late, she's already done her damage.'

'It won't happen again,' said Rachel.

'Once is enough for Fleet Street and the BBC,' said Sammy. 'They'll make a hero out of Mad Marj and I'll bet there'll be cartoons of her riding an elephant over the flattened corpse of fashion.' He growled. 'And I daresay the corpse will be covered with squashed tomatoes. I think I'll end up with a complex.'

'Not you, Sammy,' said Rachel.

'Yes, me,' said Sammy, 'I'll end up not being able to look any kind of tomato in the face for the rest of me life. And listen, don't anybody give me an elephant for Christmas.'

'Noted, Sammy old scout,' said Polly. 'Will anybody mind if I push off home now?'

'I must go too,' said Rosie. 'I'll give you a lift, Polly.'

'Accepted with pleasure, ducky,' said Polly, whose relationship with Rosie was unbreakably chummy. 'I'll see you later, Boots old love.'

'Whatever Flossie's cooking up for supper,' said Boots, 'I imagine you'll ask her very nicely to keep tomatoes off the menu.'

'Too true,' said Polly. 'For the next fortnight I'll be tortured by a horrid memory of loopy Hannibal flinging them here, there and everywhere.'

'Understood,' smiled Boots. 'But I hope it won't hurt to tell you that for those of us who didn't attend the show, everything here remained civilized.' The offices hummed murmurously to the sound of its busy bees storing honey for Sammy's balance sheets, which might be soothing to his ears when he came to. For the moment, however, his gloom was all too apparent. 'Try an aspirin, Sammy.'

'Ta muchly for nothing,' said Sammy.

He was right about the coverage of the event. That evening, BBC television featured the fracas, and there were also interviews with the young woman saboteur. However, in chivalrous fashion, any reference to her nickname of Hannibal Alsop was omitted, but flashbacks were included to the time when she attempted to free an elephant from the London Zoo.

Much was made by both TV and radio of her one-woman anti-fur campaign, and her declaration that she would eventually raise an army of supporters was emphasized. Interviews with members of the public, in Mayfair and elsewhere, revealed varying opinions.

'Well, really, Miss Alsop is a little round the twist, isn't she, poor dear?'

'I must confess I can see her point of view. Furry animals are frightfully inoffensive as long as one doesn't get too close to their young.'

'Eh, what? Daft, I call it. Me old man's worked for furriers all his life, and ain't never come across no complaints from giraffes or lions or suchlike.'

'Good luck to her, I say. It's about time all them lords and ladies come down to wearing what us workers wear, overcoats that ain't off the backs of polar bears. And what's wrong with woolly long johns if they've got cold bottoms? Yes, all right, I know wool comes off the backs of sheep, but only when they give 'em an overdue haircut.'

Alas, as Sammy had forecast, the fashion collections themselves were only mentioned in the context of the act of sabotage.

The treatment of the incident by television and radio was repeated in the following morning's newspapers. It was all front-page stuff, and all about the egg-and-tomato-throwing female. The photographs were striking, and editorial comments on the fur trade and the wearers of fur in his own daily paper were, thought Boots, impartial but ominous.

'Hornets' nest,' he said, showing the front page to Polly.

'Buzz, buzz?' said Polly. 'Oh, yes, I see, and

there's the champion of cows and beavers herself.'

'Listen, Dad,' said James, 'is there some way we can stop Gemma telling everyone in Dulwich that the family firm got caught up in yesterday's tomato bash?'

'I'm not going to tell everyone, just my best friends,' said Gemma.

'If you only tell Jessie Upchurch, that's as good as everyone,' said James. 'Then they'll all be on our doorstep by tomorrow, asking Mum if she's got any furs she'd like to get rid of for people in need, like Eskimos. Anyway, leave it to you, Dad, to cope with everyone, unless you lock Gemma up. I'm off to chemistry now. So long, folks.'

'Here, wait for me,' said Gemma, and they both got up from the breakfast table, and were on their way to the day's classes a minute later.

'There go two young people who really think yesterday was a bit of a lark,' said Polly, frowning at the headlines. 'Which it was in its way,' she added, frown turning into a little smile.

'I don't think Sammy thought so,' said Boots.

'Oh, well, ducky, yesterday may be today's news, but it's tomorrow's back number,' said Polly. 'So if I know Sammy, he won't take too long to recover.'

'As general manager, I'm slightly wounded myself,' said Boots, 'but not having actually been part of the scene, I haven't lost as much blood as Sammy.'

'I'm happy for you, old warrior,' said Polly, 'but feel for Sammy. So when you get to the office, give my regards to his bandages.'

'I said so, Susie,' declared Sammy, at breakfast with his one and only soulmate. 'Didn't I say so?'

'Yes, of course you did, lovey,' responded Susie, still as mellow in spirit as a light and balmy trade breeze. 'Um, what was it you said?'

'That none of the collections would get a mention,' said Sammy, 'and none of 'em did. Look at that.' He smacked a hand on the front page of their daily paper. 'Talk about who put the cat out and landed it in a dogs' home. All that stuff is on a par with a report on a football match full of broken legs. Our designer will cry her eyes out when she sees these headlines. I tell you, Susie, I'm mortified.'

'Buck up, Sammy,' said Susie.

'I don't often get inflicted—'

'Inflicted, Sammy?'

'Yes, with mortification, if I can borrow an educated word from Boots,' said Sammy. 'But it's happened, and I tell you, Susie, I feel seriously injured.'

'Oh, dear,' said Susie.

'Mind, I ain't actually dead,' said Sammy.

'For which we're all grateful,' said Susie.

'Me too,' said Sammy, 'I don't fancy not being able to walk about. The business will have to sit up and fight for any publicity for its winter party frock.'

'We'll go to church on Sunday,' said Susie, 'and sing that hymn, "Fight the Good Fight".'

Chinese Lady could not have offered anything more appropriate, nor laced it with a nicer touch of reverence.

'We'll fight all right,' said Sammy, and added darkly, 'I only hope Marjorie Alsop and her elephants or whatever get stuck with nothing but tomatoes for their Sunday dinners.'

As for the present circumstances of the young woman in question, she had been summoned to appear at a magistrates' court to answer a charge of causing an affray.

'Gee whiz,' exclaimed Mrs Patsy Adams, American wife of Daniel Adams, 'have you seen the front page of your *Daily Mail*?'

'Seen it? I've chopped it,' said Daniel. 'Or at least, I'm going to.' He and Patsy were at the final stage of their breakfast, their children, ten-year-old Arabella and eight-year-old Andrew, out of the house and on their way to school.

'Well, you might as well trash it,' said Patsy, 'it's sticky with marmalade.'

'Unbeknown to me at the time,' said Daniel, 'a smidgen or two slipped off my toast. But my main reason for shoving it in the dustbin is all it says about the Mayfair punch-up and all it doesn't say about the fashions. But there you are,

Patsy, bad news for business is good news for the press.'

'Daniel, I feel for the business, and for you and your pa,' said Patsy, 'but I've got to hand it to the girl for her bravery.'

'Bravery?' said Daniel. 'What's brave about chucking eggs and tomatoes at people?'

'Oh, just the fact of standing up at a classy Mayfair fashion show and doing it, I guess,' said Patsy. 'As for the headlines, well, that's how it goes the world over.'

'One day,' said Daniel, 'one day in about AD 5000, when the world is about to sink below the sea and disappear under mountains of ice, creating the worst news ever, the press and television will enjoy their heyday. They'll only come to when they realize an iceberg's sitting on top of them and freezing their outlets.'

'Think positive, honey,' said Patsy, 'with your help, your pa will soon turn the loss of a write-up into victory. So give him your best shot today. I'll be at my keep-fit classes, trying to make sure I never get to look like a blancmange or jello, which I guess would be kind of antisocial and not likely to earn the respect of one's husband. By the way, sweetie, is the firm thinking of suing Marjorie Alsop?'

'No,' said Daniel, up on his feet, 'just of dropping her into a large hole full of tomato juice.'

*　　*　　*

103

Sammy's nephew Paul, assistant in the property company, had a different kind of breakfast conversation with his wife Lulu. Paul was a typically easy-going Adams, Lulu a modern young woman who, although a wife and the mother of a little girl, four-year-old Sylvia, had no intention of allowing events or circumstances, or her husband, to turn her into a domesticated nobody.

Paul was mostly a listener rather than a participant in the first chapter of the conversation. Lulu was letting him know at lenqth that she was on the side of the young woman saboteur in yesterday's rumpus. It wasn't necessary, in any case, she said, for anyone to wear furs, since conventional overcoats for men and women were perfectly suitable for keeping out the cold. But, of course, she went on, there were always spoilt capitalists who liked to look what they were, filthy rich. Some of them even came down to breakfast in something like a mink negligee or a fur-lined dressing gown, according to their sex. If Marjorie Alsop saw that as next door to criminal, it wasn't surprising. No, affirmed Lulu, simply no-one needed to wear furs outside or inside the home.

'What about Eskimos?' asked Paul, smiling at Sylvia, who was quietly eating her cereal.

'I expect Marjorie Alsop considers they need talking to,' said Lulu, eyes earnest behind her spectacles. 'But if they eat seal meat as a natural part of their diet, their wearing of sealskins could be as acceptable as us making use of the hides off the cows we eat with our Sunday roasts. Anyway, don't ask me to feel sorry for Uncle Sammy being on the wrong end of eggs and tomatoes, because I'm pretty sure Marjorie Alsop is a true Socialist and, let's face it, he's a typical capitalist. Not that he isn't likeable. I'm really quite fond of him, and of your dad too, even if they're both addicted to profit.'

'Lulu love,' said Paul, 'I'm still a Labour voter, but business won't work unless there is a profit.'

'Somehow, some way, I'm going to work out how to eliminate it,' said Lulu.

'Profit?' said Paul.

'For the sake of the workers who don't participate in profit,' said Lulu.

'You'll eliminate business as well,' said Paul.

'No problem,' said Lulu, 'everything will be nationalized.'

'Everything?' said Paul, rising to his feet.

'Everything,' said Lulu, 'including Buckingham Palace.'

'Understood,' said Paul, dropping a kiss on his daughter's curly head. 'I'll let Queen Liz know that on my way to the office. It'll give her time to put her name down for a council flat.'

In her handsome house in Twickenham, Mrs Louise Alsop regarded her daughter Marjorie with an air of resignation. There she was, with a copy of every leading newspaper on the couch beside her. One was in her hands, and she was devouring the contents of its front page.

'Marjorie, you're twenty-six. Has nothing caught your fancy except creatures that squeak or growl in the night?'

'Mother,' said the recent torment of Mayfair, 'look at all these headlines, and remember what a smashing job television news made of the event last night. Aren't you proud of me?'

'Should I be?' Mrs Alsop pointed out that she and Mr Alsop, after Marjorie's success in securing a university degree, had expected more of her than to develop an infatuation with the welfare of animals. Worse was the suggestion that her father should pay for the acquisition of a site that could be turned into an animal farm, especially as there was a hint that this should include a paddock large enough for homeless elephants. Were there such things as homeless elephants? Mrs Alsop put that question now.

'There are stranger things, Mother,' said Marjorie, and pointed out that if she could raise enough support for the cause, this might bring in sufficient contributions to keep the farm going and subsidize a very effective anti-fur campaign. Father, she said, would only need to finance the initial costs.

'He'll be relieved to hear of that possibility,' said Mrs Alsop. 'It might have a calming effect on his bank balance.'

'We must all make some sacrifices,' said Marjorie, still absorbed in her newspaper.

'I've made mine,' said Mrs Alsop, 'I've given up my furs.'

'Shame on you, Mother, that you bought them in the first place,' said Marjorie.

'I can't recall any moments of shame,' said Mrs Alsop. She could, however, she said, recall a day of deep embarrassment when the whole of Twickenham came to know that Marjorie had conducted a demonstration outside an exclusive local ladies' outfitters. That embarrassment was compounded by an incident at the Zoo so ridiculous that Marjorie had earned herself the absurd nickname of Hannibal Alsop. 'Your father and I are having to live with that.'

'I refer you, Mother, to the old and tried adage that sticks and stones may break our bones, but words will never hurt us.'

'Well, they're not hurting you, obviously, but they're making it difficult for your father and me to smile our way around the social circles of Twickenham,' said Mrs Alsop.

'You're a good sort on the whole, Mother, and so's Father,' said Marjorie, and expressed the view that both her parents would survive.

'Thank you,' said Mrs Alsop. She then wanted to know if Marjorie was on the point of giving up all her social activities, including those she had been enjoying with a gentleman by the name of Geoffrey Webber.

'Geoffrey Webber?' said Marjorie, now gobbling up her fifth front page without any loss of appetite. That man, she informed her mother, had turned out to be a first-class cad. He had not only laughed at her enthusiasm for animal welfare, but had suggested she go off to the wilds of Africa and look for Tarzan.

'Tarzan?' said Mrs Alsop.

'Yes,' said Marjorie. 'He suggested I was Tarzan's long-lost Jane.'

'Was Tarzan's Jane long-lost?' asked Mrs Alsop.

'Oh, Mother.'

'How are you going to plead at your court case next week?'

'Not guilty, of course. If the magistrates have any real sense of justice, they'll accept that I drew the whole of London's attention to the despicable criminality of the fur trade.'

A week later, despite her plea, Miss Marjorie Alsop, the one-woman band in favour of letting wild animals keep their coats, was found unarguably responsible for causing an affray, as charged, and fined ten guineas. Alternatively, she could elect for seven days in prison. She chose to pay the fine. Or rather, she chose to let a sympathizer pay it for her. That provided her with more welcome publicity, but caused Sammy Adams of Adams Fashions to gnash his teeth with the frustration of a man who had hoped a special cell at Dartmoor prison could be found for the lady. Susie sympathized. Well, never before in the years of their marriage had she known Sammy to grind his molars and produce the sound of gnashing.

However, she was sure the incident could now take second place to plans for a spring collection. Sammy, she knew, always liked to view the future as a land of promise, and that usually offset drawbacks of the present.

The Wolf had to wait a week, not a few days, before he heard from the man who had once been an officer in Roumania's anti-Semitic, pro-Nazi Iron Guard.

The communication arrived at the hotel by registered post, and was signed for at ten forty by the receptionist, Miss Janice Browning. She herself took it up to Mr Seidler's room.

Knocking, she was invited to enter. She found Mr Seidler in the middle of a change of clothes. He was in shirt and trousers, and buttoning up the shirt. His incomplete attire emphasized his masculinity. Miss Browning was impressed.

'Oh, good morning, Mr Seidler, so sorry to disturb you, but here is a registered letter for you. I have signed for it.'

'A registered letter? That is so?' He took it from her. 'Thank you. Good.'

'I thought you would like to have it at once.'

'Yes. Thank you, Miss Browning.' His smile,

bright and benevolent, poured over her as she left. He closed the door behind her.

He opened the letter and began to read it, looking for the required information. In conveying it in this way, by registered post, his contact was, he acknowledged, indirectly advising him that he was not to call again at the house in Clapham. Well, a man like that, with his wartime pro-Nazi record, would not want anything to jeopardize his comfortable way of life in London, a long-established centre of effete democracy. That could cause a more thorough inspection of his personal papers.

So, was his information satisfactory? Yes. The Wolf realized he now had no need to go to Clapham again. He could set about the task he was here for. He required no help, nor wanted any. It was to be his pleasure alone.

He smiled again, but not in a way Miss Browning would have recognized as benevolent.

Chapter Nine

'Boots, look at this!'

Sammy's entry into his brother's office was dramatic. He waved a sheet of paper at Boots.

'Who's on fire?' asked Boots.

'I am,' said Sammy, 'can't you see the smoke? Take a shufti at that, received in my morning post.' He placed the paper in front of Boots, who noted it was a copy of a printed original.

It was headed 'WOOL OR FUR?' Beneath was the short title, 'WOOF', followed by the information that the Manager and Secretary of this organization was Miss M.J. Alsop. The address, in Twickenham, was given. So was the text.

'To whom it may concern! Beware! We exist to rid the fashion world of furs and to encourage the increased use of wool! We are ready for immediate action! Note that this warning is being sent to all fashion houses! Note too that we intend to raise an army of operatives! Unless you declare your firm to be anti-fur, we caution you to take care! Guard your windows! Guard your outlets! Reactionaries, beware!'

It was signed by M.J. Alsop and had been addressed to Adams Fashions.

'Very pungent,' said Boots.

'You mean it smells?' said Sammy. 'I didn't notice that myself, I was too concerned with me blood pressure.'

'So, then, Sammy, we haven't seen the last of Hannibal Alsop. We can expect one of her supporters, or the determined lady herself, to picket these offices?' Boots suggested.

Sammy did a good impression of an upset music maestro clutching his fevered forehead, while groaning out his suspicion that the Hannibal woman might have the offices, the retail shops and the Bethnal Green factory all picketed at one and the same time. Worse, it might mean having rotten eggs and squishy tomatoes chucked all over staff when they were either arriving or leaving.

'Which would be considerably upsetting, seeing our shops don't cater for posh, fur-buying females. Well, a coat or two with a fur collar, they're among our lines, but nothing like a mink jacket. Nothing calling for rotten eggs and tomatoes, Boots, if you see what I mean.'

'I do see,' said Boots. 'But if Mad Marj can find enough recruits to picket every dress shop, every garment factory and every fashion house in London, let alone the whole country, then Polly's a trapeze artist and I'm a wire-walker. For the time being, let's watch developments. They'll tell us when to start serious worrying, if at all.'

'Sounds fair,' said Sammy, looking and feeling a bit better.

'There's another thought,' said Boots. 'How about ensuring we don't get the lady herself picketing these offices or our factory by sending her a telegram?'

'Telling her we've all got leprosy?' said Sammy.

'File that one for possible future action,' said Boots, 'but first how about this?' Thoughtfully, he quoted from his imagination. 'MISS ALSOP STOP YOUR PERSONAL HELP REQUIRED STOP ESCAPED ELEPHANT ON THE LOOSE STOP LAST SEEN IN THE SCOTTISH HIGHLANDS SUFFERING FROM WANDERLUST STOP MAPS AVAILABLE OF THE HIGHLANDS STOP YOURS TRULY A FRIEND.'

'You serious?' said Sammy.

'Mad Marj might be, about a footloose elephant,' said Boots.

Sammy asked who Boots had in mind for Yours Truly. Boots asked if Sammy would like to volunteer.

'I didn't hear that,' said Sammy.

'Well, we could always fall back on the traditional,' said Boots.

'In this case, what's the traditional?' asked Sammy.

'Our old friend Anonymous,' said Boots.

'You'll kill me for sure one day,' said Sammy,

who, having entered his brother's office with a headache, now left it with a grin all over his chops.

Even so, he was frowning later that day when, driving back to Camberwell after a visit to the factory, he dropped in at the junkyard of his old friend Eli Greenberg. The yard was now run by Eli's two sons. He himself kept the books and looked after what cash transactions came his way. As Sammy would have agreed, cash transactions were highly valuable to a business.

Sammy came straight to the point by asking his old mate if he had heard of Marjorie Alsop, alias Hannibal Alsop.

'Sammy, Sammy,' said Mr Greenberg, raising his mittened hands, 'vhen ain't I heard of her this last veek or so? Ain't my sons had to hide anything in stock that's come off a fox or a tiger? Don't ve alvays have a tigerskin rug for sale cheap? Vhy, Sammy, if ve didn't cover up such things, it's Michal's opinion the lady vill come and set fire to our stocks and our petty cash.'

'And don't I sympathize?' said Sammy. 'I do, seeing that what's turning me grey is the thought that one day soon she'll blow up all our retail shops. I tell you, Eli, sometimes life ain't worth living. Got a cup of tea going, old cock?'

'Ain't it my pleasure to make a pot, Sammy?' said Mr Greenberg.

Over the tea, their views on Miss Marjorie Alsop as Enemy Number One coincided, which was mutually comforting, especially as they agreed there was always a possibility that the lady might get trodden on by one of her beloved elephants.

Over the course of a week or so, George Porter had persuaded himself at leaving time each day to be down at the exit door in time to say goodnight to Queenie Richards. She always responded with a pretty smile, causing George a bit of a flutter and a bit of a blush. He tried his very best to project himself beyond this gesture of goodnight, having in mind the possibility of walking Queenie to the bus stop and even sitting next to her on the journey, but, his social cowardice being stronger than his bravery, he failed to capitalize on the young lady's friendliness.

Boots was sorting through the morning post when there was an agitated knocking on his office door.

'Come in,' he called.

In rushed Queenie.

'Mr Adams, he's come back!'

'The unwanted character?'

'Yes, the rotten creep, he has! He was in our street when I got home last night, he was just standing there opposite me house, just looking.'

'Sit down, Queenie,' said Boots, 'and tell me everything.'

Queenie said she shouted at the bloke, then

some people appeared and off he went, sort of slinking away, with that cap of his turned down and his collar turned up, as always. Talk about putting her in a tizzy. It was a blessed relief to see him go, although she worried about him having been there at all. And her worry got chronic later on in the evening, because when she was in the front room and it was getting dark outside, she looked through the window and saw he was back again, on the other side of the street. She could make him out all right because the nearby street lamp was lit, and he was looking sort of – sort of –

'Menacing?' suggested Boots.

'Yes, that's it, and like a – a – '

'A ghoul?' offered Boots.

'Oh, help, yes, one of them, a sort of Dracula,' said Queenie. 'D'you think we ought to tell George?'

'George Porter?' said Boots.

'Yes, him,' said Queenie. 'Well, after the bashing he gave the bloke that time, it wouldn't surprise me if he was willing to do it again. Me mum said he'd be her first choice for an encore, and I must say me mum does talk a lot of sense.'

'So do most mums,' said Boots. 'Well, before I give you any dictation, go up and have a word with George. Put him in the picture, but first let him know I recommend standing off for the moment.'

116

'Standing off, Mr Adams?' said Queenie, puzzled. 'What d'you mean?'

'Let's see if the curse is there again this evening before George takes any action,' said Boots. 'I suggest, in fact, that last night was either an isolated happening designed to show you the menace was paying you back for the good hiding George gave him, or the start of a new campaign of intimidation. Such men can derive pleasure from frightening a woman simply by acting as her own shadow. It might never come to actually making physical contact.'

'Crikey, yes, I see what you mean,' said Queenie. 'Mr Adams, you're ever so – well, knowledgeable, like.'

'On the way to growing old, Queenie, one gets to learn something about life and people,' said Boots.

'Go on, you're not old,' said Queenie.

'Believe me, I'm well out of my pram,' said Boots. 'Right, up you go to see George.'

'He came back?' said George, gazing hypnotized into Queenie's big round eyes and remarking how anguished they were.

'Yes, like I told Mr Adams, there he was, across the street, just standing there and looking,' said Queenie, very upset indeed. Although George had given him a real bashing, she continued, the creep needed ten more like it.

George said that given the chance he'd hang him on the street lamppost.

117

'Oh, me Gawd,' gasped Queenie, 'on our lamppost, the one that's just across from our house?'

'I could do it on the lamppost in the next street, if you'd prefer,' said George. 'It wouldn't make any difference to Shifty Cecil. He's a lousy bum.'

'A whatter?' said Queenie.

'Oh, it's what Americans call dubious geezers,' said George, looking into her wide-open eyes again, and falling into them, in a manner of speaking.

'Here, Mr Porter, you ain't serious, are you?' said Queenie.

'About American bums?'

Queenie gave way to a giggle.

'Oh, Mr Porter, you know I don't mean that,' she said, 'I mean about hanging the bloke from a lamppost.'

'Well, no, I'm not that serious,' said George, 'I'm simply set on doing something that'll keep the jerk out of your life once and for all. Well, it's as I've said before, Miss Richards – '

'Queenie.'

'Oh, yes,' said George, a strange mixture to Queenie in that socially he was a kind of back runner, while in the murky world of creeps he was confident he could definitely put paid to the one who was her own bad dream. 'Yes, er, right, Queenie, it's just as I mentioned before, a nice girl like you shouldn't be pestered by – a – um – '

'Ghoul,' said Queenie, and went on to let him know that Mr Adams thought it best to first see if the bloke was there again this evening. If he wasn't, they could probably forget him, but if he was, then Mr Adams would have a word with George.

'Right,' said George. 'That's understood, Miss Richards.'

'Queenie.'

'Good show,' said George vaguely, and tried hard for the rest of the day not to let images of her big round eyes interfere with costing a new contract.

Walking home from school, fifteen-year-old Emily Chapman, Rosie's daughter, uttered a little shriek as someone popped out from behind the front garden hedge of a house in Elmwood Road, south-east London. Recognizing face and form after a split second, she gave a yell, swung her school satchel and delivered just and swift punishment. Since the satchel contained a textbook on trigonometry and a volume of Wordsworth's poems, the punishment took the wind out of the recipient.

'What d'you mean, you beast, jumping out on me like that?' she shouted. 'Think it's clever, do you?'

'Wait a bit till my head stops hurting,' said Bradley Thompson. His real name was Albert, not Bradley. Bradley was his way of presenting

119

himself as a guy who was with it, and he asked to be called Brad. At eighteen he affected a Tony Curtis quiff and, truth to tell, his looks were not unlike those of the film star. Socially, he was a Teddy boy, and dressed like one. At the moment, however, he was wearing a boiler suit, that of a plumber's mate. 'What's in that satchel of yours, bricks?'

'Books,' said Emily, as pert and precocious a schoolgirl as ever was, and a bit of a trial to her parents. 'And I'll hit you again if you don't tell me what you're doing here near my home.' Her home was in Red Post Hill, and Elmwood Road led to it.

Brad, at the gate of the house, said he was doing plumbing there. That is, his guv'nor was doing the plumbing and he was handing him tools as required and learning more about the technical ins and outs of the work. Right now, his guv'nor was enjoying another cup of tea provided by the obliging lady of the house, while he himself had popped out for some fresh air.

'On my honour, baby doll.'

'I bet,' said Emily. 'You mean you're where you are because you thought you might just catch me on my way home. Lucky for you I didn't swoon and break my neck when you jumped out like that. My dad would have sued you for your life savings.'

'Well, you can tell your pa I could sue you for hurting my head,' said Brad. 'Listen, you always look great in your glad rags, and even in your school blazer you're up with the lookers.'

'Oh, delighted, I'm sure,' said Emily. They had known each other for over a year after meeting in a Brixton dance hall, but while Brad had ideas of making Emily his number one date, Emily had no intention of becoming a fixture in the life of any Teddy boy. Her horizons were wider, far wider. In the world that was inhabited by people who had caviar as a lunchtime starter, there was always one spare millionaire or lord looking for a new wife. Brad was just an early stepping stone. Well, he did know one or two pop vocalists who might soon be up-and-coming. She would like to know some top stars, like Michael Holliday and Alma Cogan. Their kind rubbed shoulders with the rich, the famous and the racy. 'Well, I can't stop, I've got to get home or my mother will give me a talking-to.'

'I like your ma,' said Brad, brilliantined quiff shining in the afternoon light. 'She's hep like she was born for boogie-woogie. Jazzy, if I might say so.'

'Don't bother to, you're not her type,' said Emily, round school hat worn like a blue halo on the back of her head. It did something for her, such as giving her a cute look in the eyes of Brad.

'Well, anyway—'

'Young man.' The front door had opened, and the lady of the house was addressing Brad. 'You're wanted by your employer.'

'Right, coming, Mrs Eagles,' said Brad. 'See you at the usual jig on Saturday,' he said to Emily.

'All right,' said Emily, and resumed her walk home. Brad went back into the house to rejoin his guv'nor before he was bawled out and fired.

Emily was thinking not of Saturday night rock 'n' roll, but of Sir Jack Forrester, a raffish millionaire playboy highly popular with the sporting fraternity. At thirty-six he'd just divorced his second wife. Now, thought Emily, someone like him has got to be every real girl's idea of high life. Who needs a plumber's mate?

Emily was unlike her charming and agreeable mother, or her uncomplicated Dorset-born father. Her character was on the lines of me, me, me.

Later that day, near to six in the evening, Queenie Richards was on her way home after her usual bus ride. She tensed a little as she turned into Hampton Street, and her eyes took in the spot immediately opposite her parents' house. It was vacant. There was no-one there, not a neighbour, not a neighbour's kid, and not the bloke George Porter called Shifty Cecil because he sounded a bit posh. A lovely feeling of relief flooded her, and she reached home on quick, happy feet. Her mum was in the kitchen.

'Mum,' she said, 'he's not there, thank goodness.'

'Well, I've been taking a look now and again,'

said Mrs Richards, slender where her daughter was plump, 'and I can't say I've seen sight nor sound of him, which has stopped me from going out and speaking to him meself. I've told meself I've got to do that, speak to him and give him a large piece of me mind.'

'Mum, you just be careful,' said Queenie. 'I wouldn't trust him not to hit you. Thank goodness, it probably won't happen again, as Mr Adams mentioned this morning. He also mentioned not to do anything unless Shifty Cecil does show himself again.'

'Shifty Cecil?'

'Oh, that's what George Porter calls him on account of him talking quite posh,' said Queenie, 'and he couldn't be more right.' She helped herself to a home-made fruit bun from a tin on the kitchen table.

'You shouldn't eat between meals,' said her mother, 'you'll get fat.'

'Fat? Me?' Queenie dismissed that possibility with a laugh and bit into the bun.

'Well, you're on the way, my girl.'

'Me? Mum, I've just got a natural healthy figure, that's all.'

'Queenie, it's a bit more than that, so don't eat too many sweet things.'

'Mum, I know how to keep me figure in order. It's George that must've let himself go when he was younger.'

'George?'

'George Porter. I wonder if that's what's made him a bit shy and retiring?'

'I don't know about that,' said Mrs Richards, 'I only know that from what I saw of him the time he gave that horrible man a good hiding, I thought he looked a nice solid gent.'

'Oh, I suppose so,' said Queenie.

She checked the street several times during the evening. Not at any time did she see a ghoulish figure touched by the light of the street lamp.

Chapter Ten

One of the opening scenes at the Camberwell Green offices of Adams Enterprises the following morning went like this.

'Mr Adams, he wasn't there last night.'

'Pleased to hear it, Queenie. You're quite sure?'

'Positive. He wasn't there when I got home, nor at any time after. I was ever so relieved, so was me mum. Well, she was thinking she really ought to go out and let the creep know what she thought of him. I told her not to, that he might set about her. A man like that . . .'

'It could happen.' Boots mused. 'Well, let's watch events. There's still a possibility he might rise up from the dead again.'

'The dead, Mr Adams, the dead?'

'Figure of speech, Queenie.'

'Crikey, for a minute I thought you thought Mr Porter really had done him in.'

'We don't want to go quite as far as that in any circumstances. You keep an eye on developments, and see whether or not he does turn up again. Then we'll think about what to do. Now, if you want to, go up and let George know the coast was clear last night, but to hold himself in readiness.'

'Yes, all right, Mr Adams, and thanks ever so for being so kind and helpful,' said Queenie, and up she went to see George. He listened while she told him there'd been no sign of Shifty Cecil last night, not at any time, and how relieved she felt. 'And so was me mum,' she said, at which point George's eyes met hers. Hers brightened with a friendly smile. His went elsewhere and found an unplanned resting place on her sweater. He blinked and coughed. Queenie nearly told him it was time he stopped being shy, but kept her tongue to herself in case she hurt his feelings.

'Well, good,' said George, tingling a bit on account of this very attractive sweater of Queenie's being not far away from his jacket and waistcoat. 'If Shifty Cecil has decided to give up, I'll be as relieved as you and your mum.'

'Mr Adams says to hold yourself in readiness, though, just in case.'

'Oh, right, yes, I can understand what he means.' George nodded. It made him look as important as a bank manager. Queenie would have said he had the figure as well as the look of that kind of man. 'Yes, I'll be ready any time.'

'I must say I've got faith in you after what you did to him that time,' said Queenie, and that left George tingling a bit more. One day, he thought,

I might just ask her if she'd like to go out with me. One day.

Mrs Lizzy Somers, widow of Ned Somers who had died from a heart attack last year, entered Southwark Cemetery. Although she had celebrated her sixtieth birthday in July, Lizzy did not, at first glance, or even second, give the impression that she was now an old-age pensioner. But then her mother, Chinese Lady, was remarkably well preserved at eighty-two, and Lizzy undoubtedly took after her in this respect. Her chestnut hair still retained its rich tints, and for that matter, her brothers, Boots, Tommy and Sammy, showed not a grey hair between them, even though their combined ages amounted to one hundred and seventy-six years. The Adams family, thought Lizzy, were long-living, and it was still a sadness that Ned had gone when only sixty-one.

She was here to visit his grave. He had had a plot reserved for himself and for her too, not far from where Emily, Boots's first wife, had been buried. Close by were the graves of Lizzy's maternal grandparents, Chinese Lady's mother and father. Ned had once asked if Boots and Polly would share the same grave, or if Boots would be buried next to Emily, and Polly near her father. Lizzy had said that sort of thing wasn't what they ought to talk about, because it wasn't to do with anyone except Boots and Polly themselves. Privately, Lizzy thought that Emily in spirit would be waiting to reunite with Boots.

Lizzy was by no means morbid about deaths, graves and cemeteries. She simply believed in proper resting places for those who had gone, and in visits by those who were left behind.

There were only a few other people in the large, well-kept cemetery, and she was quite by herself as she arrived at Ned's plot. Its headstone, as ever, caught her eye.

NED FRANCIS SOMERS 1895–1957
BELOVED HUSBAND OF ELIZA
AND CHERISHED FATHER OF
ANNABELLE, BOBBY, EMMA AND EDWARD

'Hello, Ned lovey, here we are again,' she said in greeting. She had no pretensions as a Christian in thinking herself favoured by the Lord, so whether Ned heard her or not, wherever he was, she had no idea. She just believed that somehow her religion kept her close to him. She had brought some roses with her, blooms from her garden in a cardboard box. Now she took up the metal vase that always stood at the foot of the headstone, carried it to the nearest water tap, washed it clean and half-filled it. She carried it back and took the roses out of the box, removing the thick wet newspaper around their stems. Carefully avoiding the thorns, she placed them one by one in the vase. She then put the vase back. The blooms created a little blaze of scarlet and pink against the granite of the headstone. 'There, they're your own roses, Ned, ones from the bushes you planted yourself.' She was down on one knee, the ground dry, fussing a little with the flower arrangement until it was completely to her liking.

A shadow loomed, cutting off the sun from her back.

'My, that ain't you, is it, Lizzy?'

Lizzy turned her head and glanced up. She saw a lumpy woman, looking untidy in a loose open coat revealing a brown blouse on which buttons were askew. An old-fashioned straw hat sat on her grey head. Her face was a trifle blotchy, due, Lizzy thought, to old age or a fondness for drink. Yes, she had always liked her drink. Lizzy, recognizing her, remembered that.

'Well, goodness me, imagine seeing you, Mrs Castle,' she said, straightening up. The woman was the mother of Emily. 'It is Mrs Castle, isn't it?'

'It's me all right,' said Mrs Castle, who had been a fond wife and mother, if a somewhat blowsy woman. 'And I must say it's a nice surprise, meeting you. How is yerself? I don't think I've seen you since me poor Em'ly's funeral, the Lord rest her. I've just been to her grave and put a bunch of roses there. You've been and lost yer hubby, ain't yer, dearie? Your mum wrote about

129

it to her old friend Mrs Blake, and Mrs Blake told me when I run into her a few months ago. My, I'm that sorry, Lizzy, what a nice man he was. A heart attack, wasn't it?'

'Yes,' said Lizzy.

'Oh, I was grieved for you when I heard,' said Mrs Castle, 'and this is his grave, is it?' She peered. 'Well, so it is. Next time I come and put flowers on my Em's grave, which I do reg'lar – well, nearly every year or so – I'll bring some for your own dear departed, like. It's hard being a widow, Lizzy, and don't I know it, I've been one for over forty year.' Her husband had died of cancer in 1916.

'It's been very lonely for you, but you must have managed wonderfully,' said Lizzy, who actually had no idea what kind of a life Mrs Castle had known as a widow, for she herself had left Walworth before the end of the Great War.

'I've had me sorrows, love,' said Mrs Castle, 'but still the worst thing that could ever have happened was losing my Em in that air raid. Cruel, that was, for her and for me, and I hope you won't mind me saying so, but I took it hard when Boots went and married again so soon after. Well, it was when Em must've still been warm in her grave.'

Lizzy felt embarrassed. She knew she'd been among other members of the family who had disapproved at the time, although everyone, including herself, had eventually come round to accepting Polly.

'It wasn't quite as soon as that,' she said, 'and Boots was never born to live alone. Mind, he's never forgotten Emily, and he's never neglected her grave. He and Tim come often. Tim has Emily's eyes – he's so like her.' She hastened to change the subject. 'Are you still living in the house that was next door to ours?'

'No, don't you remember,' said Mrs Castle, 'I moved out and went to live with me sister not long after I was widowed, which was when Em started lodging with your mum. How is yer mum, dearie? Oh, I tell yer who come to see me last Saturday, Rosie's mum that was once Milly Pearce.'

'Rosie's mother?' said Lizzy, who had her memories of the woman, selfish and tarty.

'Yes, she wanted to know if I knew where Rosie 'ad moved to, which she didn't know herself. I didn't know, either, so I couldn't help her, except I did tell her to go and see Mrs Blake, who still keeps in touch with yer family through yer mum. Did I ask how yer mum is? Em was always very admiring of her.'

'Yes, I remember that, and Mum's fine, thanks,' said Lizzy. She picked up the cardboard box, in which she'd placed the wet newspaper. 'Well, excuse me, but I must go now and catch a bus back home. It's been nice meeting you again. You look wonderful for your age.' Lizzy considered that more of a politeness than a lie. 'Goodbye, Mrs Castle.'

'Goodbye, love, don't forget to let Boots know 'ow much it hurt me when he got married again.'

Lizzy hurried away, dropping the box and newspaper in the waste receptacle near the exit gates. It was hard to believe Emily's loud and beery old mum had turned up, or to know if meeting her was welcome or unwelcome when she herself was there only to commune in spirit with Ned.

Boots would have said well, luck of the draw, Lizzy.

He made one of his frequent homeward-going calls on her that evening. He had been doing so ever since the death of Ned. She told him of her visit to the cemetery and her surprise meeting with Emily's mother.

'Mrs Castle?' said Boots. 'Well, well. Surprises, however, happen to all of us. Tell me, Lizzy, how is the old girl?'

'Looking her age, and still a bit casual with her coat buttons,' said Lizzy.

'Still untidy-looking, you mean?' said Boots. 'I suppose she was always a little lazy about herself and her family, but good at heart. I haven't seen her since Emily's funeral, and certainly never at the cemetery. However, she's still alive and active, even if she never buttons her coat up?'

'Active?' Lizzy laughed. 'Boots lovey, she can

still use her tongue. She never stopped talking from the minute she recognized me.'

That amused Boots.

'Well,' he said, 'to own an active tongue in one's old age must be far easier to live with than arthritis.'

'Yes, but can her friends and neighbours keep on living with it?' asked Lizzy.

'Fortunately,' said Boots, 'that isn't something you and I need to worry about, so let's count our blessings.' He exchanged a few more minutes of small talk with his sister, then said, 'I'll push off now, Lizzy old thing, and see you again sometime.'

'Not so much of the old thing,' said Lizzy.

Boots smiled and went on his way.

Lizzy repeated none of Mrs Castle's remarks concerning his marriage to Polly. She was sure that after all this time, the controversy it had aroused was dead and buried and should stay so. The same should apply to everything about the natural mother of Boots's adopted daughter Rosie. An awful woman, if ever there was one.

The hired car was stationary, parked alongside the pavement, and from there the driver had seen a slim, spring-heeled girl enter the house on the other side of the road, a girl in school uniform. Not long after, a tall boy also arrived. He too wore a school outfit, blazer, trousers and cap. It wasn't difficult to conclude they were the children of the man in whom he was intensely interested.

A woman, crossing the road, passed the car at an angle. She glanced at the driver. He was studying a map. Not being a woman who concerned herself with car drivers studying maps, she went on. However, her glance seemed to cause a reaction, for the driver started the car and drove away only a few seconds later.

When he returned after fifteen minutes, he was on foot.

It was some time after six when a Riley, its hood down, turned into the drive of the house. Out stepped a tall man in a charcoal-grey suit.

The Wolf tensed. The man entered the house by using his key, and the door closed behind him.

So, he was the man to whom Hans had surrendered, the man responsible for Hans's death. Impressive-looking, yes, and almost certainly the father of a healthy-looking boy and girl. What was his wife like? Alive and well, probably.

Ernst Thurber chewed his lip. He reminded himself that his own wife, like his parents, was dead, his parents victims of an air raid early in the war, his wife shot by the Russians towards the end of the conflict. And his brother Hans had undoubtedly been tortured to death by the British.

The Wolf had something with which to comfort himself at this stage of his life: the anticipatory pleasure of revenge. And that pleasure was no slight thing.

He left the scene and went back to his hired car.

Queenie had a pleasant ride home on the bus. There was always a lot to see on the journey from the Green to the Elephant and Castle, especially as the main road was a shopping thoroughfare, while the market at East Street, Walworth, always looked a busy hustle and bustle. George Porter lived not far from the market, in Wansey Street. He had the same journey as she did, but usually he didn't leave the offices until a bit later, so he never shared the ride with her. Mind, a few times lately he'd been at the ground-floor exit to wish her goodnight. But he hadn't offered to walk with her to the bus. Probably too shy to. What a funny man, still shy at thirty. Some woman somewhere might fancy him, she supposed. Well, he had nice manners and a nice talking voice, even if he did look a bit like a portly bank-manager type.

She noted for the umpteenth time that although the scene from the bus was always interesting because of the shops and people, the background was never of anything except bricks and mortar, with not a tree in sight. Once more Queenie thought about her chances of meeting a decent bloke and ending up in suburbia somewhere. She wasn't the only person in crowded

South London who fancied open spaces and some roses in the back garden. It didn't mean you had to leave rock 'n' roll behind, because wherever you lived these days you could always find dance halls. Except, of course, in tiny villages. Well, she wasn't going to ask anyone to settle down with her in a tiny village. Just somewhere like New Malden would do.

Mr Adams, she remembered, lived in East Dulwich, which was posh suburbia. Not that he was posh himself. In fact, someone had told her that right up to the time when he got married, he lived in Walworth. Well, he's risen above all that, she thought, he was simply any girl's idea of a born gent.

Queenie sighed a little in her wish for her future to include some trees and some green grass.

There was no sign of Shifty Cecil when she arrived home. There were a couple of noisy kids some way off, and a woman speaking her mind to them from her doorstep, but that was all. Queenie happily reported to her mum, and her mum said well, have a cup of tea, then, but try not to eat any buns.

It was a shock when, at about eight o'clock, Queenie made a casual check of the dark street from the front room. Oh, Lord, there he was, after all, at a little distance from the street lamp, so that half of him was in light, the other half in shadow. He was looking straight across the street at her house, and with his cap turned down, his raincoat collar turned up, his face just a darkness, he really did seem a menace. Her nerves jangled. What was he after, what did he want?

She reported to her mum that Shifty Cecil had reappeared. Her mum put some knitting aside, stood up, straightened her skirt and brushed it, then walked towards the door.

'Mum, what're you doing?'

'I'm going out to speak my piece to that man.'

'No, you can't, you don't know what he might do.'

'Well, all right, in that case I'm going to look to see if Constable Purvis is on his beat somewhere.'

'Mum, let me talk to Mr Adams tomorrow. He'll know what's best to do.'

'You sure, Queenie?'

'Honest, yes, I'd always bet on Mr Adams.'

'P'raps he'll get that big man, Mr Porter, to give that nasty piece of work another good hiding, a more injuring one this time.'

'I'm sure he'll do something like that.'

'So we've got the problem back?' said Boots the next morning.

'Oh, it don't half look like it, Mr Adams,' said Queenie, 'and I'm that sorry to have to bother you again when I know you're so busy.'

'It's no bother, Queenie, not in the least,' said Boots, noting that her plump prettiness was sagging a little, her round eyes showing a worried light.

'You sure I shouldn't tell the police?' she said. 'Mum wanted to go looking for one of our local bobbies last night, but I said it would be best if I talked to you first. And she said she hoped you'd get George Porter to do Shifty Cecil a real mischief this time. I still can't get over how he did him in first off.'

'George has got muscle and brains, Queenie,' said Boots. 'Leave it with me and I'll talk to him.'

'Oh, thanks ever so, Mr Adams.'

'The only way the police could finger the ghoul would be for loitering with intent to commit a mischief,' said Boots, 'but they'd have a job to make that stick in court. We'll rely on George, shall we?'

'Oh, if you can, so can I,' said the grateful Queenie, although she was still in wonder that the portly costing clerk, who read books, could act like a real toughie.

'Understood, Mr Adams,' said the real toughie, nodding his head.

'You might have to give up the whole evening,' said Boots.

'Well, I don't have a lot of commitments,' said George.

'No lady friend?' said Boots.

'I'm not the right shape for lady friends,' said George.

138

'Some ladies,' said Boots, 'don't give a fig for a bit of weight on a man as long as he's kind enough.'

'I'll look out for that sort of lady,' said George. 'Anyway, if the action you suggest offers a sure way of getting shot of Shifty Cecil for good, I'll go for it.'

'Winding him would do no permanent damage,' said Boots.

'Right, no permanent damage,' said George. 'What's important is doing him down on his own doorstep. I take note of that, Mr Adams.'

'I leave it to you,' said Boots. 'Queenie's going to become a nervous wreck if we don't get rid of the nuisance. That is, if you don't. You're the action man.'

'I'll give it my best shot, boss,' said George (Chicago) Porter.

Chapter Eleven

Mrs Patsy Adams rode her bicycle in lithe-limbed fashion. She had always enjoyed cycling. It was good exercise, and if, at thirty-one, she wasn't quite as leggily dashing and carefree as when she'd been an all-American girl of eighteen, it was only because as the mother of two growing children she had a certain modesty to observe. When she had explained that to husband Daniel yesterday, the comical cuss said very solemnly that true modesty for mothers riding bikes could be covered by a pair of trousers.

'But you hate me in trousers,' she said.

'We'll have to rethink modesty, then,' he said.

'Oh, you're real cute,' she said. They were all alike, the Adams men, they were all amateur comics.

But then her own amateur said, 'Your car will solve the problem.'

'My car? What car?'

'The one I've ordered for you from Matthew, the one you liked in the advertisement,' said

140

Daniel. 'We can afford it now, a li'l ole Austin runabout for my l'il ole chickadee.'

'Daniel, oh, you dreamboat.' Naturally, she gave him a loving hug and a smacker of a kiss. 'But do you have to talk like someone out of Alabama?'

'Only with you, Boston lily.'

Today, she was heading for morning coffee with Grandma and Grandpa Finch. Aunt Lizzy would be there too, and so would Helene, the French wife of Daniel's cousin Bobby. Bobby had a very important job with Britain's Foreign Office, and went to work in a bowler hat and carrying an umbrella, something his twelve-year-old daughter Estelle said she was trying to live down. Certainly, Patsy could have told her that on Wall Street, New York, not even the most conservative of stockbrokers would have been seen dead in a bowler hat. But the English, of course, had their funny little old-fashioned ways, and the only regret for some of them was that Queen Victoria was dead.

Patsy smiled to herself as she cycled down Red Post Hill towards the home of Grandma Finch. She took the descent slowly, looking about her. Daniel's cousin Rosie and her husband Matthew Chapman also lived here, along with their son and daughter. Matthew was the garage owner due to come up with the car promised by Daniel.

She saw a woman knocking on Rosie's front door. She turned as Patsy came near. She called.

'Here, excuse me.'

Patsy stopped, slipping smoothly from the saddle.

'Can I help you?'

The woman moved from the door and came down to the gate, and Patsy saw her to be well past her best, although she'd made an attempt with make-up to repair the raddled effect of time and – what? Gin? She wore a cream-coloured raincoat that, like herself, had seen better days, and a blue scarf that helped to cover the lines of her neck. On her head was a pudding-basin purple hat, gaudy in the extreme. She regarded Patsy hopefully.

'D'you live hereabouts?' she asked.

'No,' said Patsy, thinking the woman absurd in the vanity of her make-up, her lips slashed with crimson. 'I'm just visiting relatives.'

'So you don't know a woman name of Chapman?'

'Chapman?' Something impelled Patsy to be on her guard.

'Yes, Rosie Chapman.' The woman sounded keen for information. 'I been told she moved here a while ago, but I can't get no answer to me knocks.' There was a hint of the cockney in her voice. 'I need to see her.'

'You know her, then, do you?' said Patsy.

'Know her? I should think I do, she's me one and only daughter, isn't she?'

Oh, my God, thought Patsy, a woman like this

the mother of a woman like Rosie? The one was a freak, the other peerless. She knew Rosie to be the unwanted child of her natural mother, and the adopted daughter of Boots. But she knew little of the original circumstances, nor of the natural mother. No-one in the family ever mentioned her, and no wonder. She had the painted looks of a one-time floozie.

'Your daughter, you said?'

'Well, wasn't it me that give her birth?' The woman made it sound like a complaint. 'She used to live with her husband in some place called Woldingham, down in Surrey. I went there once, miles from anywhere it was, and not my style, I can tell you. I like a bit of life.' The woman, having found a listener in Patsy, was not to be denied. 'Anyway, an old neighbour told me she'd moved to this district, so I looked in a phone book for her address, so I know this is the house. But it looks like she's out. You wouldn't know when she'll be back, would you? No, of course you wouldn't, seeing you said you don't live round here.' That too sounded like a complaint.

Patsy was in a dilemma. Instinctively, she was against giving this unlovely woman any kind of information, but on the other hand, what was the point of holding back? The woman would only stick around until Rosie appeared, or go off and come back later. Rosie was at work right now, but would be home from her job with the family firm not long after three. She was always there when her children arrived home from school.

'Well, I guess your daughter will be back sometime.' That was as much as Patsy could bring herself to say to the woman. To tell her exactly where Rosie was at the moment might mean the apparition actually turning up at the offices. Not to be thought of, decided Patsy. 'I have to go now.'

'Well, all right, but I don't fancy having to wait all day,' said the woman. 'I'm not in the best of health just lately.'

'But you're OK now?' Patsy couldn't help asking the solicitous question.

'Well, I've got a bit of a headache,' said the one-time Milly Pearce, now the widow of the late Mr Clarence Rainbould, music-hall magician.

'I'm so sorry,' said Patsy, and went on her way to the home of Grandma Finch, the Adams matriarch who regularly invited female members of the Adams clan to morning coffee or afternoon tea. And often she entertained one individual family or another to traditional Sunday tea. The grand old lady didn't believe in sitting quietly around waiting for something to happen, and Patsy was pretty sure that when she finally left the family to take tea with St Peter, she'd do so on her feet.

Arrived at her destination, Patsy wheeled her bike over the drive and knocked on the front door. She was admitted by Grandma's daily help, Mrs Plumstead, and found that Aunt Lizzy and Helene were already there. Greetings were exchanged, Patsy deciding to wait until coffee was served before she spoke of the woman who had insisted she was Rosie's mother.

A little later the cat was out of the bag.

'What?' said Lizzy.

'Beg pardon?' said Chinese Lady.

'I think you had better repeat yourself, Patsy my dear,' said Sir Edwin.

Coffee had been brewed and served by Chinese Lady herself, despite Mrs Plumstead's offer to do so, and now Patsy was suddenly the focus of all eyes.

Lizzy shuddered. Chinese Lady looked shocked, Sir Edwin philosophical. Helene, inquisitive, addressed the gathering.

'Is it good or bad?' she asked. Like Patsy and others of their generation, she knew little of the background to Rosie's story. Those most directly involved, Chinese Lady, Boots, Tommy and Sammy, rarely mentioned any comprehensive details. 'I only know Rosie is adopted. So I mean, is it good or bad that her natural mother wishes to see her and is even at her door?'

'It's far from good,' declared Lizzy.

'But why, Mama?' asked Helene of her mother-in-law. Bobby's French wife at thirty-seven was a picture of robust health. She still looked like

145

a farmer's daughter, but with her own Gallic temperament. 'Why is it not so good?'

'The woman just isn't worth talking about,' said Lizzy forthrightly.

'I think,' said Sir Edwin gently, 'I think, Maisie, that our younger people are entitled to some information. I'm sure Boots would have no objection, even if he's always preferred to remain silent himself.'

Chinese Lady said it had always been very private and personal, first between Boots and Emily, and then Boots and Polly. And as far as she was concerned, the less she had to do with the woman the better she liked it. Still, she went on, Helene and Patsy could be told how it all happened. Lizzy, who had long ago received all the details from Boots, said to go ahead, that she'd try to feel a bit more Christian-like about the woman, but doubted if she would.

So Chinese Lady informed Helene and Patsy of a neighbour of long ago, a woman by the name of Milly Pearce, who had a baby girl in 1915 by a man no-one knew about and who never put in an appearance. At the age of five, the little girl, Rosie, was a neglected and unloved child. Boots befriended her, cared for her, and when the mother went off to live with some man no better than herself, he saw it as a downright selfish desertion of her own flesh and blood. He and Emily, man and wife then, took Rosie in and eventually adopted her, much to the child's happiness, although it cost Boots a scandalous amount of money before Milly Pearce would sign the adoption papers. That woman had since turned up once or twice to ask for more money, and if she was knocking at Rosie's door now it was certain she wasn't there out of love for Rosie. Milly Pearce had only ever loved herself.

'Such a dreadful woman, selling her own child,' said Helene, 'but I think Bobby once told me that Rosie's natural father was much, yes, much different from the mother.'

'A gentleman he was, Helene love, that never knew he'd fathered Rosie until he found out years later, when she was a young woman,' said Chinese Lady. 'He offered to give her a home with himself and his wife, but Rosie simply never had a single thought about leaving Boots and Emily.' Chinese Lady mused a little before adding, 'I remember her saying to me once that she thought of Boots and Emily as her natural parents, which of course was what she'd have liked. She won't like it that that woman has turned up again.'

'Grandma,' said Patsy, 'I'm sure she won't like finding her on her doorstep.'

'That, Patsy, means Rosie should be warned,' said Sir Edwin. 'I wonder now, do you all think I should phone her at the office?'

'Let me do that,' said Lizzy.

'Yes, Edwin, let Lizzy,' said Chinese Lady.

*   *   *

'Hello?' said Rosie into her office phone.

'It's Aunt Lizzy here, Rosie.'

'You're a nice surprise, then.'

'I'm not sure you'll think so when you hear what I've got to tell you. Can I talk? I mean, is someone with you?'

'Rachel's here. We share this office. But you can go ahead.'

Lizzy went ahead with the prior details, details that came down to the unpalatable fact that Patsy had seen an unwelcome woman knocking on Rosie's front door.

'And not too long ago, Rosie.'

'An unwelcome woman?' said Rosie. 'What does that mean?'

'Well, Rosie love,' said Lizzy, speaking very quietly, 'I'm afraid it means your mother was seen on your doorstep, and that you might find her there waiting for you when you get home from your work.'

Rosie said nothing for long moments, then asked Lizzy if this was really true. Lizzy said Rosie could believe she wouldn't joke about Milly Pearce or Milly Rainbould, or whatever her name was now. So what would Rosie do?

Rosie, collecting herself, said, 'I must definitely make sure I get home well before Giles and Emily arrive from school.'

'You'll face up to her, Rosie?'

'I must,' said Rosie, 'and you're a dear, Lizzy, for warning me.'

'We owe Patsy some thanks,' said Lizzy. 'Rosie, if that woman gives trouble or is the worse for drink – '

'I'll manage,' said Rosie, knowing the one thing she had to do was to keep the woman away from the children. Nothing would rock them more than the sight of a raddled creature claiming to be their grandmother. That was how she had looked on the last occasion Rosie had seen her. Raddled. She was a woman whom Rosie had never been able to acknowledge as her natural mother. Giles and Emily knew she had been adopted, and they also knew how it had come about, but so far had never worried her with intimate questions. They were contented that her adoptive father was Grandpa Boots.

'Are you still there, Rosie?' asked Lizzy.

'Yes, and thanks again for phoning me,' said Rosie. 'I'll be in touch.'

When she put the phone down, she hesitated, then informed Rachel she was going to see Boots for a few minutes.

'Take your time, Rosie,' said Rachel.

'Jesus Christ,' said Boots.

'Amen,' said Rosie.

'The harridan has been knocking on your door?' said Boots.

'Lizzy says Patsy's description sounds just like her,' said Rosie.

'What d'you propose to do?' asked Boots. He

149

still had Queenie's problem on his mind, but this new one was a genuine curse. He could visualize Rosie's natural mother materializing regularly out of her alcoholic mists until the day she died, and perhaps on that day itself, so that Rosie would be forced to pay for her funeral. But then, Rosie would give her natural mother that last favour without question, however indifferent she felt towards her.

'I wondered if I could leave thirty minutes early,' said Rosie. 'If she's there, at the house, I want to have time to deal with her before Emily and Giles get home.'

'Rosie, shall I come with you?' asked Boots. 'After all, it's almost certain she thinks I'm the one who should pay the piper.'

'Dear man,' said Rosie, 'you're the only one she's frightened of. You know more about her past and her behaviour than anyone, and she knows you know. If you arrive home with me, she'll disappear, but she'll turn up again on another day, and heaven knows at what time. I want to avoid either Emily or Giles answering the door to her, and having to see what she's like.'

'Rosie, it's probably inevitable that one day—'

'I'd like to fight the inevitable,' said Rosie, 'so I'll face up to her, and hope I can do so before Emily and Giles are home.'

'She'll blackmail you again,' said Boots.

'Perhaps,' said Rosie. 'But you won't mind if I leave thirty minutes early?'

'Why not go now?' said Boots. 'I don't think you'll like living with the problem from now until this afternoon. You'd rather do what you can as soon as you can, wouldn't you, Rosie? Yes, of course you would, so buzz off now, poppet.'

'Thanks, old sport,' said Rosie. She leaned over his desk, lightly ruffled his hair and delivered a kiss on his forehead. 'There's a sweet man you are, and you've been that all my life.'

Chapter Twelve

'Kiernik knows where he is now?' said a senior Polish government official to a colleague of slightly lesser status.

'Yes, he knows.'

'It was a pity, of course, that the man slipped through your fingers in West Berlin.'

'I did inform you that in West Berlin I was being watched. My chances of a strike were minimal.'

'Probably because in West Berlin you are too well known. I sympathized with your failure.'

'A hiccup, Comrade Kommissar, not a failure.'

'Of course. However, Kiernik is not under surveillance?'

'We've never had reason to believe British Intelligence was ever interested in him. He runs a very innocuous business.'

'From which he has been a loyal and obedient servant of our advancing nation?' Poland was Communist.

'Extremely. He's waiting now only for your approval of his intended strike.'

'Very well. Inform him he may proceed.'

Rosie was home before her mantelpiece clock chimed twelve noon. There was no-one on her doorstep, nor any sign elsewhere of the mother for whom she bore no affection. Sometimes she told herself she should feel guilty about that, but all she did feel was pity for her and her empty life. It was pity that had induced her, with Matthew's blessing and co-operation, to finance an allowance sufficient to cover the woman's rent and living costs. That allowance, by arrangement, was paid monthly through a bank.

So if she had reappeared, what was her reason?

Rosie thought about phoning Matt to let him know her mother had been seen on the doorstep. But the moment she entered the house she was struck by an uneasy feeling that she was not alone, that the woman had somehow advanced from the doorstep and had actually found a way in. A sudden faint noise sounded like confirmation.

'Who's there?'

No answer. Gritting her teeth, Rosie tracked her way towards the noise, and it took her into the lounge, where it came to her ears as a clear tapping sound.

And there she was, outside the French windows, tapping on them with her knuckles.

Her lips were moving and she was obviously saying something. Resignedly, Rosie opened up the windows, and mother and daughter faced each other.

'Rosie—'

'What are you doing here?'

'Rosie . . .' The name slipped out in a slightly tired way. 'Rosie, your mother's ill.'

Rosie sighed. This was a new tack. Yet she conceded the eyes looked dark and faintly rimmed, and the powdered cheeks a little sunken. Further, the habitual brashness seemed to be missing.

'You had better come in,' she said.

'Oh, that's kind.' The voice wavered a bit. 'I've been waiting most of the morning, with me head getting worse all the time.' The woman stepped in, eyed a very inviting armchair and tottered herself into it. 'Oh, bless you, Rosie love, I do need a long sit-down. I heard you round at the front, I've been round at the back for a while, but yer garden seats are all a bit damp.' A long sigh, a little shiver and a hand to her hat. Off it came, revealing a frizzy mop of dyed auburn hair that made Rosie wince. The hand touched a lined forehead and tenderly rubbed it. 'Rosie love, did I mention I'm ill?'

Whether she was ill or not, Rosie could only feel pity for a woman who seemed so beaten down.

'Yes, you did mention it. Tell me about it.

Would you like some tea or coffee first?'

'Oh, a cup of tea would save me life. Well, for today, I suppose.'

'What d'you mean, for today?'

'I'm really ill, Rosie. Not like you, I never saw you looking more healthy. Or more prosperous.'

More prosperous? Very meaningful, thought Rosie, and her pity dropped a few notches.

'Are you suffering a headache?'

'It's chronic. Rosie, could you get me that cup of tea? Then I'll talk to you.'

'Stay there,' said Rosie, comforting herself with the knowledge that it would be about four hours before Emily and Giles arrived home from school. She had plenty of time to deal with whatever the woman was after.

The woman. Not since she was a small child had Rosie been able to call her mother. Going to the kitchen she wondered if it was not time to forgive and forget, to let Emily and Giles meet her before they did begin to ask leading questions. Something might set them off one day.

The tea quickly made, Rosie carried the tray into the lounge. The woman had hardly moved, except that her head was bent and to one side. Wheezy breaths escaped her. She was snoozing. Rosie suspected then that the woman really was unwell. However, she woke up as the tea tray was placed on a small table. She blinked, she saw the teapot, and the cups and saucers.

'Oh, bless yer, Rosie, and I'll have two sugars.'

Rosie poured. She handed cup and saucer to the woman, then sat down to enjoy her own share of the pot.

'I'm sorry about your bad headache,' she said. 'Perhaps it's due to worry about a debt. Is it?'

The woman, gulping hot tea, gave Rosie a sorrowing look.

'Don't I wish it was, Rosie love,' she said. 'Rosie love' could have pointed out that that endearment had never been addressed to her as a child, but she was long past any desire to indulge in recriminations. 'Me head's really bad. It sometimes feels like there's a hammer going at it.'

Again a hand touched the forehead, pressing, and a painful sigh issued above the lifted teacup. The lined eyes darkened.

Rosie felt a return of pity.

'What exactly is wrong?' she asked quietly.

'I'm ill, Rosie.'

'How ill?'

The woman put her cup back in its saucer, and sighed again.

'Rosie, I've got a tumour,' she said.

'A tumour?'

'It's what me doctor and the specialist said.'

'Dear God,' said Rosie. One could not wish that on one's bitterest enemy. 'Is that really true?'

'Don't I wish it wasn't?' The woman went on to say that through her doctor she'd been in hospital several times, had seen a specialist, had had various tests and X-rays, and been told she

156

needed a very special operation before a tumour reached the nervous system of her brain. Her doctor had recommended a French surgeon operating in a place called Lyons in France. He excelled in removing tumours of the kind she'd got, and he had a high success rate. But it would cost as much as one thousand pounds for him to do the operation for her. Her National Health specialist had backed up her doctor in recommending the Frenchman. 'Look, here's the letter he sent me after he wrote to me doctor.' She fished in her handbag, extracted an envelope and handed it to Rosie, who was listening in silence.

Rosie took the typewritten letter from the envelope and read it. It was headed, 'W.R. Wainwright, FRCS', with a Tulse Hill address, and sure enough it gave Mrs Rainbould information concerning a renowned French brain surgeon, René Saint-Denis, and a recommendation to consult him with a view to having the necessary operation, providing she could meet the cost, which would be in the region of one thousand pounds. This, unfortunately, could not be avoided, since Mrs Rainbould wasn't a French citizen. The letter ended, 'Be assured you would be in the care of a surgeon more advanced in this field than any other known to me.'

Rosie looked up from the letter.

'I'm sorry, so sorry, that you're as ill as this,' she said.

'Rosie, I don't have nowhere near a thousand pounds. You and your hubby, you've been good to me, making me a regular allowance, and I don't like asking for something extra, especially all that much, but – '

'Speak to your doctor,' said Rosie. 'Tell him you'll go to France as soon as necessary, that you'll have the operation, and that Matt and I will pay for everything, including all travelling expenses and any hotel bills.'

'Rosie, d'you mean that?'

'Yes, as long as you'll first do something for me.'

'Rosie, you just say.'

Rosie hesitated for a moment, then spoke firmly.

'You are to have your hair returned to its natural colour, even if it's now grey, and suitably restyled. You are to use modest make-up and to buy new clothes suitable for your age. The costs will all be taken care of, along with the other expenses.' She supposed she was being cruel, but in order to be kind she continued. 'In France, you must know, they expect women who are getting on a bit to look and dress as if they're growing old gracefully. Do you understand?'

Mrs Milly Rainbould bit her lip.

'Rosie, ain't I – haven't I – I mean I've only always done me best to make the most of me looks.'

'You've tried, yes, and I daresay you've been happy with the results, but it's been going on for too long. Favour me, and settle for being your age.'

'I'll do what you want, Rosie, honest. Rosie, are you and your hubby really going to pay for everything?'

Rosie, her tea cold, faced facts. Whatever the character and way of life of this woman, one unalterable fact persisted. Milly Pearce that was had given birth to her, given her life, and out of that life had come years of supreme happiness. Who could not be grateful for that life, who could not overlook the unhappy beginnings? As for the cost of the operation and incidentals, Matt's garage business was doing well, and she herself had been enriched by the money left to her by Sir Charles Armitage, her natural father, sixteen years ago. That inheritance would easily provide the necessary funds.

It was time now to forgive and forget.

'Matt and I will be happy to pay for everything. Tell me, are you still in pain?'

'Oh, not like I was.' The woman still sounded fragile, but there was obviously a sense of relief at her daughter's generosity and lack of quibble. 'It's always like that, the worst pains sort of come and go, and they're easing a bit now. I'll be all right, I'll find me way back to me lodgings in Brixton in a while.'

'I'll drive you,' said Rosie.

'No, I'll be all right, specially now you've taken a lot of worry off me shoulders.'

'I'll drive you,' said Rosie firmly, 'but first let me make another pot of tea. This one is cold. And I'll make some sandwiches too, for both of us. More tea and some sandwiches will fit you up for the ride to Brixton.' She knew her mother now had a bedsit in Effra Road.

'I don't hardly know how to thank you, Rosie.' The woman looked and sounded repentant about the past.

Rosie made a decision.

'After you come back from France and are well enough, and yes, growing old gracefully,' she said, 'I'll pick you up and bring you here one Saturday.'

'You'll bring me here? What for, Rosie?'

'By then,' said Rosie, 'it'll be time for you to meet your grandchildren.'

'Rosie, say all that again,' said Matthew over the phone forty minutes later. He was at his garage in Peckham.

'I'm sure you heard, ducky,' said Rosie.

'Well, like you, I have to be sorry for the old girl,' said Matt, 'and you can count on me to stand with you. You say you're now going to drive her back to her Brixton lodgings?'

'Yes, and I've plenty of time before Emily and Giles get home,' said Rosie.

'You'd still prefer them not to meet her?' said Matt.

'Not as she is now, painted and powdered. She's freshening up at the moment, but I doubt if she'll take off much of the paint. But I've made her understand it's something she's got to work on before she leaves for France, and keep working on after she returns. I'm never going to let our children see her while she's looking like an— well, you know.'

'Yes, I know,' said Matt. Like an old bag, he thought. He assured Rosie he'd back her all the way in the matter, and would add his own persuasions to her mother in getting her to look presentable, and not like mutton dressed as lamb. Although she was obviously suffering a dangerous condition, he liked the fact, he said, that her National Health specialist's recommendation was a positive one, and good enough to go by. 'We have to wish the old lady well, Rosie, never mind her history.'

'Yes, of course,' said Rosie. 'Well, I'll see you later, ducky. I thought I'd let you know about events, and that I'm driving her back to Brixton.'

'Good luck,' said Matt, 'and give the old lady my regards. After all, I do owe her a lot more than a get-well card.'

'Do you?' said Rosie.

'Yes,' said Matt, 'I owe her for you.'

This confirmed Rosie in her decision to forgive and forget.

* * *

'Had an exciting day at the office, Mum?' said Giles on his arrival home from school.

'I hardly noticed the passing hours,' said Rosie, whose drive to and from Brixton had given her more time with her mother, but had otherwise proved uneventful. She placed a slice of fruit cake in front of her son, following that with a glass of his favourite beverage, bottled apple juice. 'Where's Emily the incorrigible?'

'Oh, she'll be here in a minute,' said Giles, dark and sinewy like his dad. He was sixteen. 'She's outside, gassing with friends. It beats me, the way she gasses all day one day and has still got plenty left over for the day after. Did you never stop talking when you were young?'

'Hardly ever,' said Rosie, filling the teapot with boiling water.

'What did your mum and dad say?' asked Giles, and Rosie knew he meant Boots and Emily. The other persons were only a vagueness to him, and to his sister too. 'Did they tell you you ought to be seen more and heard less?'

'Not a bit of it,' smiled Rosie, 'they both agreed that my conversation was brilliant.'

'Well, I give it to you, Mum, it still is,' said Giles, enjoying his cake. 'Well, nearly.'

Emily came in at that point. Entering the kitchen, she dumped her satchel on the four-wheeled tea trolley, placed her school hat on top, sat down at the table and announced that Sadie Wheeler was a drag full stop. Giles suggested his sister ought to say hello to their mum before knocking Sadie Wheeler, whoever she was.

'Is there any tea going?' asked Emily, glancing at her mother.

'As usual, yes,' said Rosie, pouring a cup for her daughter and then cutting her a slice of cake.

'Ta,' said Emily, one of an increasing band of young people currently questioning the attitudes of parents. Parents were inclined to be interfering and bossy. Some teenagers, those with very advanced minds, were asking if parents were actually necessary, and if an alternative was available. Few parents regarded that kind of revolutionary offspring seriously, and put their weird talk down to growing-up pains, the kind that would disappear without trace once they were adults. 'I'm going to the Streatham dance hall tomorrow, not Brixton,' said the revolutionary daughter of Rosie and Matt. Tomorrow was Saturday.

'I'm not against that,' said Rosie, 'as long as you're home by ten thirty, as usual.'

'Don't fuss,' said Emily.

'It's my responsibility to fuss a little,' said Rosie, 'and it's your responsibility to listen a little. Say at least once a week.'

'All right, once a week,' said Emily. 'Say on Saturdays about me getting home on time.'

'Very well,' said Rosie equably, 'let's agree on that.'

163

'Emily, I wish you wouldn't always get at Mum,' said Giles.

'I'm not getting at her,' said Emily, 'I'm just having my say, that's all.'

'Well, now and again,' said Giles, 'try putting a sock in it.'

'Who's a mummy's boy, then?' said Emily, but under her breath. As far as Rosie was concerned, all she asked of her son and daughter was the same kind of healthy outlook shared by their father and most of their Adams relatives. Rosie could never dissociate the best things and best moments of life from her years of growing up among her favourite people, and her wartime years of getting to know Matt.

If Emily were to develop an individuality entirely her own, nothing would be wrong with that as long as she did not become the odd one out in an unlikeable way.

After supper, and while the children were doing their homework, Matt took Rosie aside to suggest they should phone Mr Wainwright, the surgeon who had written to her mother.

'I'd like to know if he really is confident that the operation has a great chance of success.'

'Matt, even if there's only a fifty-fifty chance, we can't pull out,' said Rosie.

'Wouldn't dream of it, but any brain tumour is a dodgy proposition for the operating surgeon,' said Matt soberly.

'Well, perhaps an honest opinion would help us to know what we can really expect to face up to,' said Rosie. She hesitated, and then added, 'And what the patient can expect.'

'If it's not as promising as the letter says, we don't tell her,' said Matt, 'we let her live in hope.'

It was Rosie who made the phone call, the Tulse Hill number being included in the letter-head. If the address was his surgery, then Mr Wainwright would almost certainly not be there. However, she dialled the number.

'Hello?' A man's pleasant voice.

'Is that Mr Wainwright, surgeon?' enquired Rosie.

'Who is calling, may I ask?'

'I'm Mrs Rosie Chapman, and my widowed mother is Mrs Milly Rainbould.'

'Really? I had no idea Mrs Rainbould had a daughter. She has never mentioned you, although she's been a patient of mine for about two months, ever since her GP sent her to me. Are you phoning in connection with her condition?'

'Yes.' Rosie said she had the letter he had sent to her mother, and that although it was of a generally optimistic content, would Mr Wainwright care to tell her what he truly believed about the chances of success? She did not in the least mean to imply his letter was an exaggeration, but did he understand her wish to know for certain what the chances were?

'My dear lady, taking your word for it that you are indeed Mrs Rainbould's daughter, allow me to say that what I truly believe is reflected in the letter, that the chances of success are excellent. Excellent, yes, indeed.' The voice was reassuring, and mellow with maturity. 'It's a great pity that Mrs Rainbould— but no, it's not for me to discuss her financial situation.'

'I've told her to go ahead with the necessary arrangements, and that all expenses will be taken care of by my husband and myself,' said Rosie.

'Really? I am to believe this?'

'I assure you,' said Rosie.

'Then I'm delighted, Mrs Chapman, delighted, and I'm certain it will raise your mother's spirits high, always a good thing for anyone awaiting an operation.'

'And I'm sure your confidence in the outcome will have helped her already,' said Rosie. 'Her main worry has been the cost.'

'I really am delighted at the generosity of you and your husband. Thank you for phoning.'

'Oh, before you ring off,' said Rosie, 'who will let me have a detailed account of all the estimated costs, you or her GP?'

'I'll do it myself, and with pleasure.'

'Thank you, Mr Wainwright,' said Rosie, and gave Matt the salient details of the conversation. Matt said he liked the fact that the invoice covering the estimated costs for the whole thing would come from Mr Wainwright.

'Yes, I do like it,' he said.

'Why do you make a point of it?' asked Rosie.

'Well, sweetheart,' said Matt, 'knowing the old girl as I do, I don't think getting the details from her and sending her the cheque would be the wisest thing. Much as she knows she needs the operation, I wouldn't put it past her to pay the cheque into the bank and then draw a bucketful of the dibs to go on the binge.'

'Dear man, my sentiments entirely,' said Rosie.

Chapter Thirteen

When Queenie arrived home that evening there was no sign of the creep. But he had left his mark, in the form of a note enclosed in an envelope inscribed 'Kitten', and dropped through the letterbox. Mrs Richards had opened it, and she showed the note to Queenie almost as soon as her daughter walked in.

'Just look at that,' she said. 'It's from him all right.'

Queenie looked. The wording was in capitals.

'KITTEN, YOU'RE JUST MY TYPE. WHEN CAN WE GET TOGETHER?'

Queenie felt a cold shiver run down her back.

'Ugh,' she said, 'that's spoiled the day for me, that has.'

'You'll have to go to the police now, my girl,' said Mrs Richards.

'No, I'll talk to Mr Adams on Monday, and I expect he'll talk to George,' said Queenie, who liked that idea better than going round to the police station. 'And I'll keep me eyes open just in case the creep shows himself later this evening.'

'I hope he don't,' said Mrs Richards. 'Queenie, what're you looking for?'

Queenie was now inspecting the larder, looking for something tasty enough to make up for the lousy blow the note had dealt her.

'Oh, nothing much, just one of your fruit buns, Mum,' she said.

'Well, you can stop looking, I've hid the cake tin,' said Mrs Richards.

'What for?'

'For the sake of your figure,' said Mrs Richards, who had the supper potatoes on the boil. She'd mash them, adding margarine, pepper and milk. 'You don't want to get to be a big girl, do you, big like that George Porter, by eating too many fruit buns in between meals? Mind, big like he is suits a man more than it suits a young woman.'

'Well, I know that,' said Queenie, quite sure her figure was a help to her chances of ending up with a nice feller in a suburban semi-detached. 'But I'm never going to get personally big in the way you're talking about.'

'Well, as your caring mum, I'm going to see you don't,' said Mrs Richards, who had slightly over-optimistic hopes for her daughter, based on a special kind of young man, like one of the Cambridge boat-race crew, all six-footers and ever so civilized. 'So I don't want no more eating between meals.'

'But after the shock of reading this note – ' Queenie read it again and made a face. 'Well, I just feel I need a nice little snack. I bet Mrs Adams wouldn't starve her daughter when she was having a bit of a crisis.'

'Mrs Adams?'

'Me boss's wife.'

'What's she like?'

'Mum, I don't know what she's like to talk to, I've only ever seen her once, when she came to the office to see Mr Adams about something. But I do remember she looked ever so elegant in a light brown coat with a dark brown fur collar.'

'Fur?' said Mrs Richards, checking the apple pie that was baking in the oven. 'Well, I don't know if that would've pleased that woman that messed up your firm's fashion show a while ago.'

'Oh, some people are born normal and some a bit daft,' said Queenie. 'And some get their knickers in a twist every Friday the thirteenth. Oh, did I tell you one of the girls told me Mrs Adams had been an ambulance driver in the Great War?'

'No, you didn't tell me,' said Mrs Richards, 'and I don't know I'd have believed it, anyway. I mean, in the Great War? She must be nearly ninety by now, then.'

'Mum, you never could add up,' said Queenie.

Later that evening, she had a look at the street from the front room, and was shocked to see, just touched by the light of the lamp, her bad dream himself. She froze. She hadn't really expected this, she'd thought the note alone had been enough. But it was him all right. His cap, as usual, was turned down, his raincoat collar turned up. He must have known she was there, at the window, for he offered a wave before walking away. It took her a few seconds to come to, then anger boiled up and she rushed to the front door. But when she ran out into the street, intending to catch him up and confront him, come what may, he was gone.

She said nothing to her mum, who was worried enough. As for herself, as soon as she cooled down she started to get the shivers again. She thought, however, that she could just about manage to live with them until Monday, when she'd talk to Mr Adams and George Porter. Yes, that was what she'd do. She had a feeling that these two men could arrange to rid her of Shifty Cecil once and for all.

'Where is Miss Browning?' asked the German visitor as he handed his room key to the male receptionist the following morning.

'She's off duty for the weekend, sir.'

'Ah, so? Good. Weekends are for play, *ja*? Not work, eh?'

'Some of us have picked the short straw, but have an enjoyable time yourself, sir.' The receptionist watched the long-legged German leave the hotel, although not with the same interest Miss Browning always showed.

Reaching his parked car, the hired vehicle, the Wolf paused for a moment. There were things to get, to buy, but the day was fine and clear, if cold, and a drive out of London's crowded centre might be more satisfying than shopping. He was in no great hurry to complete his self-appointed mission. Taking one's time to reach the moment of execution was always pleasurable. He had known that kind of pleasure many times as a loyal servant of Himmler.

He entered the car, watched by a young man with a wealth of well-dressed hair. The car moved off, and the young man crossed the road.

'Ready, troops?' called Boots from the hall.

'Ready,' called Gemma from the lounge.

'Ready,' called James from the living room.

'Unready,' called Polly from somewhere up above.

'Seven days CB,' called Boots.

'"Oh, when this blooming war is over, how happy we shall be,"' sang Polly, '"we'll kiss the sergeant major when he brings our morning tea . . ."'

'There you are, Daddy,' said Gemma, joining him in the hall, 'as soon as you stop bawling at Mummy, she'll stop singing and give you a kiss.'

'Who's bawling?' asked Boots.

'Well, have a go, Pa,' said James, also appearing, 'and see what happens.'

'Coming, coming,' called Polly, and in only a half a minute more she was running down the stairs in a fur-collared coat and fur hat. The autumn day, though fine, was chilly.

It was a little after twelve noon, and they were due at the home of Tim and Felicity for lunch. Everyone was keen to see how Felicity's life had changed with her restored sight. Last time they'd visited, Tim had said she was so giddy with new life that on some days she was spinning like a top with no need for anyone to wind her up.

A little way down on the other side of the road, Ernst Thurber watched them leave their house from the seat of his car. His eyes almost glowed. There they were, the whole family, husband, wife, son and daughter. It was the first time he had seen the wife, and in his brief glimpse he acknowledged her to have the air of what he presumed to be a typically aristocratic Englishwoman. He supposed, accordingly, that she considered herself superior to all other beings. Didn't she know that the only race superior to the rest had been Hitler's Germans? The world would one day realize what a mistake it had been to allow them to be beaten not by a greater people, but simply by countless hordes of Russian termites.

So, then. A man with an aristocratic wife and a

son and daughter. All of them would go. Yes, to avenge the undoubted death by torture of Hans and to strike a post-war blow for the SS, the whole family of the one-time Colonel Robert Adams of the British army would and must go. Again the Wolf reminded himself that it was Colonel Adams who had been responsible for Hans landing up in the hands of British interrogators in London, where he had met his death. The underground SS organization had discovered that, and he himself had found the home of the man and his family.

He watched as their car passed him. He formed the impression that they were in an animated mood. Well, a weekend was for enjoyment, yes. Payment was for another time.

'Felicity, everything is still marvellous?' said Polly, a few minutes after the family's arrival.

'Everything, Polly, is miraculous,' said Felicity.

'That includes me,' said Jennifer. 'Well, out of billions of people all over this globe, I'm the only one who's me, and that's a miracle for sure.'

'So's the fact that she's got a boyfriend,' said Tim, a tough ex-commando with a soft-hearted approach to the whims of his wife and the wiles of his daughter.

'At thirteen?' said Polly. 'At that age I was still working out how to spell rhubarb, and having my hair put into pigtails and ribbons. Pink. A boyfriend at thirteen, Jennifer?'

'Oh, he's really only someone who walks me home from school,' said Jennifer.

'Gemma gets walked home by half a dozen someones,' said James.

'Well, over lunch,' said Felicity, eyes clear and bright, 'Gemma can tell us about all six of them. Is that number a record for a sixteen-year-old?'

'I fancy it's a definite record for Gemma,' said Boots.

Over the lunch, Jennifer asked what about James, didn't he have a girlfriend? Gemma said well, he'd had Cathy Davidson and Cindy Stevens, but Cathy went off to Paris with her mother, and Cindy was collecting other boys by the dozen. So he's only a bit of an also-ran, said Gemma.

'Oh, what rotten hard luck, James,' said Jennifer.

'Very trying,' said James. 'Would you pass the salt, Jennifer?'

'Your social life must be awfully dull,' said Jennifer, pushing the cruet forward.

'Not good, no,' said James. 'Usually on Saturday mornings I'm restricted to being taken shopping by Cindy or doing a spot of drill with our cadet unit.' The cadet unit of his school was long-established. 'Were you ever taken shopping by a girl, Dad?'

Boots's memory had no difficulty with this one. He recalled an outing in former times with Emily, the girl next door at the time.

'James, old chap,' he said, 'when I was only a few years older than you, I was taken by a girl into Gamages ladies' underwear department, but not until we reached the counter did I realize it was to help her choose some frillies.'

'Never,' said Felicity. 'Never been known, never will be.'

'Fact,' said Boots.

'News to me,' said Tim, grinning widely.

'And me,' said Polly.

'What happened, Daddy?' asked Gemma.

'Everything went blush-red,' said Boots. 'Up until then I think I'd have passed as a fairly normal young feller, but if you've ever heard your grandmother refer to me as a hopeless case, you'll understand what that experience did to me.'

'I can imagine the scene in days of old,' said Tim. 'It's a wonder you weren't arrested. Incidentally, who was the girl?'

'Oh, some neighbour's daughter,' said Boots, preferring not to reminisce by name about his first wife in the presence of Polly. One simply didn't do that.

'Well, whoever she was, Boots, she left you with certain memories of ladies' frillies,' said Felicity.

'She sounds to me as if she was a bit potty,' said Gemma. 'I mean, only a girl slightly round the twist would need a boyfriend to help her choose – well, whatever it was.'

'There's probably more to this than met your eye, Boots old love,' said Polly.

'I pass,' said Boots.

The lunch went on in this easy atmosphere without either Boots or Polly having the faintest notion that they and the twins had been marked down as fodder for the maw of a psychopathic ex-SS guard, known to his concentration-camp colleagues as the Wolf.

Chapter Fourteen

That evening at a dance hall in Streatham, an area somewhat superior to good old cockney Brixton, Emily Chapman was swinging with boyfriend Brad to the music of a band called the Bopcats. It was a band with a very individual appeal, composing its own music and writing its own lyrics, and reckoned by the pundits to have a great future, along with its own legion of fainting fans. Fainting fans were impressionable teenage girls who, carried away by hysterical adulation for their favourite stars, keeled over during a concert. This trend had originated with the female fans of Frank Sinatra. Frank had seen thousands faint right in front of his microphone. Most hoped to be carried to his dressing room to be revived by the great star himself.

Certainly, the Bopcats were reckoned to be heading high. And they had class as well as promise. They were well dressed, well groomed, and devoid of either acne or pimples. And, as

Brad kept saying into Emily's ear, their music was smooth, man, smooth.

Emily and Brad were close to the stage, along with bunched ranks of other young people, including more than a few ready-to-swoon girls, all sinuously vibrating with their eyes closed. Emily, however, had her eyes open, keeping the bandleader, the guitarist, well in her sights. His open-necked white shirt was worn with midnight blue pencil-slim trousers that made his movements thrillingly sexy. Of course, no star's movements were quite as sexy as Elvis Presley's, but it was great to note there was talent here in Streatham.

The moment became ecstatic for Emily. The guitarist caught her eye. He delivered a slow wink and a come-on smile, and so, as the number, a dreamy one, cruised sweetly to a finish, Emily fainted. That is, she sank to her knees and then flopped.

Sensation at the front of the swaying ranks. Officials arrived.

'Stand back.'

'Stay clear.'

'Here, give over,' protested Brad as he was pushed aside, 'she's my girlfriend.'

'Just stand back, sir.'

Brad took a poor view of that. He was wearing his best Saturday night outfit, a dark green hip-length velvet jacket, yellow pearl-buttoned waistcoat, brown drainpipes and his Tony Curtis quiff. He expected all that to be noted, as well as his social relationship with Emily, but it wasn't, and while he was held back she was borne away to a reviving chamber, to wit, the Bopcats' dressing room. To re-settle everyone, the next number began, and Brad was caught up in swarms of swingers.

Emily opened her eyes. All was light and sparkle and mirrors. She was comfortably at rest on a couch, and above her was the singularly handsome face of a man dressed in a roll-neck white sweater and tan slacks.

'Better?'

'What happened?' asked Emily, deliciously engaging in a white broderie anglaise blouse, a full skirt and flat black pumps.

'You fainted.'

'I didn't, did I?' She hadn't, of course, although she'd made a very convincing job of it. 'Well, I've never fainted before.'

'Oh, it happens at some concerts with some girls.' The man was reassuring, his smile gently concerned. 'The point is, how do you feel now?'

'Oh, I think I'll live,' said Emily. Being in the Bopcats' dressing room, the object of the exercise, and wanting to stay, she added, 'Except I'd like a few quiet minutes to help me recover. Well, I still feel a bit dizzy.'

'You're welcome to take your time.' This was said with the easy air of a man who knew more

180

about the world than callow youths did. 'There's no hurry. Would you like, say, a pick-me-up?'

'D'you mean an aspirin or something?'

He laughed. Gently.

'I mean a pick-me-up. But you can have an aspirin, if you prefer, with a glass of water.'

'Oh, I don't prefer any aspirin,' said Emily, feeling sure she needed to make a more wordly choice in order to impress this fascinating man. 'I think I need something to get over the shock of collapsing.'

'I see, we're suffering a sense of shock, are we?' The smile became quizzical.

'D'you think a little brandy might help?' suggested Emily in her worldly guise.

'Young lady, how old are you?'

'Seventeen,' said Emily, who had been fifteen in August.

'I see,' said her doctor of the moment. 'A little brandy, then. That's always the best kind of pick-me-up in a case of shock.'

'Oh, thanks,' said Emily, and made ready to brace herself for what a sip of brandy might do to her inexperienced tonsils.

The smiling face went away, and in a moment she heard the clink of a glass. She felt her fainting act had brought her to the edge of that thrilling world most people only ever read about. This retreat, with its dressing tables, its mirrors and its lights, was the home this evening of the classy Bopcats, which really was exciting. At the moment it was uncrowded, and that made her highly sensitive to the intimacy of being alone with the handsome man. Who was he?

Returning with a measure of liquid in a glass, he must have read her thoughts, because he said, 'By the way, I'm Ross Featherstone, manager of the Bopcats. Here, have a sip of this.'

'Oh, man,' breathed Emily in sudden awe. Of course, Ross Featherstone. Everyone had heard of him. Well, most pop fans had. He'd been seen on television, and in newspapers, in company with smart people on big social occasions. He was said to be on very close terms with a famous female vocalist. With her pulses jumping about, Emily gazed dizzily at him, recognizing that here was an actual celebrity, the kind who could open for her the door to real life. 'Oh, man,' she breathed again.

She sat up and took the glass. The contents glittered with splashes of reflected light, and the light danced in Ross's eyes as he leaned over her, as if he meant to ensure she spilt none of the contents. She quivered and thought about how to make sure she was allowed to stay until the concert was over, when the Bopcats would arrive from the stage, with every one of them breathing and alive.

'Oh, I'm Emma Chapman,' she said, having suddenly decided Emma was more glamorous than Emily, 'and thanks all over for being so kind, Mr Featherstone.'

'You're welcome, young lady,' said Ross Featherstone. 'Try the pick-me-up,' he encouraged, and seated himself on the edge of the couch, close to her feet.

Emily took a cautious little sip, while opting to forget that her parents would not have put a glass of brandy anywhere near her hand. She expected the sip to bite her at the back of her throat and to make her cough, because that was what it did to people in novels, and to Hollywood stars like Doris Day in films. Instead, there was only a little tingling effect, even a refreshing one. So she took a further sip. More little tingles.

'Oh, I think it's doing me good,' she said.

'In that case, finish it,' said Ross Featherstone.

With what she thought was a very worldly air, Emily finished the rest in one go. The effect was sort of fizzy.

'Oh, thanks,' she said.

Ross Featherstone's smile was that of a man easily in charge of the situation. His eyes travelled from her feet up over her nyloned legs, over her skirt to her blouse and on to her own eyes. There was an exciting little clash of glances for Emily, exciting little disturbances.

'Better now?' His soothing voice was mesmerizing.

'Oh, it really did me good, that brandy,' she murmured dreamily.

'That brandy, young lady, happened to be Canada Dry ginger ale,' said Ross Featherstone.

'Ginger ale?'

'You can believe it.' He was far too sophisticated to take risks – any kind of risks – with an overexcited, under-aged teenage girl. He knew everything there was to know about concert hysteria, and what it could lead to.

'Ginger ale?' said Emily again.

'Ginger ale.'

'Not brandy?'

'Not brandy, no,' he said. He took the glass from her and placed it aside. The strains of music reached their ears. He laughed, very softly.

'Where the hell is she?' Giles was fed up. His sister could be a burdensome trial to him on their Saturday night outings. His was always the ultimate responsibility of ensuring she behaved herself reasonably and arrived back home by ten thirty. Emily thought such a time demand by parents in this day and age to be on a par with the regulations of Victorian workhouses. Giles was more understanding of parental principles. That is, those of his own parents. 'You saw her disappear, Brad, you said?'

In his searching journey around the hall, he had just bumped into Brad. They were to one side of the dance hall, and not far from the stage. Brad had been close to Emily when she flopped, but Giles had seen nothing of that, only the subsequent surge of people near the stage. Giles could always trust the good-natured Teddy boy to help keep an eye on Emily, thus relieving him of much of his brotherly chore. Brad also helped to ensure Emily arrived home on time.

'You bet I saw her,' said Brad, brilliantined quiff looking a bit out of shape. 'Passed out, didn't she, on account of getting a come-on from the bandleader.'

'A come-on?' said Giles, searching the massed ranks of vibrating boppers.

'Eyeball contact,' said Brad. 'As I mentioned, man, she was carried off to wonderland, while someone put the boot in on me.'

'Don't make me suffer,' said Giles, 'give me some idea of where you think she is. It won't be wonderland.'

'Dressing room, you bet,' said Brad, 'and being treated for hysterics. Well, that's what makes these cookies fall over their footgear if the music gets to them. Hysterics. It pains me, y'know, that your sister's caught the complaint. I mean, aside from that, she's up with the best.' He went on to say he'd twice managed to get to the door of the dressing room, but each time a hairy guy as big as a Soho club bouncer had blocked him.

Giles grimaced. The magic of the music was lost on him for the moment, and the swaying mass of teenagers caused him to feel even more fed up. Everyone ought to be worried about Emily, but he and Brad alone were turning grey.

'Come on, pal,' he said, 'let's get round to the

dressing room together. Two can make it better than one.'

'Sure, let's give it a go,' said Brad, and they made their way out of the hall and round to the rear entrance. No big bloke was there to damage them, and as the door wasn't locked they went in, taking the indicated route to the star dressing room. Dance halls hoping to acquire any real importance in the world of pop had to have a star dressing room these days.

'Seventeen, you said?' murmured Ross Featherstone, well aware that this teenage girl had the quivers. Female teenage quivers were dangerous both to the quiverer and to himself. 'Seventeen? I doubt if your parents would agree.'

Emily knew then that she was being laughed at. She went hot all over. There came a loud knocking on the door. And raised voices penetrated.

'Emily, you there? Come on out, you hear?'

That was Giles.

'Emily? Come on, baby.'

And that was Brad.

She slipped off the couch, feeling sick that the Bopcats' manager had merely been amusing himself at her expense. However, by no means a mouse, she summoned up a touch of pride and delivered an arrow.

'I thought only small boys acted childishly,' she said.

Ross Featherstone rode that, and made no move to stop her as she walked swiftly to the thumped door and the raised voices. She turned the handle. The door wasn't locked. It opened and there stood Giles and Brad.

Brad, catching sight of Ross Featherstone, called, 'Hey, man, what's been going on?'

'Who are you?'

'I'm her boyfriend,' said Brad.

'And I'm her brother,' said Giles.

The Bopcats' manager smiled and said to Emily, 'Tell your boyfriend and your brother what's been going on.'

'I needed some reviving refreshment,' said Emily, 'so he gave me a drink of ginger ale.'

'Really?' said Giles.

Ross Featherstone came to the door.

'Goodnight, young lady,' he said to Emily. 'Goodnight, fellers,' he said to Brad and Giles, 'and take better care of her next time she's at a concert.' And he closed the door.

'What happened in there?' demanded Giles of his sister.

'I told you,' said Emily, 'a drink of ginger ale to revive me.'

'Listen,' said Giles, 'he's got a reputation that's nothing to do with ginger ale.'

'More like a Mickey Finn,' said Brad.

'Oh, blow that kind of talk,' said Emily. 'Let's get back to the dancing.'

But once they had returned to the hall, Brad

and Giles kept her out of the action. With Brad pouring questions into her ear, they tried to mentally torture her into coming up with what they considered must be the truth. They could not equate ginger ale with the truth. They both knew Emily, how precocious she was, and how she could let the excitement of a pop concert run away with her. However, she persisted in denying that anything had happened, beyond what she'd said in the first place. A rest and a drink of ginger ale. In the end they had to accept that.

'Listen, baby,' said Brad, 'I just naturally worry about girls like you getting locked in by fly guys like Ross Featherstone.'

'Well, don't,' said Emily, 'just be your age. I wasn't locked in. Now, d'you want to swing a bit or not?'

Brad fell in with that, and Giles fell back in with a group of his contemporaries.

And when Emily reached home later that evening, neither Brad nor Giles said anything to her parents about her entry into the ranks of fainting female pop fans. She'd said she'd kill them if they did. The threat wasn't actually necessary, for her boyfriend and her brother weren't the kind to split on a girl, anyway.

'Well,' said her dad in greeting, 'how did the evening go at Streatham?'

'Great,' she said.

'A bigger great than your usual Brixton venue, or smaller?' asked Matt.

'Oh, just great,' said Giles. 'The Bopcats performed.'

'Bobcats?' said Rosie.

'The band,' said Giles.

'The Bobcats?' queried Rosie again.

'Not that outfit, lady,' said Brad, an admirer of Emily's ma. 'That outfit, the Bobcats, happened to be a pre-war Dixie band. We're talking about the Bopcats. Bop, as in bebop.'

'Matt,' said Rosie, always willing to be introduced to the language of teenagers, 'do we know about bebop?'

'Well, personally, I know about Noah's Ark,' said Matt, 'but I think I've fallen behind since then.'

'Well, just get up to date, Daddy,' said Emily. 'Bop, which is short for bebop, means dancing to pop music.'

'Fact?' said Matt. 'Well, what about dancing to a foxtrot, then? What's that called?'

'Mr Chapman,' said Brad, his quiff restored to the perpendicular, 'I guess that's called the dodo.'

Rosie laughed. She quite liked the Teddy boy and his reliability as joint guardian with Giles of Emily, who, frankly, wanted to run after life instead of first learning to walk with it.

'Well, young man,' she said to Brad, 'let me thank you for helping Emily to enjoy one more dancing evening, and for bringing her home.'

'Pleasure, Mrs Chapman,' said Brad, 'she sure is a hepcat, your daughter.'

'Hepcat?' said Matt, unrivalled when it came to understanding a car's innards, but definitely falling behind in respect of teenage lingo. 'Hepcat?'

'Lover of modern music, Dad,' said Giles.

'Hepcat?' smiled Rosie, her wealth of hair as much of a golden crown as it had ever been, and accordingly much admired by Brad. 'I suppose that's the opposite of dodo.'

'You bet it is, and more,' said Brad, which was a hint to Emily that he still had his doubts about what she had got up to with Ross Featherstone. 'Goodnight, all.' And he departed homewards.

For some reason, the last thing Emily thought about that night, as she put her head on her pillow, was not the moment when the Bopcats' worldly manager let her know he'd been having a game with her. No, she thought of Maureen, the daughter of Freddy and Cassie Brown, and the fact that she had made it into the exciting world of glamour. She was now quite a well-known pin-up. Yes, so she was. Well, imagine that . . .

Chapter Fifteen

Sunday afternoon.

Ernst Thurber was taking advantage of a fairly pleasant day, weatherwise, to play the tourist. He was presently viewing the Houses of Parliament, but not with any admiration for the nobility of the architecture. No, he was remembering the day when Dr Goebbels made the announcement by radio that the Luftwaffe, in one more night raid on London, had smashed the House of Commons, the seat of Britain's elected government and the place where their warmongering Prime Minister, Winston Churchill, made his pitiful speeches.

Unfortunately, the raid hadn't flattened the place beyond repair. There it was, rising up from the river in sneering triumphalism, and damned if Churchill himself wasn't still posturing around the world. Himmler had gone, so had Goering and Goebbels, and the Great One too, the Führer. And so had the American, Roosevelt. But Churchill had had the luck of a black Russian cat, or that of a favoured idiot gaping at an avalanche while all around him were swept away.

The Wolf's strong teeth grated for a moment. Then a ghost of a smile flitted. If he was not in a position to eliminate Churchill, he was very well situated to do away with one of his ex-army officers, together with wife and children.

Content with that, he strolled away.

On the corner of Whitehall, scene of Churchill's wildly acclaimed appearance on VE Day, stood a young man with a handsome head of rich black hair. His name was Andre Kiernik, and he was the son of a Polish hairdresser, Emil Kiernik.

He watched as Ernst Thurber moved on.

Rosie's Sunday newspaper contained items and articles that broadened the mind and increased one's knowledge of the world and its teeming masses. Her liking for its educational value had been born when she and Boots shared the reading of it during her college days.

Matt's Sunday newspaper was of a livelier kind, one that did not deal overmuch with the burning questions of the day. It was in lighter vein and carried very informative bits and pieces concerning cars.

This afternoon, while he was replacing old plugs with new ones in Rosie's runabout car, Emily had her nose in his paper. Her whole attention was fixed on one of the feature pages. It actually contained an illustrated article on Ross Featherstone, describing him not only as the imaginative manager of the Bopcats, but also as the darling of the teeny-boppers. The illustrations included a photograph of him outside the door of his scenic farmhouse in Bucks, where he had his own recording studio. There was also a shot of the current Rank starlet in his life, plus a photograph of the Bopcats, and at once Emily noted the good-looking guitarist. Finally, she took in the fact that their next concert was on Saturday at the Hammersmith Palais, a great joint for gigs.

'What's catching your attention, darling?' asked Rosie, curled up in Sunday afternoon comfort on the settee.

'Oh, there's a write-up here on the Bopcats,' said Emily. 'You know, the band we danced to last night in Streatham.'

'I know they impressed you and Giles,' said Rosie, 'just as most of these modern bands seem to. Your dad, of course, is still a Jack Hylton fan.'

'Mum, that music is out of date,' said Emily.

'I think he knows that,' said Rosie, and murmured, 'I think I do, too.'

Matt appeared then, along with Giles, who had been helping him with Rosie's car. They were both wearing tatty old clothes and showing slightly oily hands.

'Afternoon, all,' said Matt, 'how about some tea?'

'How about some soap and water?' smiled Rosie.

'Will do,' said Giles. 'Who's going to put the kettle on?'

'Not me,' said Emily.

'Who's a sweet girl, then?' said Giles.

'There's an old Dorset saying,' said Matt.

'Oh, help,' said Emily.

Rosie had a smile on her face as Matt began.

> "Down in Dorset, so they say,
> Mums be busy every day,
> So be girls, along the way,
> You'll find 'em in the summer hay."

'Very funny, I don't think,' said Emily.

'Spot on, Dad,' said Giles.

'I'll make the tea,' said Rosie, rising.

'Oh, all right, I'll get the cups and saucers out,' said Emily.

That evening she phoned Maureen Brown. As Maureen's father was Aunt Susie's younger brother, Emily counted Maureen as a kind of cousin. On a Saturday afternoon in August, they had paired up at an open-air pop concert in Battersea Park. Maureen, by then a glamorous pin-up, had looked gorgeous, and it was no wonder she was right on the edge of the exciting world one dreamt about. Emily, having reminded herself of that, enjoyed a happy phone conversation with her cousin from Walworth.

Boots woke up in the middle of the night. There was no apparent reason for it, no jerking from the embrace of a nightmarish dream, simply a sudden transition from oblivion to consciousness. There had been no dream at all, in fact, yet here he was, wide awake, with Polly sleeping soundlessly beside him.

The house was quiet, the quiet of night after one more busy day. Outside, there was neither wind nor rain, neither gale nor storm, although one was conscious that chill winter was pushing at late autumn.

He turned onto his back, reflecting on the quirks of life. It was a quirk to pull a man so suddenly from sleep and offer him no reason for it. Or was there a reason he could only guess at? That thought alerted him to possibilities. He turned again, towards Polly. Polly the inimitable, a comrade of both world wars, wild in her ways as a young woman, but now his cherished wife for seventeen years, and the only woman who could have made up for the loss of Emily.

She was in total slumber, breathing easily and evenly. The twins? He could not help himself. He slid quickly but quietly out of bed, put on his dressing gown and made his way to Gemma's bedroom. With his eyes used to the darkness, he put no light on. Very gently he turned the handle of her door and insinuated himself into the room. He picked out the bedclothes that shaped her body. He went close, looked down at her and saw her face resting on the pillow, her hand cupping her chin. She too was breathing easily and evenly. No crisis there. But what about James? Making no sound, he left Gemma's bedroom and hastened to see if her brother was in similar peaceful repose.

James looked as if he, at least, had been having a bad time. He was lying on his back, sheet and blanket flung down to his waist, one arm bent on his pillow, hand under his head. Nevertheless, he was asleep, healthily so. Boots gently covered him up. James murmured happily, as if conscious of restored warmth, but he did not wake up.

So here I am, fussing like some old mother hen, thought Boots wryly, and I'm more awake than ever. There's only one thing for it, a breaking of the wakeful pattern. That means the kitchen and a cup of tea.

Down he went. Reaching the kitchen, he switched on the light. Familiar surroundings embraced him. He put the kettle on and prepared the teapot.

Fifteen minutes later.

'Boots?'

Polly was at the open kitchen door, clad in her dressing gown, her eyes regarding him anxiously.

'Hello there, old girl,' said Boots, 'come and join me.'

'Not before you tell me why you're down here in the middle of the night,' said Polly.

'Woke up, couldn't get to sleep again,' said Boots.

'That's all?' said Polly, still not sure there wasn't cause for concern. 'Darling, you're not ill, are you?'

'Ill? No, not a bit,' he said, 'unless drinking tea at three o'clock in the morning is a serious complaint. Like to join me, heroine of World War One?'

Polly was swift to move then, and to help herself to a cup and saucer. She sat down opposite him at the table, put milk in her cup, and watched him as he filled it with hot tea. If she had felt alarm at waking up to find him gone, that was over now. He was perfectly himself, and his reference to the war of the trenches reminded her of their shared past.

'What did wake you?' she asked.

'No idea,' said Boots, 'unless it was an uneasy conscience.'

'Piffle,' said Polly, and drank her tea. The night was still quiet, the murmurings of dawn hours away. 'Uneasy conscience is no go, ducky, so what else could it have been?'

'Ask me another,' said Boots, 'but it did give me a few quiet moments to think about my life, and to tell myself that in all I've had and been given, I can count my blessings, as Lizzy sometimes reminds me.'

Polly wondered if he counted his four years of blindness as a blessing. No, the blessing in that context would have been the existence of Emily, his first wife, for she had given him care and devotion all through his dark days. Polly knew of those years, and wished she herself had been that woman.

'Boots, old soldier,' she said, 'I've had my own moments of good fortune.'

'Well, you count as a leading example of mine,' said Boots, and there was affection rather than whimsy in his smile for her.

'You must know,' she said, 'that very few women are completely satisfied with what they have. What I have is all I've ever wished for from the time we first met.'

'Then you and I are both in clover,' said Boots. 'Incidentally, what woke you up?'

'The cold bed,' said Polly. 'It's always cold when you're not there.'

'Well, dear girl, you deserve warmth and a cuddle,' said Boots, 'so when we've finished this tea, we'll go back up again, shall we?'

'Your wish, ducky, is ever my command,' said Polly.

'Is that a truthful statement?' smiled Boots.

'It's the best I can do at half past three in the morning,' said Polly.

* * *

The Wolf was asleep in his hotel bed, dreaming of the great days of Himmler and the SS, when he himself, as sergeant in charge of a platoon of guards at Auschwitz, had the authority to play God.

He woke up, languorous and full of well-being, and dwelling immediately on the pleasurable anticipation of playing God again, this time by virtue of his own authority.

He wondered if ex-Colonel Robert Adams and his family were enjoying sound sleep. If so, let them make the most of it, for quite soon they would be sleeping their last. It would not be difficult to acquire the means to extinguish them.

He turned over and sank easily back into his dreams.

Ex-SS Sergeant Ernst Thurber was without the conscience, compunction or feelings of a civilized man.

Chapter Sixteen

Monday morning.

Alarm bells rang for Adams Fashions, when Tommy, the moment he reached the factory, telephoned through to Sammy to tell him a large poster had been plastered on the gate. Its message was a diabolical liberty. Further, it wasn't even true.

'PEOPLE OF LONDON! TAKE NOTE! THE OWNERS OF THIS FACTORY MANUFAC-TURE COATS MADE OF ANIMAL SKINS! STRIKE A BLOW FOR ANIMAL HUMANITY! BOYCOTT THIS FACTORY AND ITS OUT-PUT!'

'What the hell's animal humanity?' asked Sammy.

'How the last fanackapan do I know?' said Tommy. 'All I do know is that it's upset our machinists and drawn a gawping crowd.'

'Now, Tommy, use your loaf,' said Sammy, 'tear it down.'

'Easier said than done, mate. It's plastered on,

and needs hot water and a scrubbing brush to get it off.'

'Well, get someone to put the kettle on, for Christ's sake,' said Sammy.

'Listen, mate, don't try teaching me how to suck lemons,' said Tommy, 'I'm long past being simple and gormless. Incidentally, the name and address of this daft, one-eyed organization was on the bottom of the poster.'

'Scrub it off now,' said Sammy.

'I said was, not is,' bawled Tommy. 'It's already been blacked out. Now we've got a fellow scrubbing his best to make the whole poster vanish. Listen, talk to Boots and ring me back sometime.'

'First off, I'll ring one or two of our competitors,' said Sammy, 'and find out if Mad Marj has put posters up outside their premises. And might I point out I don't have to rely on Boots every time there's a strange cat in the alley?'

'Boots is a natural at sorting out problems we don't want,' said Tommy. 'And listen, watch out that Tarzan's jungle mate doesn't paste a poster on the front door of your offices. It'll send Camberwell Green lopsided. You don't want your windows broken by the kind of people who consider elephant fur sacred, do you?'

'Elephant fur my Aunt Fanny,' said Sammy, 'didn't you do geography or something at school? Mad Marj is on about bears and leopards and suchlike, not elephant fur, of which there ain't no such thing.'

'You think I don't know it?' said Tommy. 'Of course I bloody do. Listen, ask Boots to get stuck in on the problem of animal humanity, which is a new one on me as well as you.' And he rang off to spend the next two minutes bawling out his maintenance man for taking too much time scrubbing off the libellous poster.

Sammy phoned a London competitor, and his alarm took a turn for the critical when told that two of those posters had been stuck on their office frontage.

'Bloody hell,' he breathed.

'Excuse me, Mr Adams,' said the director to whom he was speaking, 'but I happen to be a Sunday school teacher.'

'Apologies,' said Sammy, 'I'm Church of England meself.'

He phoned a second competitor, and his alarm went off bang when he was told of more posters.

'Holy Moses,' he whistled, 'she's conducting a war.'

'Come again, Sammy?'

'Her. Mad Marj. She'll be our death unless we can get her certified and locked up. So long, Izzy.'

Rachel entered his office as he put the phone down.

'Good morning, Sammy.'

'Don't I wish it was,' said Sammy, and acquainted her with the news.

'My life, we should worry?' said Rachel.

'Well, Tommy ain't exactly celebrating,' said Sammy, 'and nor am I. I know we're not furriers, and nor do we sell fur coats, but we do turn out cosy items trimmed with fur. Mad Marj put us on her list because of the Mayfair show, which is upsetting me considerably.'

'Of course, there are people who wouldn't wear furs at any price,' said Rachel, 'but they don't usually kick up a fuss about people who do.'

'What's going to worry the trade is if Mad Marj starts getting more publicity,' said Sammy. 'It could mean Adams Fashions having to think about cutting out anything in the nature of fur trimmings, which would upset certain Brixton customers who like to look expensive. It's what furs or fur trimmings do for female women. Might I quote you the fact that our shops sell a steady number of stylish winter coats with dinky fur collars, all at affordable prices?'

'Sammy,' said Rachel, who herself always looked stylish when wearing fur, 'if any such coats feature in our shops' window displays, can we expect posters to be stuck on the windows overnight?'

'Well, frankly,' said Sammy, 'I'm hoping Mad Marj will end up trying to convert Australian Eskimos. I mean, that should keep her busy for a few years.'

'Sammy, there are no Eskimos in Australia.'

'Well, all right, so there aren't,' said Sammy. 'I was naturally thinking Australia is as far away as we could get Mad Marj. Now I'd better have a word with Boots.'

'George Porter and Queenie are with him at the moment,' said Rachel.

'Don't tell me Queenie's still got problems with a kook,' said Sammy.

'Could be,' said Rachel. 'My life, Sammy, there's never a quiet day here.'

Queenie had begged Boots's attention first thing, and with George Porter present, she had told of Friday's happenings: the arrival of an unsigned and unaddressed note, and the presence of the creep in the street late in the evening. She went on about what it was doing to her, turning her into a bag of nerves. Boots thought about it, while George offered sympathy from the bottom of his heart. Queenie responded to that by declaring it was a godsend to know that some men were human beings.

'Especially men like you and Mr Adams,' she said.

'Oh, don't mention it,' said George. 'I mean, for myself – well, what man wouldn't sympathize with a – a –'

'A nice young lady like you, Queenie,' said Boots, who had been studying the note.

'Oh, charmed, I'm sure,' said Queenie, 'but

what about this creep? Me mum's on again about telling the police.'

Boots suggested that if George was free, he should spend the evening waiting for Sick Sid to appear.

'Meaning Shifty Cecil?' said George.

'There are all kinds of names for men like that,' said Boots, and went on to suggest further that if the nuisance did appear, George was to deal with him in the best way possible, as previously agreed.

'We're applying psychology?' said George.

'I don't know my mum would like the sound of that more than the sound of a copper laying a hand on the bloke,' said Queenie.

'Trust George,' said Boots.

'Tell you what, Mr Adams,' said George, 'I'll make it my business to be on the spot every evening this week until he does turn up. Miss Richards – Queenie – might I suggest I – um – ride on the bus with you in the hope of catching him as soon as we reach your street?'

'Yes, course you can,' said Queenie, and Boots complimented George on coming up with a first-class suggestion. It would mean stopping the shifty character in his tracks if the man intended at last to confront Queenie, and also give George the opportunity to pin him to the wall, in a manner of speaking.

'Understood,' said George.

'Oh, help,' said Queenie, 'the neighbours will

come rushing out if you start breaking his legs.' If that possibility concerned her, it didn't alter the fact that she now had quite a bit of respect for George, never having forgotten what he was capable of in a rough house. 'Still, me mum won't complain.'

Boots said to see what the evening would bring, and Queenie went back to her desk to prepare for her day's work. Boots had a few more minutes of conversation with George, and then the cost clerk went back to his office.

Boots, addressing himself belatedly to his share of the morning's mail, suffered a second interruption in the form of Sammy and a declaration that Mad Marj was at war with Adams Fashions and other companies. Boots was given details of the poster campaign, along with Sammy's personal hope that somehow someone somewhere might get Mad Marj to conduct a save-the-kangaroo lark in Australia.

'And I've got to tell you, Boots old cock, that Tommy and me coincide in looking at you.'

'Well, Sammy,' said Boots, 'if I were that someone somewhere I'd be delighted somehow to get the lady on a one-way trip to down under. But I'm not.'

'All right,' said Sammy, 'so think of something else, mate. But don't include any telegrams about an elephant looking for its dad in the Scottish Highlands.'

'Try sending her a donation,' said Boots, 'with

a letter saying the firm supports the cause of – what was it? Oh, yes, animal humanity. Yes, try that, Sammy.'

'Hold on,' said Sammy, 'exactly what is animal humanity?'

'Oh, teaching foxes to be kind to little lambs, I suppose,' said Boots. 'Anyway, do your best to convince her Adams Fashions is on her side. Oh, and ask her to send some posters.'

'Eh?' said Sammy.

'Yes, good idea, Sammy, give her the impression the firm's going to use them on her behalf. Now, if you don't mind, I'd like to start work.'

'Half a mo,' said Sammy, 'what's that bit about posters?'

'Better to have them in your desk drawer than stuck on the factory gates,' said Boots. 'Sign the letter "Yours truly". No, perhaps not "truly". Make it "Yours sincerely".'

'Pardon me if I'm looking cross-eyed,' said Sammy.

'Worry not,' said Boots, and finally got down to inspecting his mail.

'Good morning, Mr Seidler,' said Miss Janice Browning, the daytime receptionist.

'Good morning, Miss Browning.' The German gentleman, who was wearing his hat and rain-coat, offered a smile hugely benign as he handed in his room key. 'But the day is not so good, is it?'

'It's raining, I'm afraid,' said Miss Browning, hanging the room key on its hook. 'London rain.'

'So?' Mr Seidler seemed willing to chat. 'That means it is more wet than Berlin rain?'

'I've never encountered Berlin rain,' said Miss Browning. 'Well, I've never been there.'

'But your RAF pilots have, *ja*?' The smile lost its element of good humour for a fleeting second. 'Many times, I think.'

'Oh,' said Miss Browning, taken aback. One did not mention the war to German visitors, nor expect them to. 'Oh, the war's been over for years now, sir, and we're all grateful for that, aren't we?'

'Everyone is pleased?'

'Naturally. Are you going to the City again today, Mr Seidler?' The question was asked out of politeness.

'No, most of my business in the City is done, so see, I have my London guidebook and am going to that famous place – *ja*, Trafalgar Square – to feed the pigeons.' He left then, his raincoat and hat guarding him against the weather.

It was not, thought Miss Browning, the best kind of day in which to stand around feeding the pigeons of Trafalgar Square. His reference to the wartime bombing of Berlin had been very unexpected and out of place. After all, it was the Germans who had started the terrible practice of bombing cities.

The Wolf saw feeding London pigeons as one

more way of dwelling pleasurably on revenge. He did not drive to Trafalgar Square in his hired car. He took a taxi. The question of expense did not concern him. He had salted away a fortune when it was obvious Germany was going to lose the war. The fortune, of course, had been made up of Jewish gold and jewellery, and since his release from prison a Swiss bank had been providing him with all the funds he needed.

The dark young man with the handsome head of hair happened to be around as the Wolf entered the taxi. He then made a phone call from a public booth.

'Sammy,' said Rachel during the afternoon, 'you wish me myself to type this letter and to see that it's posted?' She had a sheet of notepaper in her hand, given to her by Sammy, a written communication to a Miss Marjorie Alsop.

'Yup, leave it to you to keep it confidential,' said Sammy. 'We don't want all the staff to know we're playing ball with a female nutcase. I'll sign the letter when you've typed it. Oh, and don't forget to enclose the donation, which, as you can see, is in the form of the firm's cheque made out for ten quid.' He handed her the cheque.

'You say this is Boots's idea?' said Rachel.

'You're asking serious?' said Sammy. 'Who else could have cooked it up but my educated brother? And all done without blinking an eyelash. I tell you, Rachel, by the time he was five my dear old ma must have wondered if she'd given birth to one of those Persian oracles. And I tell you again, by the time he was ten the street kids were already calling him Lord Muck. And that was before he'd been seriously educated.'

'My life, Sammy, never will I hear a word against Boots,' said Rachel. 'If he thinks this is the best way for us to deal with Miss Alsop, we should both go along with him.'

'Might I point out I'm doing so?' said Sammy. 'Who else put that letter together if it wasn't me? And who else is going to type the letter confidentially if it ain't you? We're both going along with Boots right enough, but I get a feeling sometimes that one day his brains are going to unwind and finish up as loose ends. I hope this ain't the day.'

'Sammy, that might happen when he's a hundred,' said Rachel, 'but not while he's still in his prime.'

'In his prime?' said Sammy. 'Rachel, he's over sixty.'

'Some men are still in their prime at seventy,' said Rachel. 'Some men. Well, I'll go and type this letter. Will you mind if I show it to Rosie?'

'OK,' said Sammy, 'but no-one else. I don't want any of the staff to find out. They'll think the firm's executives have gone demented. They'll lose confidence and worry about their jobs.'

'I shall worry not, Sammy,' said Rachel.

'He said that,' muttered Sammy.

'Who's he?' asked Rachel.

'Houdini,' said Sammy.

At Bethnal Green, the Adams factory and its workforce had settled down after an agitated morning. The poster on the right-hand gate had been soaked and scrubbed off, and Tommy had been told by Sammy just how he was going to deal with Mad Marj, which was as recommended by the family prophet, otherwise Boots. Tommy was prompted to remark that Boots must be having an off day for once. However, he assured Sammy he was prepared to wait for results.

Towards the end of the working day, Jimmy, Sammy's younger son and the factory's personnel manager, looked in on his Uncle Tommy, wanting him to know there were a few termites in the woodwork. Tommy said to clarify that.

'I'm referring to some of the seamstresses,' said Jimmy, who, like others in the family, was disinclined to take life too seriously.

'What about some of the seamstresses?' asked Tommy.

'They agree with the lady,' said Jimmy.

'D'you mean Marjorie Alsop?' said Tommy, slight thunderclouds darkening his brow. 'She's no lady, she's a ruddy menace. We run a nice line here turning out fur-trimmed coats and suchlike, and she's out to sabotage it.'

'I know,' said Jimmy, 'and it seems some of our

staff go along with her. They're mostly the ones who keep cats and whose kids keep rabbits. Well, that was what Lily Packer whispered in my ear five minutes ago.' Lily Packer was a seamstress.

'Now look, sonny,' said Tommy, 'it's knocking-off time in fifteen minutes. You trying to send me home with a headache that'll put me off me supper by telling me we've got traitors in the machine shop? Tell Lily Packer to tell 'em we don't skin leopards or alligators ourselves, nor cats and dogs – all right, hamsters.'

'Don't worry,' said Jimmy, 'they're not likely to risk their jobs by marching behind Miss Alsop, but I thought they might just ask you one day if fur-trimmed clobber is really necessary to our range.'

'Well, ta for the thought,' said Tommy, 'but I ain't playing.'

Chapter Seventeen

'Oh, er – right, there you are,' said George Porter as Queenie emerged from the office building. The working day was over and he was waiting for her on the pavement. Queenie was wearing a coat and knitted hat to ward off the cold of the evening, George a coat and trilby. It had to be said that the coat gave his thickset body quite a handsome look, and the trilby kept the wind from ruffling his hair. 'I think – um – I think we agreed to travel together,' he said with his customary diffidence.

'That's right,' said Queenie, not a bit diffident herself, even if Shifty Cecil did make shivers run down her spine every time he intruded into her life. 'So come on, let's walk to the bus stop.'

Along with other workers, they began their walk to the junction, the chill of late autumn offset by a clear night sky.

'It's a nice evening,' said George, imagining himself as a private eye and Queenie as the imperilled and innocent daughter of a Mafia boss. 'Just the kind to bring Al Fascioni out of his hideaway.'

'Who?' asked Queenie, her quick perky footsteps keeping up with his deliberate strides.

'Eh? What?'

'Al Whatsisname, how did he get in?' asked Queenie. 'Don't you mean Sick Sid, like Mr Adams called him?'

'Of course, yes,' said George, 'I tripped over my tongue. Well, here we are.' They were at the bus stop, fastening themselves onto the end of a queue of waiting passengers. Almost at once a bus came along, and the queue surged forward.

'Now hold yer horses, friends,' called the conductor, 'passengers off the bus first, if yer don't mind. It's me responsibility to see they don't get trodden on. That's it, stand back, don't climb over them, there's plenty of room for all.'

When they did board, Queenie and George found seats together on the lower deck. They settled down, Queenie's rounded hip communicating silently but warmly with George's firm hip, which made him quiver a bit in a pleasant way. He paid for both of them when the conductor came round asking for fares.

'Well, ever so kind of you,' said Queenie.

'Don't mention it,' said George, beginning to feel less diffident. 'It's a relief to find spare seats at this time of the day. Mind, I've got ideas about— Well, I won't talk about them here.'

'No, all right,' said Queenie, and chatted inconsequentially with him. There were too many ears close by for them to talk other than casually, and certainly not about private matters or Shifty Cecil. However, as soon as they alighted from the bus at the Elephant and Castle, George became confidential.

'Yes, going back to finding spare seats,' he said, as they began their walk to Hampton Street, 'I hope eventually to avoid the crush and crowds of London buses, and do my work journeys from a place where there's room to breathe. Like New Addington, not far from Croydon.'

'New Addington?' said Queenie. 'I've heard of that, ain't it nearly out in the country?'

'Yes, nearly,' said George.

Crikey, he's got the same wish as me, thought Queenie, he's got ideas about living where there's trees and green grass.

'I suppose you mean when you're married,' she said.

'Oh, I don't know about that,' said George, 'I'm not much of a catch for a woman.'

'Oh, you mustn't put yourself down,' said Queenie. 'You've got to have belief in yourself, and why shouldn't you, seeing how you sorted out Shifty Cecil that time? I don't know I ever saw anyone get sorted out quicker. The wonder is that he's asking for more. Well, he is, writing me intimate notes and watching me house. Oh, crikey, now me nerves are all ragged again just thinking about him.'

'Now don't get worried,' said George, a large reassuring figure as he escorted her past shops and people. 'If he's there, all the better in one way, because I'll be able to deal with him on the spot.'

However, when they arrived at Queenie's home, there was no sign of the man in the dark street, so George said he'd stick around for an hour or so in case he did turn up and put himself underneath the lamplight like Lili Marlene of the war. He'd promised Mr Adams he'd do that, stick around, and he'd do so every evening until he struck lucky. Queenie said it was news to her, that anyone could think it lucky to meet up with a creep. George replied that it would be lucky for himself and unlucky for the creep. Queenie said she was ever so admiring of his self-confidence. George said a man needed to be positive when dealing with people like Chicago mobsters.

'Chicago mobsters?' said Queenie, gazing up at him out of large round eyes that looked larger by night. George gulped a bit.

'Er – dubious geezers,' he said. Queenie understood that kind of language.

'Look,' she said, 'Mum and me wouldn't want you to wait out here, so you'd best come in and meet her and have a cup of tea.'

'Well, that's nice of you, Miss – um – Queenie,' said George.

Mrs Richards was more than happy to meet George face to face, to take note of his physical largeness, and to take absolutely no notice of his shyness and nervous coughs. She told him that, like Queenie, she was very admiring of the way he'd set about that pest of a man who kept bothering her daughter, and that it was a relief to know he'd come to set about him again if he showed up.

'And that reminds me, Queenie, look what I found on the mat only about half an hour ago,' she said, and produced another anonymous billet-doux. Queenie read it.

'I DREAM ABOUT YOU, YOU SEXY ANGEL. SOMETIME WE'VE GOT TO MEET. I WANT TO SEE MORE OF YOU IF YOU KNOW WHAT I MEAN.'

Queenie made faces. She'd have shivered if George hadn't been there.

'There, look at that,' she said to him, and handed him the missive. George read it and handed it back.

'He's sick all right,' he said, 'and the best place for him is a large hole at midnight, with a truckload of wet concrete poured on him to serve as a blanket.'

'Beg pardon?' said Queenie, startled.

'He'd end up a stiff,' said George.

'Well, bless me, you're a man after me own heart,' said Mrs Richards. 'That's the place for a man like him, under a load of concrete. I'll put the kettle on now and we'll have a cup of tea before our supper. I hope you'll stay, Mr Porter, it's a lamb casserole, the kind that used to be called a meat stew when I was a girl. People use fancy names now for dishes. Sit down, you too, Queenie, and let's hope that after supper Mr Porter will get the chance to do what we'd all like. If your dad was home, Queenie, he'd mix the concrete.'

'Mum, you're not talking about doing the bloke in for good, are you?' gasped Queenie.

'That's up to Mr Porter,' said Mrs Richards, putting the kettle on, 'but I don't suppose there'll actually be any funeral. I don't like funerals, anyway, they're gloomy.'

'Well, no, we don't want any funeral,' said George. 'Nor any blood,' he murmured as an afterthought, and Mrs Richards gave him an appreciative look. Queenie just blinked. Her mum and George Porter as an alliance were taking her breath away.

It even made her feel excited in a strange kind of way. It even made her hope the creep would turn up.

He did. At almost precisely eight o'clock he materialized out of the dark night and placed himself on the edge of the light cast by the street lamppost. His peaked cap was turned down low, his raincoat collar turned up, and his shadowed eyes gleamed as he took in the outline of a house in which lived a girl who excited his peculiar leanings. One day, perhaps – no, one night – he might indeed see more of her, if he could somehow get round to the rear of these houses and view her bedroom from there. She would almost certainly occupy the back bedroom. Front bedrooms were always the prerogative of parents. He supposed she didn't go to bed earlier than about ten thirty, and he'd have to overcome his parents' dislike of him being out late, or slip unseen from the house.

He imagined the girl entering her bedroom, switching the light on and beginning the routine of undressing. But would she draw the curtains and shut herself off from him? He could only hope not. As for that pot-bellied oaf who'd interfered last week, he was out of the picture now. Well, he hadn't seen the lout since.

For this evening it was enough just to be standing here and watching her house, while imagining what she might be doing. Looking at the telly, perhaps, if her mother had one, or listening to the radio. He'd found out, from asking a few casual questions of a local grocer, that the father was away in the navy. Absent fathers were preferable.

In the front room, unlit, George murmured to Queenie.

'That's him right enough.'

'Yes, and as creepy as ever,' said Queenie, eyes fixed on the figure half in light, half in shadow. 'What're you going to do?'

219

'Wait,' said George.

'Wait? Wait?' said Queenie. 'What for?'

'The chance to follow him,' said George, who had enjoyed a very nourishing supper as a welcome guest.

'Follow him?' said Queenie. 'But I thought from the way you and Mum were talking that you were going to jump him and leave him half-dead.'

'No, that would risk upsetting all your neighbours,' said George, conscious in the darkness that the innocent daughter of the Mafia boss was close to him. Well, something like that. And she was certainly close. Her rounded hip communicated its warmth again, as on the bus. He told himself to file his pulse rate and concentrate on the job in hand, as befitted a top-class private eye. 'When Shifty Cecil makes a move for home, I'm going to sit on his tail.'

'You mean follow him?'

'That's it,' said George. 'And tackle him on his own doorstep. Injure him a bit. Well, getting injured and found out, if that doesn't make him stay away from you, we'll have to think seriously about that large hole and the load of wet concrete.'

'Oh, go on, you don't think I believe that, do you?' said Queenie, who didn't feel half so intimidated by the creep while George was beside her. It still amazed her that he could talk and act so tough about the bloke, when he was otherwise all shy and awkward.

'Queenie?' Her mother was calling. 'Is anything happening?'

'Yes, he's there, Mum.'

'That horrible pest?'

'Yes, he's across the street, and looking.'

'Looking?'

'Yes, straight at our front door.'

'Oh, he is, is he? And what's he expecting, that you'll pop out in a naughty nightie? That's what men like him are after, and in a downright queer way. Is George still there with you?'

'Yes, Mum.'

'Well, like he said, I hope he'll do the man a bit of mischief, enough to see him off for good. If not, I'm just going to have to go to the police.'

'Leave it to me, Mrs Richards,' called George.

'Well, all right, George ducky,' said Mrs Richards, having taken to him.

At that moment, Queenie nudged George with her elbow and breathed, 'Look, he's going.'

The man was leaving the patch of light, walking in the direction of Walworth Road.

'Right,' said George, 'time for me to sit on his tail.'

'But suppose he gets on a bus?' said Queenie, as she followed him out of the room to the front door.

'I'll think of something,' said George. Opening the door, he slipped quietly out into the night. Queenie watched for a minute or two, then closed the door with the merest click of the lock.

*　　*　　*

The man walked in his furtive way, face still half-hidden. He was constantly vanishing in stretches of darkness and reappearing in the patches of light cast by street lamps. George followed at a sensible distance to ensure he was not breathing down his quarry's neck. Not that they were alone. There were people about, and the evening traffic was fairly busy. George was in his element, playing the part of Mike Finnegan, the private eye who never failed to nail his man.

By the light of a corner lamp, he saw his quarry turn into Heygate Street. That looked like the end of the pursuit, for when George turned into the street himself, everything seemed to be swallowed up by darkness. Certainly, the man had vanished. He had gone from the light of the corner lamp into blackness. George, momentarily frustrated, thought quickly. What would Mike Finnegan do now? There were no sounds of footsteps. Had the man actually entered a house as soon as he turned the corner?

No, there he was, emerging from the pall of night into the light of a lamp further down. George hastened, passing houses with dim light showing behind glass-panelled front doors. He guessed, from the complete lack of sound, that his prey was wearing rubber-soled shoes. Much to be expected.

The man turned again, this time to put himself on the doorstep of a house. He produced a key.

George, moving at speed now, caught up with him as he slipped the key into the lock of the door.

'Got ya, punk,' said Mike Finnegan. That is, George Porter.

The man whipped round, breath hissing. Only the light dimly showing through the glass panels illuminated the two faces. One was livid with shock and fury, the other showed a satisfied smile.

'How dare you follow me?'

George confirmed his first opinion, that the speech was not that of a cockney, but of a fairly well-educated man.

'Cut the crap, pal,' he said, 'and let's get informative. Right, name? Age? Occupation? Address? No, scrub that, we've got your address. Start with your name.'

'None of your business.'

'Face it, punk, you're nabbed, so let's have some info I can hand to the cops down at the precinct. Or do I beat your brains out?'

'Get out of here!'

'You've spent the last month or so upsetting a certain young lady we both know. Is your wife home? Let's get her to the door, shall we?' George reached for the knocker. The creep hit his hand away and attempted a punch. George parried it. 'Feeling a mite frisky, are we?' he said. 'Want to mix it?' He showed a balled fist. It was large and had an aggressive look. 'Later, perhaps, but first let's have another go at getting your wife to the door, shall we?'

The man suddenly spilled rushes of words.

'There's no wife. I'm not married. I live with my parents. They've come down in the world. They rely on me to always be there. My father makes me an allowance for that. It's not my fault I've got certain problems.'

'Problems like following young ladies and frightening the life out of them?'

'I can't help myself.'

'You punk, of course you can help yourself. You don't have to give in to it, you lousy earwig. You hear me? Take up crossword puzzles, or I'll come round and knock up your parents to let 'em know what kind of a hobby you've got.'

'No, don't speak to my parents.'

'Well, you watch yourself.' George knew he had his man. 'I'm going to keep an eye on you, and any time I spot you wearing that peaked cap with your coat collar turned up, I'll know you've got some other poor female in your sights. Then I sure will blow the gaff to your parents. And the cops. You get me, Cecil?'

'Yes, all right.'

'It had better be all right and some more,' said George, and suddenly the door opened and an elderly woman stood there, showing a grey head in the glow of the passage lamp.

'Hubert?' she said.

'Oh, I'm just having a few words with a friend, Mother,' said the discovered Hubert.

'A friend?' The woman stared at George. 'Do your father and I know him?'

'I'm a passing acquaintance, actually,' said George. 'Goodnight, madam. Goodnight, Hubert.' And off he went to deliver to Queenie and her mother the details of how he'd copped the dodgy bloke on his own doorstep, and that Queenie definitely wouldn't be bothered again.

'You're really sure?' said Queenie, round eyes aglow with relief and not a small amount of new admiration.

'I'll bet a monkey on it,' said George.

'A monkey?' said Mrs Richards.

'Five hundred dollars – er, pounds,' said George.

Mrs Richards laughed.

'You didn't need any load of wet concrete, like?' she said, giving the hero a playful push.

'No, I agreed with Mr Adams that doing him down on his own doorstep would be good enough,' said George.

'Well, I should think so and all,' said Mrs Richards. 'Queenie, I must say I've never met any man I've been more admiring of than George. Let's all sit down and have a nice pot of tea now, and some fruit cake.'

'Let's,' said Queenie, thinking for some reason of George's intention to move to a suburb one day. Well, he could afford it, he had a good job with Adams Enterprises, and the Adams brothers weren't stingy in respect of the wages they paid, providing you gave them good value.

In the house in Heygate Street, Mr and Mrs Williams were berating their son Hubert. They told him they knew what he'd been up to, giving in to that failing of his, which was why he was safer staying indoors all the time, except when doing a bit of shopping. Who was that man on the doorstep with him?

'Oh, just someone wanting to know where the Old Kent Road was.'

'He's lying,' said Mr Williams to Mrs Williams.

'That's another of his failings,' said Mrs Williams.

'Best thing we can do to help him is lock him in his bedroom again for a month,' said Mr Williams.

'On bread and water?' said Mrs Williams.

'With an occasional helping of hot rice pudding,' said Mr Williams.

'Yes, you like hot rice pudding, don't you, Hubert?' said Mrs Williams.

No answer.

Chapter Eighteen

'Well done,' said Boots the following morning, and made it very clear that he considered George had handled Queenie's troublesome problem in the best possible way. No blood, no hospital involvement and no questions. 'Yes, very well done, George.'

'Oh, I think so too,' said Queenie, and wondered who'd have thought it of George Porter, when he was so retiring and only read books. 'Mum said she was never more admiring of anyone, and that she was only sorry she wasn't actually there to see Mr Porter wipe the floor with the creep.'

'Tell her I'm using my imagination,' said Boots. 'Once more, well done, George.'

'Well, it's been a pleasure, Mr Adams, helping to get an unhealthy character out of the life of a nice girl like Queenie,' said George. 'Her mother's just as nice.'

'I'm sure,' said Boots, whose confidence in George had been based on many years' experience of his fellow men. 'So as you're now an un-worried young lady, Queenie, can I get you to take dictation in a little while?'

'Oh, you bet, sir,' said Queenie, and left his office in company with George. In the corridor, George stopped and cleared his throat. Queenie stopped too. 'You're saying something?' she said, her large round eyes luminous.

'Well – er – ' George stumbled, despite his determination to be firm. 'Well, I was thinking – that is, I wonder if I could take you to the flicks one evening this week – there's a Humphrey Bogart film on. Of course, if – '

'Crikey,' said Queenie, thinking not of Hum-phrey Bogart but of the possibility that trees and green grass might be in the offing, 'I thought you'd never ask.'

'I've had a donation of ten pounds,' said Marjorie Alsop, self-elected champion of animal humanity.

'I had no idea you needed donations,' said Mrs Alsop, 'I thought your father and I gave you free board and lodging, and that you earned a little from your articles for that nature magazine.'

'Mother, the donation is not for myself,' said Marjorie, 'it's for my organization.'

'Thank heaven for that,' said Mrs Alsop, 'neither your father nor I could bear to think you were one of the starving poor. Who sent you such a generous amount for your wildlife work?'

'The managing director of Adams Fashions, a Mr S.W. Adams, from their head office in Camberwell,' said Marjorie. 'They have a factory in Bethnal Green. We postered it, myself and a helper. Well, before I bank this cheque, I shall beard Mr Adams in his den to satisfy myself it isn't an attempt to buy us off. They've no morals, these fashion houses, when it comes to the commercial skinning of animals. Yes, I shall call on Mr Adams.'

'I shall pray,' said Mrs Alsop.

'For hunted polar bears?' said Marjorie.

'No, for Mr Adams.'

'Mother, how absurd.'

'Well, I beg you won't take a bomb with you.'

Matt took a phone call that evening. He summoned Emily, who was doing her homework on the kitchen table.

'Emily, you're wanted. Teddy's on the line.'

'I don't know any Teddy,' said Emily.

'Yes, you do, pet, Teddy boy Brad.'

'Oh, him,' said Emily.

'He's nice enough under his fancy waistcoats,' said Matt, 'so come on, buck up.'

Emily came to her feet, went into the hall and picked up the phone.

'Brad?'

'Hi there, girlie, how's your rolling hips?'

'Have you rung me up just to ask a soppy question like that?' said Emily.

229

'Well, no, more to enjoy a talkie with you,' said Brad.

'Well, I'm doing my homework,' said Emily, 'so I can't talk now.'

'Hold on, baby, how about our usual Saturday gig? Back to Brixton?'

'You can, if you want,' said Emily, 'but I'm going out with a cousin of mine.'

'Eh?' said Brad, and Emily explained that it was a girl cousin, that they had a lot in common and a lot to talk about. Brad asked how come it was going to be a Saturday evening talk? Emily said a Saturday evening was as good as any other evening. Brad said he thought Saturday evenings were kind of exclusive. Emily asked exclusive to who?

'Yes, come on, who?' she insisted.

'Me and you, you and me,' said Brad.

'Listen,' said Emily, 'I'm a free individual, I'm not exclusive to any feller. Crikey, you dope, I'm still at school.' That wasn't something she'd have admitted to any of the Bopcats. 'I've got to get back to my homework now, so phone me next week, if you want. But don't take me for granted.'

'Hey, baby, listen,' said Brad, but the line was already dead. 'I could worry about that young lady,' he murmured, replacing the receiver, 'and I probably will, except that I've got a plumbing manual to study.'

* * *

Rosie received a phone call later. From her mother, who wanted her to know everything had been arranged for her journey to Lyons. 'Lions', she called it. Everything, in fact, she said, had been done as quickly as possible because of her condition.

This prompted Rosie to ask, 'Exactly how are you at the moment?'

'Oh, just one of me usual headaches, Rosie. They come and go, like I told you, but it's not too bad just now.' The widowed woman sounded as if she was making an earnest effort not to feel sorry for herself. 'Me doctor and Mr Wainwright have been ever so good. Well, all the arranging's been done by them, and I'll be leaving on Wednesday week.'

'The sooner the better,' said Rosie. 'But you're surely not going all the way by yourself, are you?'

'Oh, no, Mr Wainwright's providing me with a nurse to make sure I get to the French hospital all right.'

'I think you'll need that kind of help, very much,' said Rosie. 'Look, I'll be coming to see you on Saturday morning just to make sure about how you look. You understand?'

'Oh, I know what you mean, Rosie. It's all right, you'll see that I've had me hair done, but I don't know I like it as it is, all grey. Still, they styled it quite nice, and I've bought new clothes with the money you gave me when you drove me home. Rosie, I expect you'll get a letter any day now from Mr Wainwright, asking if you could send a cheque to cover all the costs, like you promised. Will that be all right? I mean, it might be a lot, considering the operation itself is near to a thousand pounds, and then there's what the nurse will cost, which wasn't mentioned before.'

'My promise that Matt and I will meet all the costs is still good, so don't worry about them,' said Rosie.

'Well, I'm grateful, Rosie, to you and your hubby, and I won't forget what you're both doing for me.'

'Expect me on Saturday morning about ten thirty,' said Rosie.

'Oh, I'll wear some of me new clothes,' said her mother.

'Take care,' said Rosie in natural compassion. Like Matt, she was sure the operation was going to be tricky. That, perhaps, was putting it mildly. Replacing the phone, she rejoined her family.

Giles wanted to know who she'd been talking to. Rosie said to someone she had known far back in her Walworth days. Was that, asked Giles, before or after Grandpa Boots adopted her? Before and after, said Rosie, at which point the nine o'clock news opened up on the television, and the subject relating to her early days died a death.

Emily might have provoked a new talking point, because she declared the news was always boring, especially when it was about politics, and especially about the politicians themselves. Politicians, she said, were so boring they must have been born like it. Nobody, however, took her up on this. Mother, father and brother were all inclined to agree with her. However, a footnote to the news drew her serious interest. It concerned Elvis Presley the Great, and the fact that, having been called up for army service, he was presently stationed with his unit in West Germany. The newsreader went on to say what a hit he was with all the American troops there, although he was greatly missed back home, and on concert platforms. His fans all over the world considered his call-up a diabolical blow struck at the very heart of rock 'n' roll. It was as if a collection of ancient Yankee fuddy-duddies had pernicious ideas of bringing down the rock 'n' roll monarchy.

'Elvis ought to have been excused,' said Emily.

'Well, he is,' said Giles, 'he's excused every time he wants to leave the room. Well, I suppose he is.' He thought. 'Barrack room, I mean,' he added.

'Oh, you're a scream, you are,' said Emily.

'Nice to know you two are the best of friends,' said Matt, who later received from Rosie the news that her mother was to begin her journey to France a week on Wednesday, and that Rosie was going to see her on Saturday. Matt said he hoped that with the help of the nurse, the old girl would survive the journey all the way to Lyons. Her personal history, he said, might not be angelic, but he supposed she could still be counted as a human being.

'Yes, let's agree on that,' said Rosie.

She spoke about her mother to Boots in his office the following day. Boots made his own point about the principle of doing what one could for any human being facing up to so serious an operation. It was a principle, he said, based on love thy neighbour and to do to him – or her – the good you hope someone would do to you. It's unfortunate, he said, that it's not easy to love all our neighbours, but certain feelings need not interfere with a willingness to help.

'Am I sounding like an old humbug?' he asked.

'Not to me,' said Rosie.

'Or an old woman?'

'Are you asking for compliments?'

'No, just an assurance that we think alike on this matter,' said Boots.

'The next time you and I seriously differ,' said Rosie, 'will be the first.'

Boots lightly touched her shoulder.

'Well, poppet, I sincerely hope there'll never be a first,' he said.

At fifteen minutes to eleven, after the coffee break, the Enquiries bell of the general office was pressed by a visitor. A clerk, one Vanessa Finney, answered the summons by opening up the hatch.

She found herself looking at a youngish woman dressed in a baggy sweater and battered jeans. Her pleasant features seemed not unfamiliar.

'Good morning, can I help?'

'I hope so,' said Miss Marjorie Alsop. 'I wish to speak to your managing director, Mr S.W. Adams.'

'Our Mr Sammy Adams?' said Vanessa, whose cockney parents, on registering her birth, gave her what they thought would advantage her. To wit, a posh name instead of one like Ada, Edie or Annie. Vanessa was still living with it. 'Do you have an appointment?'

'No, no appointment,' said the creator of WOOF. 'In fact, I don't make appointments, I prefer to make impromptu calls. It catches the enemy unprepared.'

'Enemy?' said Vanessa, groping a bit.

'Oh, I'm not saying your Mr Adams is the enemy,' said Marjorie, physically and mentally robust. 'In fact, I've had a very nice letter from him.'

'Oh, have you?' said Vanessa, knowing nothing about any letter, and certainly not the one typed confidentially by Rachel.

'Yes, and it's that which I wish to see him about. My name is Alsop, Marjorie Alsop.'

Vanessa knew then why she felt she had seen the lady before. Marjorie Alsop, yes, she was the person who'd ruined the winter fashion show and had got herself onto the front pages of newspapers. Crikey, Mr Sammy reckoned she was as barmy as a cross-eyed pigeon going backwards.

'Well, I don't know if he'll see you without an appointment, he—'

'Don't be negative,' said Miss Alsop briskly, 'just tell him I'm here and that I've come all the way from Twickenham for the pleasure of having a friendly chat with him.'

'Well, I'll let him know you're here, but I can't promise he'll see you,' said Vanessa, quite sure she wasn't going to be the one responsible for landing the tomato-chucker in Mr Sammy's lap.

'Look, lovey, I'm not going until he does see me,' said Miss Alsop. 'It's either that or battle stations. If you're not aware of it, I happen to be a champion of furry animals, and I'm always ready for war. Incidentally,' she added, eyes raking the general office and its female staff, 'I hope none of you young women wear furs.'

Oh, help, thought Vanessa, has she got a bagful of rotten eggs or squishy tomatoes tucked away somewhere?

'Furs? Us? No, course not, furs are for—'

'Vanessa?' Queenie, typing from her shorthand notes, turned her head. 'Mr Sammy's in conference with the property company directors, but Mr Adams is free.' She was referring to Boots, and giving Vanessa a hint that maybe he'd be able to deal better with the problem than Mr Sammy, known to bite pencils in half at the mere mention of the female fire-eater. 'Ask Mr Adams if he'll see Miss Alsop, like.'

'Oh, yes, all right,' said Vanessa. She excused herself to the unwelcome visitor, and went to see Boots. Boots said to bring the lady in, and then to go and warn Mr Sammy of her presence. On returning to the waiting champion, she said, 'Our Mr Robert Adams will see you, Miss Alsop.'

'Robert Adams?' said Miss Alsop. 'Who's he?'

'Our general manager.'

'Well, watch out if he's just the office boy. I don't deal with office boys.'

'No, all right. Would you like to follow me?' Vanessa took the lady to Boots's office, then went to warn his brother of the caller. Mr Sammy was in his office with his son and nephew, the joint managing directors of the property company. He was in good form until Vanessa gave him the message.

'Blimey O'Reilly, not her in person, not Mad Marj herself?' he said.

'It's all right, Mr Sammy, Mr Adams said you can leave him to deal with her for a bit. He said you can make an appearance in about ten minutes or so.'

'If I said I can't wait, I'd be lying like fifty con men rolled into one,' growled Sammy.

Chapter Nineteen

Miss Alsop, having bustled into the office of the general manager, pulled up short as the man at the desk rose to his feet in acknowledgement of her entrance. She'd expected a kind of busy-looking individual, jacket off, collar loose, shirt undone, and cigarette ash all over his desk and person. Instead, she saw a man of distinction in a tailored charcoal-grey suit. Unexpected too were the fine mouth, deep grey eyes and a hint of whimsy in his light smile of welcome.

'Miss Alsop? Miss Marjorie Alsop? Sit down, won't you?'

The power behind the public emergence of WOOF lost a few watts as the mellow baritone reached her ears. Well, really, who would have bet on encountering a gentleman in any hive of the throat-cutting garments industry? As for men of the furrier trade itself, they were anything but gentlemen.

'Mr Adams?'

'Yes?'

'Mr Robert Adams?'

'None other, Miss Alsop.'

What could one say next when the deep grey eyes were offering immediate friendship?

'I'm Marjorie Alsop.'

'Yes, so I gathered. Would you like to sit down?'

'How kind, yes, thank you.' Gratefully, she lowered her fine, if temporarily faltering, body into a chair. She then found herself seated opposite him, he on one side of the desk, she the other. It seemed extraordinarily intimate. 'I – that is – my organization – pardon me, but is it a little close in here?'

'The temperature?'

'Pardon? Yes, the temperature.'

'I fancy about sixty-five.'

'Sixty-five?'

'Sixty-five Fahrenheit. The staff find that comfortable.' Boots was gentling her along, while wondering about her hesitancy. Although he'd never met her before now, first-hand reports had led him to believe she was neither a hesitant nor an uncertain young woman. Far from it, in fact, according to Sammy and the press. 'But is it too warm for you, Miss Alsop?'

'No. No, not at all. It's a sensible working temperature. Mr Adams, where was I?'

'Before you arrived here? On a bus, perhaps?'

'No, I meant where had I got to in our conversation?'

239

'Only as far as the room temperature. However, if you'd like to let me know why you've called, I'll be happy to listen.'

'Oh, yes. Yes. Thank you. Let me see – oh, yes, I've had a letter from your managing director.'

'That would be my brother, Sammy Adams.'

'Sammy?' Miss Alsop was in mesmerized eye contact with the man on the other side of the desk, and out of a kind of haze came the realization that his left eye was of a darker grey than the right. How strange. 'I see. Yes.'

'Yes?'

'Of course, I remember now. The letter contained a donation of ten pounds to my organization.'

'Sammy is a supporter of good causes. So am I, and so is the firm.' Boots smiled. 'It hasn't bounced, has it?'

'Good Lord, no.'

'Then add it to your funds.'

'Thank you, but let me see, I really wanted to know if you – if your firm – your factory – that is, do you produce fur garments?'

'Such as fur coats or jackets?'

'Exactly. I could never accept a donation from any firm trading in fur.'

'We've never been involved in such expensive lines as fur coats or jackets, Miss Alsop. We cater for the everyday customer, and our main lines are garments affordable to high street shoppers, not Bond Street.'

'Really?'

'I assure you. Is that the reason for your visit?'

His eyes seemed to hold no secrets, and his light smile was encouraging, but she still felt slightly dazed.

Wavering, she said, 'Pardon?'

'Is your concern for the welfare of brown bears and so on the reason for your call?'

'Oh, yes. Yes, precisely.'

'Very commendable, Miss Alsop.'

'Thank you, Mr – Mr – '

'Adams. Robert Adams.'

'Oh, yes.'

The door opened and Sammy entered.

'Here we are, here's my brother,' said Boots.

Miss Alsop, disoriented, looked up and met a new pair of eyes, eyes of electric blue that made her feel no better at all. She was used to coming up against people either obsequious and ingratiating or aggressively contemptuous. Again, expectations were confounded, and she wondered if she was where she had reckoned to be, in the offices of one of the firms that had exhibited at the Mayfair Gallery a while ago, when the ultimate had been the new line in winter furs.

Sammy had thought to say, 'Gotcher, you female Turk, you're in my back yard now.' Instead, noting she looked confused, and also remembering he and Boots were operating a bluff, he issued a polite greeting.

'Well, good morning to you, Miss Alsop, pleasure to see you.'

'How kind.' Miss Alsop, her physical and mental robustness buckling, blinked. 'I've been talking with your brother.'

'I talk with him a lot,' said Sammy. 'Sometimes I win, sometimes I lose. How did you get on?'

'Get on?'

'With my brother.'

'Oh, very well, I think.'

'Miss Alsop is happy about everything, Sammy,' said Boots, 'and will bank the cheque you sent as a donation.'

'Right, then I'm happy too,' said Sammy.

'Let me have the pleasure of seeing you out, Miss Alsop,' said Boots.

The confused originator of WOOF allowed Boots to see her down the stairs to the front door of the offices, and he even stepped out onto the pavement with her in order to shake her hand in full view of passers-by. With another smile, he remarked on how nice it had been to meet her.

'Thank you, yes, thank you.'

Miss Alsop tottered away. Boots went back to his office, where Sammy awaited him.

'No fireworks, Boots?'

'None.'

'Bust my braces if you don't still have a way with females,' said Sammy.

'What way is that, Sammy?'

'How do I know?' said Sammy. 'If I did know,

I'd have a go meself every time I needed to. Anyway, she went happy on her way?'

'Apparently.' Boots mused. 'But allow for the fact that she might be back.'

'Eh?' said Sammy.

'For some reason,' said Boots, 'she seemed a little vague. But she'll recover. It's in her blood. So don't be surprised if she does turn up again.'

'Me, I won't be here,' said Sammy, 'I'll be somewhere else. She'll be all yours, old mate.'

'Am I flushed?' Marjorie Alsop asked the question of her mother after arriving home from Camberwell.

'Flushed?' said Mrs Alsop.

'Do I look feverish?' asked Marjorie.

'You look your usual self, my dear,' said Mrs Alsop, 'although I think your appearance could be improved. Isn't it time you retired that sweater of yours to an old sailors' home? Not that I'm sure they'd accept it.'

'I dress for comfort or for practical purposes,' said Marjorie. 'Apart from that, are you sure I look my usual self?'

'Why do you ask?'

'Frankly, I feel slightly detached from reality,' said Marjorie. 'I went ready to do battle, if necessary, with a firm called Adams Fashions, but the blighters diddled me.'

'Diddled you?' said Mrs Alsop, 'What on earth do you mean?'

'I've no idea,' said Marjorie, 'it's all hazy.'

'You're being absurd,' said Mrs Alsop.

'I told you, I'm not in the real world.' Marjorie frowned. 'But I'll have recovered by tomorrow.'

'I'm sure you will,' said Mrs Alsop. 'By the way, there have been two or three of the usual kind of phone calls from people willing to help. I jotted down their names and phone numbers on the pad.'

'Yes, tomorrow,' murmured Marjorie.

'Marjorie, aren't you listening?'

'Tomorrow,' mused Marjorie, 'I'll be designing our new posters.'

'Oh, dear.'

'I wonder if he'll like them?'

'If who will like them?'

'Mr Robert Adams,' said Marjorie.

'I'm afraid I'm not with you,' said Mrs Alsop.

'That makes two of us not quite our usual selves,' said Marjorie.

'You're dining out again tonight, sir?' said Miss Janice Browning, accepting the room key from the hotel's German guest. The time was six o'clock and she was due any moment to hand over to her replacement.

'Tonight, yes,' said the man she knew as Rolf Seidler. 'That is fine by you, Miss Browning?'

'Oh, I didn't mean to be critical, sir.'

'Perhaps you will be going out with your young man, eh?'

244

'Not tonight, sir,' said Miss Browning. 'He's on duty.'

'Duty?'

'He's a CID officer at Scotland Yard.'

'CID? Ah, a policeman, *ja*?' The Wolf's expression of interest gave no indication of his wish for the British police to keep their long noses out of his business while he was here in London. 'A detective he is?'

'Yes, sir.'

'Well, I hope he will catch many bad men.' He himself had been caught by British Redcaps in 1946 at a time when he was expecting to join other comrades on the secret SS escape route to South America. Not that he classed himself a bad man. There were no bad men in the SS, only loyal Germans faithful to the Party then, now and for ever. 'Goodnight, Miss Browning.'

His smile was mellow as he emerged from the hotel into the evening darkness, which meant there was only a little glimpse of his teeth.

He's gone to Simpsons in the Strand,' said the young man with a handsome head of hair. He was using a public phone box. 'By taxi. I heard him speak to the driver.'

'You understand all is now ready?'

'Yes, I understand.'

'You are to make sure you keep in touch with me.'

'I won't let you down, Papa.'
'Good.'

The Wolf returned to the hotel at just after ten, but did not go in. Instead, he entered his parked car, sat there for a few minutes, then started the engine and drove away. He motored carefully through the illuminated night life of London, a night life returning to a pre-war level due to the departure of austerity, the re-entrance of well-lined pockets, and the new exciting entertainment phenomenon being created by the stars and the music of rock and pop.

Leaving the West End behind after a while, he drove to the Surrey side of the river by crossing Waterloo Bridge, and entering an area that lacked the bright lights of theatreland. Here, the street lamps were practical rather than enlivening, and most shops were shut, apart from the occasional fried-fish-and-chips establishment. He knew his way by now, but still drove carefully. Not on any account did he intend to have a traffic accident, not on this night or any other.

Five minutes past eleven.

'Heigh-ho, old love, I'm for the sack,' yawned Polly.

'I'm ready,' said Boots, switching off the late-night radio news.

'Why is it I can no longer stay the pace?'

'D'you want an answer to that?' said Boots.

'I know the answer,' said Polly, rising from her armchair. 'Oh, well, sweetie, I accept that giddy youth is past, and that midnight frolics around Trafalgar Square are for others. Bed calls and I like the thought of it, especially as Hemingway's *Farewell to Arms* awaits me. What are you reading in bed?'

'Goldilocks and the Three Bears,' said Boots.

'What?'

'I missed out on that story when I was young,' said Boots. 'However, as our wise ones say, it's never too late.'

'You're not fooling me,' said Polly. 'Listen, who's going to put the cat out?'

Since they had no cat, that was always interpreted as 'Who's going to put out the lights?'

'I will,' said Boots.

'Good old reliable,' murmured Polly, and went up to the marital bedroom.

Seated in the car on the opposite side of the road, the Wolf was watching. He had been parked there for quite some time, and had taken note of the gradual extinction of lights in various houses. The night was closing down for families. It was now closing down for ex-Colonel Adams and his brood. Yes, their lights were being extinguished, all but one, that of what the Wolf assumed was the front bedroom. It glowed dimly behind drawn curtains, and remained so for all of twenty minutes. Then it went out, leaving the house a darkened bulk in the night.

Not until a further forty minutes had passed did the Wolf move. He came silently out of his car, closing the door with only the faintest of clicks. Just as silently he crossed the road, a deserted thoroughfare now, and walked a little way before turning into a wide drive. He noted the dark outline of a car. He eased around it and advanced to the front door. Torchlight sprang from his hand, illuminating the letter box. That was the crucial element of the planned attack. Very carefully indeed, he pushed at the metal flap. It yielded without a sound, and the light played over the yawning mouth.

Good, very good. A long length of petrol-soaked linen, weighted, could easily be inserted and lowered to the floor. And the nozzle of a large brass syringe could just as easily spray petrol all over the hall. No entrance into the house was necessary. It could all be done from the Englishman's doorstep.

Well, the cans of petrol had been obtained, and so had the strip of linen and the syringe. All he needed now was a night as fine and quiet as this one. The conditions at this moment, the absolute quiet and the sleeping house, were so perfect that he almost wished he had opted to strike now. But no. Although linen, petrol and syringe were in the locked boot of the car, the box of matches had yet to be bought. Had he been a smoker, he would have had matches on his person, but he had never allowed the nicotine habit to affect his physical fitness in the slightest way. Well, the pleasure of execution was only delayed. Silently, he removed himself from the doorstep.

Not a person showed up, and not a light went on when, a few minutes later, the Wolf began the drive back to the hotel in Bloomsbury.

The front of the hotel was deserted, and he entered like a late-night reveller, insisting that the sleepy porter join him in a glass of schnapps. The porter, however, begged to be excused, and then saw him up to his room.

In the darkness of the car park, a young man ghosted into being.

Chapter Twenty

On Thursday morning, Rosie picked up a letter from the mat. It was addressed to Mr and Mrs M. Chapman. Opening it, she found it had come from W.R. Wainwright, FRCS, and contained a detailed summary of expenses covering Mrs M. Rainbould's forthcoming operation in Lyons, France. The sum amounted to sixteen hundred and seventy-two pounds, which included the costs for the accompanying nurse, Alice Newman, SRN.

Once Emily and Giles had finished their breakfasts and were away to school, Rosie and Matt had time together. Matt's garage in Peckham did open at eight, mainly for petrol sales, but this was looked after by an assistant, enabling Matt to enjoy breakfast with his family.

Rosie produced the letter, Matt read it, and they then spent a short time discussing it. Matt thought the amount reasonable, considering what was involved. Rosie agreed. They were not, in any case, disposed to quibble. If, by this financial outlay, they were able to help the operation come about, well, that was the object of the gesture.

'I note Mr Wainwright says receipt of our cheque can be anytime between now and next Tuesday,' said Matt. 'Your mother departs on Wednesday, doesn't she?'

'Yes,' said Rosie.

'OK, Rosie, put a cheque in the post to Mr Wainwright today,' said Matt. 'Send it with our compliments and thanks. And when you see your mother on Saturday, let her know we've covered the costs with a cheque to her specialist. And we'll also cover any necessary extras once the final bill is received.'

'There's a good man of Dorset you are,' smiled Rosie. The fact that he was as tolerant of people as Boots, and just as droll at times, counted for much in her book. 'I'm glad we met.'

'Thunder and lightning,' said Matt, 'where would I be if we hadn't? Still repairing farm tractors, probably. Did I ever tell you about a certain old Dorset saying?'

'I've time to listen to one more,' said Rosie.

Matt declaimed.

'Down in Dorset, so they say,
'Tis lucky a man will be
To find himself the kind of wife
Who's just the same as 'ee.'

Rosie laughed and said, 'I've heard worse.'

They were on their different ways to work ten minutes later.

During the morning, Rosie looked in on Boots.

'Busy, old soldier?' she said.

'I can always make time for you, Rosie.'

'There, then, what d'you make of that?' she asked, and gave him Mr Wainwright's letter to read.

Boots took his time to thoroughly digest the contents, then said he rather thought she and Matt would go along with the required outlay. Rosie said she was putting a cheque in the post today.

'Well, that will send the old girl on her way and into the care of the French specialist,' said Boots. 'For the rest, let's keep our fingers crossed.'

'Matt and I thought the amount reasonable,' said Rosie.

'It's more than most people could afford,' said Boots, 'but outside the National Health Service, we know how expensive medical treatment can be. In that respect, you'll be able to reassure the old girl that everything is being taken care of when you see her on Saturday.'

'Yes,' said Rosie, her smile understanding as she noted he did not say, 'your mother'. But then, they both only ever thought of Emily as her real mother. 'Yes, I'll reassure her.'

*　　　*　　　*

'Well, are you going to alarm me?' asked Mrs Alsop of her daughter Marjorie. It was five o'clock, and Marjorie was just back from town where, with four helpers, she had been picketing the House of Worth, well known in the world of fashion design.

'Alarm you? What do you mean?' asked Marjorie, removing her navy blue windcheater. The day was cold.

'I mean, my dear,' said Mrs Alsop, 'that if you're going to tell me your demonstration turned into a brawl and stopped the traffic, then I shall be seriously alarmed. I shan't listen to the news tonight or read my daily paper tomorrow. I shall have to speak to your father about moving from Twickenham to the Outer Hebrides.'

'Mother, you're absurd.'

'I don't agree. After all, your father and I naturally hope we're acceptable to our friends and neighbours, and not part of your design for a troublesome living.'

'That's even more absurd,' said Marjorie, and put her mother in the picture. The demonstration had passed off quite peacefully, although the police did ask them to keep moving and not cause an obstruction. So they simply circled around, with their placards high. Each placard read JOIN WOOF AND STOP THE CULT OF WEARING FURS. Of course, continued Marjorie, people did gather and look on, and there was a bout of clapping when someone from the House of Worth came out with a tray and five cups of tea.

'Cups of tea?' said Mrs Alsop.

'I suppose one could have called it a peace offering from the enemy, hot tea on a cold day,' said Marjorie, frowning, 'but it was, of course, an attempt to make us look inconsequential and irrelevant. I saw that at once, and refused the offering. It hurt, believe me, when my four helpers all grabbed cups.'

'And what happened to the refused cup?' asked Mrs Alsop.

'One of my helpers had that as well,' said Marjorie, 'and at that point I felt like Colonel Custer, standing alone, while all around me lay the fallen.'

'Oh, dear,' murmured Mrs Alsop. 'In my father's day, it was Buffalo Bill who performed heroics. Marjorie, did any reporters arrive? '

'Only one,' said Marjorie.

'From a national newspaper?' asked Mrs Alsop, alarm lurking.

'No, from a French weekly magazine,' said Marjorie.

'Oh, then my worries aren't too critical,' said Mrs Alsop. 'I don't think many people in Twickenham read French magazines. What, my dear, is your next move?'

Marjorie said that on her way home she'd been thinking about the firm called Adams Fashions, and it made her remember that not only had their managing director sent a donation, he had also invited her to let him have some posters. For what purpose, Mrs Alsop asked. Marjorie said she supposed it was to display them in support of the cause. Mrs Alsop reminded her she had called on the firm to find out if that support was sincere, and had returned in a disoriented pickle.

'Yes, I remember that,' murmured Marjorie, and went into a kind of trance.

'Are you still with me?' asked Mrs Alsop after a long minute of silence.

'Pardon?' said Marjorie, coming to with a little jerk of her shoulders. 'Oh, my call on Adams Fashions, was that what we were talking about? Yes, I think my next move should be to let them have some posters. Let's see, yes, the FIGHT WITH WOOF FOR ANIMAL HUMANITY one, and others. I'll take them myself.'

'Marjorie, you'll go all the way to Camberwell to deliver them yourself?' said her mother. 'My dear girl, shouldn't you ask an underling to do errands for you?'

'Underling?' said Marjorie. 'Mother, ours is a democratic organization, not a totalitarian one. There are no underlings. We're all equal.'

'Is there no-one in charge, then?' asked the whimsical Mrs Alsop.

'Only me,' said Marjorie.

* * *

'Uncle Sammy's still worried,' said Paul over supper that evening. He was enjoying the meal of poached fresh haddock in creamy fish sauce. Sylvia was tucking into her little plateful, too. The sauce contained shrimps, which the child loved. 'And Dad's not too happy.'

'Excuse me?' said Lulu, glasses perched on the end of her nose. That gave her a professorial look, which she favoured. 'I mean, what are we talking about?'

'Furs,' said Paul. 'Finished already, Sylvie?' His daughter nodded. She had been named after Lulu's engaging stepmother, but her parents had slipped into the way of calling her Sylvie.

'Furs?' said Lulu.

'Yes. And Hannibal Alsop.'

'Who?'

'The odd female who bombarded the winter fashion show with eggs and tomatoes.'

'Odd female?' said Lulu. 'Cut that sort of talk, mate, I don't go for it.'

'Marjorie Alsop of WOOF, then,' said Paul.

'WOOF?'

'Yes, something to do with using wool in place of fur,' said Paul. 'Incidentally, this fish and the sauce are just the job, Lulu.'

'I'm never sure I trust your compliments,' said Lulu. 'I'm never sure they aren't a cunning way of inducing me to fall into the trap of permanent domesticity. Just remember it's your turn to cook next Sunday's dinner, and that my number one

256

goal is a Labour Party seat in the House of Commons. I'm still young yet.' She was twenty-seven. 'Anyway, what about Marjorie Alsop?'

'Well, there's a feeling the firm hasn't seen the last of her,' said Paul. 'Dad and Uncle Sammy have still got the wind up.'

'Paul, do you mind not bringing trivialities home from the office with you?' said Lulu.

'Listen, even Uncle Boots doesn't think Marj Alsop is a triviality,' said Paul. 'Even he thinks she might turn up again, especially if she finds out that our retail shops sell fur-trimmed garments. Not mink fur, of course, or anything else that's painfully expensive. Fox fur mostly—'

'Oh, really?' said Lulu. 'I'm not interested in furs or anything else outside the limited pockets of the workers, except that I recognize furs as typical symbols of the upper classes. As for Marjorie Alsop, I did tell you she strikes me as being a natural Socialist. A pity she's bothering about furs, and worrying Uncle Sammy and your dad, when she could be doing super work for the Labour Party.'

Sylvia gazed with interest at her mother while chewing almost absent-mindedly on her second helping of fish, which seemed to indicate she was already fascinated by the possibility of becoming a working-class champion.

'Well, nice to know you've got sympathy for Dad and Uncle Sammy,' said Paul.

'I always feel your dad and Uncle Sammy and

Uncle Boots could have been great as a collective unit in favouring the nationalization of everything,' said Lulu.

'Hear that, Sylvie?' said Paul. 'Your mum's talking like the UK Communist Party. Tck, tck, I don't know what James Maxton's going to make of her, do you?' James Maxton, a Scot, was notable as a fiery left-winger, but not on a soccer field. In Parliament.

'Pudding?' said Sylvia hopefully.

'You're right,' said Paul.

The Wolf hadn't been out all day, apart from a brisk walk after breakfast when, in passing a Bloomsbury bookshop, something caught his eye. He turned back. There, amid several other books on display in the window was a copy of the English edition of Hitler's *Mein Kampf*. He stayed looking for long moments, the title taking him back to his early years with the SS, the years when Hitler and Germany seemed destined to turn the whole of Europe into a German Empire.

He entered the shop and bought the book, a second-hand copy. Taking it back to the hotel, he stretched out on his bed and absorbed himself in it. While his spoken English was good, if very guttural, taking in the written word he found laborious. Nevertheless, his absorption was such that the interruption for lunch in the hotel restaurant was almost an irritation, a nuisance. He might have passed it by, but he was a man for

258

his victuals, and his stomach had its own way of calling for sustenance. However, he made short work of the meal and then returned to *Mein Kampf*.

Reading each word, he relived his years in Nazi Germany. On entering the SS he had been able to say yes, of course he had studied Hitler's autobiographical masterpiece, although he had in truth only read parts of it. Strangely, this English version held his interest to a compulsive extent, although he had never been much of a reader of books outside popular German fiction. He had also read equally popular magazines.

All through the day, and the evening too, he devoured Hitler's rambling account of his life, his ambitions, his reasons for living and his condemnation of the Jews as a menace to Germany and German culture.

At a little after ten he roused himself to take a walk, and perhaps to decide whether tonight should be the night. The act would go well with his mood, which was one of nostalgic memories of the Party and the Führer, with a hatred of Churchill and the British thrown in. However, as soon as he stepped out of the hotel he encountered weather wet, wild and windy. It put him off any night drive through London, and on the left side of the road into the bargain. He made his way to the nearest pub, spent fifteen minutes there in company with two double whiskies, then returned to the hotel and went to bed. He had made no use whatever of his hired car all this day. But tomorrow, yes, there was always tomorrow.

On Friday morning, by first post, Mr W.R. Wainwright of Tulse Hill, south-east London, received a cheque covering in full the estimated costs for an operation on Mrs Rainbould in Lyons, France. He telephoned the sender at once, and caught her just before she left for work.

'Mrs Chapman,' he said, 'I can't tell you how delighted I am that you and your husband have made it possible for your mother to have this very necessary operation. I want you to know that I really do have faith in the French surgeon. His record is one to emphasize and to give all of us sincere cause for optimism. I know I've already said so, but it's worth repeating.'

'And success is worth everything,' said Rosie.

'You'll pardon me for phoning you so early?'

'I'm happy to hear from you,' said Rosie.

'Splendid. Goodbye for the time being, Mrs Chapman, and on behalf of your mother, thank you again.'

'You're very welcome,' said Rosie, and mentally prepared herself for her visit tomorrow to the woman who meant little enough in her affections, but who nevertheless had given her birth and her entry into a world that became precious to her.

As Matt had said, one did owe her for that.

*   *   *

A call came through to the office during the morning.

'Adams Enterprises. May I help you?'

'Isn't that Adams Fashions?'

Adams Fashions, Adams Enterprises or Adams Property Company, the switchboard girl could speak for all. Simply, however, Adams Enterprises was the senior company and the daddy of all.

'Adams Fashions, yes. May I help you?'

'This is Miss Alsop, organizing manager of WOOF, and I—'

'Pardon?'

'WOOF.'

'WOOF? Oh, yes.' The switchboard girl remembered then, and not without a flutter for Mr Sammy's well-being. Mr Sammy was known to look ill whenever Miss Alsop was mentioned. 'Yes, Miss Alsop?'

'Please give Mr Adams a message for me.'

'Mr Robert Adams or Mr Sammy?'

'Robert, yes.' A slightly higher inflexion affected the caller's voice. 'Tell him I'll be calling on Monday afternoon about three to deliver some posters. I was invited to supply them, and I'm bringing them myself.'

'Posters?'

'Yes, posters advertising the cause. Tell Mr Adams about three on Monday. That's all. Goodbye.'

The switchboard girl knew she would have to pass this on to Boots. She told the general office girls about it.

'Oh, he'll know what to do,' said Queenie, now a much happier young lady, and with a beau in tow – to wit, George Porter. 'Go on, go and tell him.'

The switchboard girl, Jane Reeves, did so. Boots accepted the message threat philosophically, telling Jane there was always hope that it was only posters the lady would deliver. Jane said she thought it would still worry Mr Sammy. Boots said that over many years Mr Sammy had survived all crises so well that, despite any worries he was now admitting to in respect of Miss Alsop, it was a dead cert he'd survive the lady, and her posters.

'Shall I tell him she's coming, Mr Adams?'

'No, I will,' said Boots.

'Eh?' said Sammy. He was about to treat himself to lunch, in company with Rachel and Daniel, in the office cafeteria, as it was sometimes called. Half the office staff, including directors, lunched between twelve and one, the other half between one and two. 'Mad Marj is doing what?'

'Coming here at about three on Monday afternoon to hand us the posters you invited her to send,' said Boots.

'I'd like to point out that was at your suggestion, matey,' said Sammy.

'Well, certainly, it's me she's asked to see,' said Boots.

'Serve you right if she brings something a bit more hurtful than posters,' said Sammy. 'Still, I wish you luck, and request you not to point her at me. Twice I've seen her in action, once in the Gallery and once in the street, and I ain't keen on a third time. And listen, chum, don't answer any questions that might make her sniff around our shops, with our window displays full of fur-trimmed winter numbers. Just give her whatever it was you handed her before and let her go home happy.'

'Anything else, Sammy?' said Boots mildly.

'Yes, tell her she'd like Australia,' said Sammy. 'Recommend it.'

During the late afternoon, when Boots was reading and signing the letters Queenie had expertly typed for him, there was a knock on his office door. He invited whoever it was to come in. It turned out to be Tommy's younger son Paul, the only member of the extensive Adams family to have married a dyed-in-the-wool Socialist. However, no-one had actually been rendered speechless, which wasn't surprising since it was unheard of for any Adams to be lost for words. Chinese Lady, of course, had asked a question or two in the hope that the answers would allay her misgivings about the possibility of Bolshevism hitting the family. Every answer had been reassuring.

'Can you spare a couple of minutes, Uncle Boots?' asked Paul, assistant to cousins Daniel and Tim of the property company.

'Just a couple,' said Boots, 'so fire away pronto.'

'It's about Uncle Sammy's present headache,' said Paul. 'Marjorie Alsop.'

'Keep going,' said Boots.

Paul said he thought he knew how to divert the young woman from her campaign for animal humanity, whatever that was, and get her to point her talents elsewhere. Lulu, he said, was convinced Miss Alsop was a natural Socialist, with a large talent for organizing, and just the kind of gifted activist the Labour Party could do with if they were to get back into power after a whole seven years out of it.

'Get me, Uncle Boots?'

'In this little citadel of private enterprise, I get you,' said Boots, 'but I doubt if your Uncle Sammy has any great feelings for the hopes of the Labour Party.'

'Couldn't agree more,' said Paul. 'Still, there's always a chance, if you'll pardon my Labour leanings. Point is, would you like to let Lulu try converting Miss Alsop? I believe she's coming here on Monday afternoon, so I'll have the whole weekend to talk Lulu into action. I've got a feeling she'll see it as a challenge, and if you knew Lulu like I do, you'd know she might find it irresistible. Uncle Sammy would sleep a whole lot better if Lulu managed to distract the lady from harassing furriers, and turned her into a Socialist activist.'

'Done,' said Boots.

'It's OK with you?' said Paul.

'Lulu can have the use of my office for her conversion job,' said Boots.

'Excellent,' said Paul.

'Tell your Uncle Sammy that the present cloud may have a silver lining,' said Boots, and Paul went off to inform Sammy of what was being planned for Monday and to quote the bit about a silver lining. Sammy said Boots had been his brother for as long as he could remember, and accordingly he could believe his mention of a silver lining. He only hoped it would stay put. If it didn't, he said, then a cloudburst might well pour down on his brother's educated head from a great height come Monday afternoon.

Chapter Twenty-One

That evening, George Porter had supper, by invitation, with Queenie and her mum prior to taking Queenie up west to the Lyceum ballroom, where he thought he'd show her how well he could trip the light fantastic in a one-step, and where Queenie showed him how far he'd fallen behind in preferring to read books instead of shaking his hips. George mumbled something about that kind of activity not being a feature in the life of Mike Finnegan, private eye or Chicago cop, but once he'd taken off his jacket and tie and paid the cloakroom attendant to look after them, he performed with a promise that pleased Queenie no end. Portly he might be, but physically unfit he was not. His shirt front kept close company with her sweater, and sometimes the twain almost met.

At home, James took a phone call from a friend of Gemma, one Judy Braithwaite, and after the exchange of a few friendly words he said if she'd hold on he'd fetch his sister. Judy said, 'Who wants to talk to your sister when I'm already talking to you?' So James had several more friendly exchanges with her, which induced her afterwards to work out how many weeks it would be before 14 February arrived, when she could send him a Valentine card. James, generally modest, would have been flattered to know it took her quite some time to work it out and that she persevered to the end. He was still focused more on his education and his sports than girls. He was on friendly terms with several but serious about none. He believed a feller should wait until he was fully adult before getting serious about any girl, and his sister Gemma was of a similar opinion in respect of her own love life. Reminding himself he would be seventeen in a few weeks, James reckoned he'd then be getting on towards adulthood. This made him remember that his dad had married Emily Castle when he was twenty. Twenty, yes, by the example of one's dad a feller was fully adult by then. Wasn't he? Well, his dad must have been, because no-one in the family had ever said he'd made the kind of mistake associated with still being wet around the ears.

In the home of Paul and Lulu Adams, Paul was enjoying supper with his wife and daughter. He introduced the subject relating to Monday afternoon and the expected arrival of Hannibal Alsop.

'Who?' asked Lulu, pushing her horn-rimmed spectacles to the top of her nose. The lens made her eyes look big and all-seeing. 'Who?'

'You know, that young woman who—'

'Yes, I know,' said Lulu, 'but do you have to call her by that ridiculous name fastened onto her by Fleet Street misfits? Sometimes I wonder if it wouldn't be a favour to civilization if someone blew it up.'

'Fleet Street?' said Paul.

'Why not?'

'Be a bit messy,' said Paul. 'I mean, arms and legs and bits of machines all over the place, as well as mountains of paper confetti and shredded editors. No, listen, what I wanted to mention, Lulu love, was the possibility that you might be willing to do a good turn for Uncle Sammy, my boss and the provider of a monthly salary that keeps you and me off the breadline suffered by underpaid workers.'

'There are always too many underpaid workers,' said Lulu sternly, 'and always will be until we get a Labour government back. Still, I will say the firm's factory workers at Bethnal Green seem to think Uncle Sammy treats them fairly, so what good turn do you have in mind for him?'

'Getting Marjorie Alsop off his back and away from our shops and their window displays full of winter cosies like fur-trimmed coats,' said Paul. 'Uncle Boots is of the opinion—'

'Objection!' cried Lulu dramatically, which

caused Sylvia's bottom lip to quiver, a sure sign that tears were on their way.

Paul came to the rescue by giving her a little pat and saying, 'No, not you, sweetie, nobody could object to you, especially not your mummy. You're her pride and joy, and she loves you as well. It's just that she's got a bee in her bonnet about Uncle Boots.'

'There, there, Sylvie,' cooed Lulu, giving the child a reassuring smile, 'I only meant that it's best not to get involved with Uncle Boots. He's got devilish ways of undermining people, especially women.' Sylvia, lower lip no longer quivering, gazed fascinated at her articulate mother. 'He could undermine Auntie Karl Marx herself, and I don't know how many times he's undermined me about my own sacred beliefs. And he does it all with just a word or two. And a sort of harmless smile. But it's not harmless, so watch out for it when you're older, my pet. Still,' she said, turning to Paul, 'what was his opinion?'

'That you, and only you, could convert Marj,' said Paul, thinking it best not to say he'd put the idea into Boots's mind himself. 'From campaigning against the wearing of furs to becoming a first-class Labour Party activist. You did say a while ago that you thought she sounded a natural.'

'We're always in need of people who are obviously good organizers and enjoy undertaking projects,' said Lulu. 'They're born for the

Labour Party, but not all of them know it. Well, go on, persuade me.'

'You like Uncle Sammy, and the fact that he gives all his workers a square deal, don't you?' said Paul. 'So come to the office on Monday afternoon and do your best to turn Marjorie Alsop into one of your activists. I agree with Uncle Boots. If anyone can do it, you can.'

'I regard his compliments with suspicion,' said Lulu.

'Why?' asked Paul, helping Sylvia to some minted peas. 'Why?' he asked Lulu again.

'Compliments from Uncle Boots undermine me, I told you,' said Lulu, 'and that's not good for my kind of woman. I need a hundred per cent self-belief.'

'But let's face it,' said Paul, 'he admires you for your principles and the way you battle for your cause, even if he's not a political animal himself.'

Lulu, pushing her empty plate aside, contemplated her small daughter as if debating the wisdom of letting her know, at a very early age, of the traps set in the way of women by crafty men. However, she replied to Paul.

'Well, naturally, I wouldn't want to see your family firm suffering from bad publicity. But did Uncle Boots really say that if anyone could turn Marjorie Alsop away from her anti-fur campaign and get her to campaign for the Labour Party, I could?'

Paul again refrained from confessing that

Uncle Boots had merely agreed with his own convictions. Lulu, he knew, was more likely to be persuaded by Uncle Boots than himself.

'He's got faith in you, wifey, and so have I.'

'Ugh,' said Lulu.

'Ugh what?'

'Don't call me wifey. It sounds like middle-class twee talk.'

'I take it back,' said Paul. 'Well, you and me both, we want to avoid any middle-class labels. It could undermine our credibility as genuine Labour supporters. So could some of my office suits, I suppose. What's a quick way of making them look shabby?'

'Oh, very witty,' said Lulu. 'Sylvie, your dad's grandma often talks about her family being full of amateur comics. She's right, we've got one sitting next to you. Well, fair enough, Paul,' she went on, 'I'll get my stepmother to look after Sylvie for Monday afternoon while I talk to Marjorie Alsop at the offices.'

'Good on yer, Lulu, you're still me fav'rite bit of fluff,' said Paul in good old cockney style.

'Huh,' said Lulu in good old scornful style.

But a little smile came and went.

Elsewhere, Rosie and Matt's son and daughter were having an after-supper altercation. And they were having it in the living room while their parents shared the chore of washing up the supper dishes in the kitchen.

Giles was appalled, for Emily intended to go all the way to the Hammersmith Palais tomorrow evening, in company with Maureen Brown, daughter of Aunt Cassie and Uncle Freddy. She further intended to let her parents think she was going to the usual Brixton venue, except with Maureen this time. And now, because she knew Dad would say no to Hammersmith, she wanted Giles not to let the cat out of the bag, and to back her up. No, said Giles, certainly not. He pointed out that she'd never get back from Hammersmith by ten thirty. More like eleven thirty, and their mum and dad just wouldn't stand for that. Hadn't Emily told Maureen she always had to be back home by ten thirty?

'Oh, Maureen said we'd go there and back by taxi,' said Emily. 'Well, she's nearly famous as a glamour model and doesn't use anything as common as buses.'

'Buses aren't common, you dope,' said Giles. 'Listen, doesn't Maureen know you're only fifteen? She ought to know, she's been a second cousin long enough.'

'What she does know, what we both know, is that girls these days are much more grown-up than our mothers were at fifteen,' said Emily. 'No, come on, you've got to back me up. The Bopcats are doing their stuff at the Hammersmith Palais, and I want to see them again, and besides, Maureen knows their manager, the man I met last Saturday when I passed out.'

'I question passed out,' said Giles, 'and as for you thinking you're more grown-up than our mum was at your age, that's a laugh, that is. Look, if you want to tell her fairy stories about tomorrow evening, you're on your own. I'm not going to give you away, but also I'm not going to back you up. Anyway, what about Brad, won't he be calling for you?'

'Oh, I told him I'm going out with Maureen, and not to come,' said Emily.

'I don't know why you can't be your age and wait a while before wanting to act twenty,' said Giles. 'I'm not in any hurry, so I don't know why you are. Where are you going?'

'To do my homework,' said Emily, 'I hate having to do it over the weekend, and just remember you and me don't tell on each other.'

She went up to the quiet of her room. Giles could only shake his head at her silliness.

Saturday morning. Matt was at his garage on his busiest day of the week, and Emily and Giles were out with schoolfriends. That left Rosie free to make her promised visit to her mother in Brixton.

It was a few minutes after ten thirty when she arrived at the Effra Road house where her mother rented three upstairs rooms, bedroom, living room and kitchen. The rent came out of the monthly allowance provided by Rosie and Matt.

The one-time Milly Pearce of Walworth had

done her best to make her abode look present-able. She was no great lover of domestic tasks, and never had been. However, Rosie thought the flat looked fairly tidy, even if there were magazines poking out from under settee cushions in the living room, and a duster lay temporarily forgotten on the mantelpiece. Her main concern at this juncture was with her mother's appearance, and that, thank God, was much improved. Natural grey replaced the dye of her hair, which was quite nicely styled, and there was an absence of garish make-up. Also, she wore an obviously new grey costume with a conventional white blouse. True, the woman looked her age, but considering her illness, that was to be expected. In any case, she was far more acceptable to the beholder than when made up in a doomed attempt to recapture her youth.

After exchanging conventional niceties, Rosie said, 'Well, you really have improved your appearance, but tell me, how are you?'

'Oh,' said Milly, 'it's a relief that I don't have one of me bad heads just now. I said to meself when I got up this morning, thank goodness, I said, that with Rosie coming I won't be a nuisance. Well, I know how it is when I've got that hammer going behind me forehead, I'm a nuisance to everybody, meself as well. Oh, won't yer sit down, dear?'

Rosie seated herself in an armchair, the woman on the settee.

Rosie said, 'You shouldn't think of yourself as a nuisance.'

'Well, of course I try me best not to be.'

'Think of the possibility of how much better life is going to be for you on your return from France. Mr Wainwright has been very encouraging about the chances of success.'

'Oh, that reminds me, he told me yesterday afternoon that he'd got a cheque from you, a cheque that's going to look after all the expenses. I'm that grateful, Rosie, I don't know what to say. Mind, I'm pleased you said I looked improved. What d'you think of me new costume and me new hairdo, are they what you like?'

'They're nicely suitable,' said Rosie.

'Oh, would you like a cup of coffee, dear? I can make some for both of us.'

'I'll do it,' said Rosie.

'Oh, would yer, love?' said the Milly Pearce of old, always ready to dodge the boredom of the simplest domestic acts. 'It'll save me strength, and there's a jar of instant somewhere in the kitchen. On one of the shelves, I think.'

Rosie found the jar. It was standing in the middle of the kitchen table, the lid off. She gave it a wry smile. One had to concede the woman was presently a trier, but still basically indolent. As Matt had once said, in a moment of unusual cynicism, it's no good giving a new broom to the old witch, she'll only change it for a port and lemon.

Rosie put the kettle on and looked around for two coffee mugs. She found one in the sink that needed washing, and a second in a wall cupboard. In the small fridge she found one full bottle of milk and two empty ones.

She made the coffee, filled the mugs and took them to the living room.

'Here we are,' she said.

'Oh, it's ever so good of you, dear.'

'There are two empty milk bottles in the fridge.'

'Two? Oh, yes, sometime I've got to put them out on the back step for the milkman to pick up.'

Rosie said she'd do that when she left, then over the coffee some acceptable conversation took place. Acceptable, thought Rosie, in that her mother did not talk incessantly about herself and what a hard time she'd suffered since the death of Mr Rainbould. No, most of what she had to say concerned the influx of West Indian immigrants into Brixton, and how it was changing the area, which she hoped would turn out to be for the good. Eventually, Rosie asked about friends and neighbours. Her mother said oh, she had some nice friends and knew some nice neighbours. Only just lately, well, for the last couple of months or so, she just hadn't felt like entertaining anyone or even going out much. She got tired a bit quick sometimes, and then her blessed head would start thumping.

'I'm sorry it's become so painful,' said Rosie.

'Oh, it's honestly not so bad this morning, and it's been a real godsend to me peace of mind knowing you and your hubby sent Mr Wainwright all that money so's I can have the operation,' said Milly, but then a little sigh escaped her, and Rosie saw the signs indicating that her visit ought not to last too long. Well, from the moment of her arrival she'd seen that her mother's changed appearance was very much for the better, and her main reason for coming had been to make sure that this was so, and that the woman did not travel through France looking like a frizzy-haired and painted absurdity. What Mr Wainwright must have thought of her as mutton garishly dressed up as lamb was not hard to imagine.

'I'll just wash these coffee mugs, and then be on my way back home,' she said.

'Oh, all right, Rosie dear,' said her mother. 'It's been ever so nice seeing you, and I'll drop you a line from the hospital when I get there. I'm pleased you like me new costume and me new hairdo, even if it does make me look all grey. I'll have a bit of a lie-down when you've gone – oh, and thanks ever so much again for all you and your hubby are doing for me. Let's hope I'll be a new woman when we next meet, which I'm sure I will be, and which me doctor and Mr Wainwright told me I will.' She rattled on for a few more moments, and then sank back on the settee with all the sighing relief of a woman tired out.

Rosie cleaned the mugs and left them standing upside down on the draining board, since the only tea towel in evidence looked overdue for a wash. She took the empty milk bottles out of the fridge, washed them clean under the tap, and after putting her hat and coat on she said good-bye to her mother and wished her a not too tiring journey in company with the nurse, and a comfortable and successful stay in hospital.

'And I'll see you when you get back.'

'Oh, I'll let you know just as soon as I do get back, Rosie, and I'll have me lie-down now.'

Rosie left then, putting the milk bottles on the step outside the back door, while wondering how long they might have stayed stained and neglected in the fridge. Then she walked to her car. Instinctively, she looked up at the first-floor windows of the house, and there was her mother showing herself and giving a wave. Rosie returned the gesture.

As she drove away, a sense of pity for the woman returned.

Not until Matt was home at a quarter to six did she mention the visit. She still did not want to speak openly of her mother to Giles and Emily. There was too much of the undesirable to be told. Matt, however, knew everything and under-stood everything. Entirely the attentive listener, he was happy to know her mother's changed appearance was acceptable and that, apart from some obvious tiredness towards the end of the visit, she seemed fit to make the journey.

'The nurse is the key element here, Rosie.'

'Yes, she can't possibly make it on her own.'

'Let me ask you something. If no-one else had been available, would you have volunteered to go with her?'

'I wonder, Matt, do I owe her that much?'

'Well, do you, Rosie?'

'Looking at the life I've had, I suppose I do.'

They sat down to supper then, calling for Giles and Emily to join them.

Chapter Twenty-Two

'Ah, Miss Browning.'

'Yes, Mr Seidler?' said Janice Browning, ever the politest and most helpful of receptionists. She had watched the German guest descending the hotel staircase in his usual lithe fashion. 'May I be of assistance to you?'

'Will you be a good young lady?'

'I hope, Mr Seidler, that I don't give the impression of being bad.'

'Eh? Oh, yes, I see. Funny, yes. I have heard of English humour. But no, who would think you bad, Miss Browning? Not myself, no, no. I apologize. It is my faulty English, I think.'

'Your English is very good,' smiled Miss Browning, and if Ernst Thurber had been a different kind of man, he might have asked her if she would like to show him the sights of London's theatreland one evening, never mind that her young man was a police officer based at Scotland Yard. However, the Wolf's hatreds and fanaticism, as well as what his sadistic treatment of helpless

Jews and ten years in prison had done to his soul, had long driven out any normal feelings.

It was ten minutes to six and he asked Miss Browning if she would be good enough to let the evening receptionist know that he was going to visit friends, and would not be back until well after midnight. Miss Browning said that that would be quite all right, even if he didn't return until three o'clock in the morning. Guests did not have to ask permission to stay out late, but it was kind of him to let the hotel know he would not be going early to bed. And it was Saturday again, and the right day for seeing friends and enjoying oneself.

'Ah, yes. Yes, it is a cold but fine evening. *Ja*, I will enjoy myself, Miss Browning. Goodnight.'

He smiled. It was a smile full of white gleaming teeth, and Miss Browning had an extraordinary feeling that he would like to eat her. She watched him leave the hotel, and experienced an odd relief that she was not alone with him.

He walked to his parked car, the hired vehicle. He hadn't used it yesterday, having spent the morning reading *Mein Kampf* and giving himself the kind of physical exercise his body demanded in the afternoon. He had walked miles around Central London and through the royal parks, while dwelling on what he intended to do on Saturday. He could wait no longer, indulge his fantasies no further.

So here he was, beside his car. But, of course,

there was no point in going now, not when the deed had to be done when the area was totally quiet and the family sound asleep. He estimated it would take him more than a few minutes to soak the hall in petrol, delivering it through the letter box by means of the brass syringe. He would have to keep refilling the syringe from two nine-litre cans, the entirety the German equivalent of four English gallons. Only in that way could he be sure that when he dropped the lighted rag in through the letter box, it would take just a few seconds for the hall to explode in flame and fire. The house would be half-consumed before the family were aware of it, and well before they were out of their beds.

Yes, he needed complete quiet in the surroundings, he needed the whole area to be asleep. Everything he required was in the boot of the car, including a little wooden wedge to keep the letter box flap open, but he would not drive to his destination now. Not until after eleven, say. When he arrived in the area, he would spend whatever time was necessary to ensure he would be neither interrupted nor discovered. He would aim for beginning the deed at no earlier than one in the morning.

Accordingly, he took himself off for a brisk forty-minute walk before ending up in an Italian restaurant in Charing Cross Road, where he could pleasantly while away time until about eleven. Yes, good.

* * *

At seven fifteen, Emily was ready for her usual
Saturday evening excursion into the realms of
teenage Utopia, also known as the world of pop,
its powerhouses lubricated by Coca-Cola. Rosie
thought how attractive her daughter looked in a
white dress with dark brown polka dots that
matched her hair.

'Emily, you'll outshine Maureen,' she said.

'Well, hardly, Mum, she's really glam,' said
Emily, although she hoped she'd make a hit with
the Bopcats' sexy guitarist, if she could get close
enough.

'You'll be home as usual by ten thirty?' said
Rosie. She and Matt were steadfastly opposed
to their daughter staying out later, whatever
latitude other young teenage girls were allowed.

'Oh, in a taxi I'll easily be home by then,'
said Emily, too taken up with exciting prospects
to draw back. If she did get home a lot later
than usual, which she felt she might, she'd think
up an excuse. Certainly up to now she hadn't
mentioned Hammersmith to her parents.

'Maureen's definitely calling for you in a taxi?'
said Matt.

'Yes, the driver's going to give three toots on
his horn when he pulls up outside,' said Emily,
putting on her coat. 'And you might like to know
a taxi's all part of Maureen's life as a glamour
model.'

'By the way, Emily,' said Rosie, 'isn't Giles

being invited to share the taxi with you and Maureen to Brixton, or is he having to do the usual bus journey?'

'Oh, he's going with Cindy Stevens,' said Emily, which wasn't quite true. Giles would simply meet Cindy at the hall, as he and other fellers usually did.

Giles, in blue shirt and jeans, overcoat over his arm, remained silent. He was listening for three toots of a taxi horn and wondering if his sister really would dash out and ride all the way to Hammersmith with Maureen without informing Mum and Dad.

The door knocker sounded.

'Who can that be?' asked Rosie.

'Brad?' suggested Giles, and Emily gave him a discouraging look.

Matt answered the summons, and there on the doorstep was Maureen herself, known indeed by the family to be making a name for herself as a pin-up and a calendar girl. Sparkling with glamour and outlined against the dark night, a fur jacket round her shoulders, she gave Matt a brilliant smile.

'Well, hello,' said Matt, and out into the hall came Rosie, followed by Giles and Emily. Rosie expressed pleasure at seeing Maureen, while Giles complimented her looks by issuing a low whistle. As for Emily, she looked confused.

'Maureen, we thought your taxi was going to toot,' said Rosie.

'Oh, having arrived outside your door, I thought I must knock and say hello to all of you,' said Maureen. It had been Emily who'd suggested the three-toots signal. Then she could dash out and not keep the taxi waiting with its meter running, she'd said.

Now, putting aside confusion, she spoke quickly.

'Oh, glad you're here, Maureen, and let's get going, shall we, now you've said hello to my mum and dad. So long, Mum, so long, Dad, see you later.'

'Hammersmith Palais, here we come,' said Maureen. 'We'll—'

'Did you say Hammersmith?' asked Matt.

'Yes, the Bopcats are the hot stuff at the Palais tonight,' said Maureen, oblivious to Emily's frantically rolling eyes.

Giles hid a grin. The game was up for Emily. He knew it, and from her expression, so did she.

It proved to be up with a vengeance. Matt and Rosie would certainly not allow Emily to go all the way to Hammersmith unless Giles went too and Emily was back by half past ten. Maureen could have said that Emily hadn't mentioned any time restriction, but kept her peace. Rosie pointed out that Emily was only fifteen. Maureen, almost twenty and mixing as she did these days with nearly famous people, wasn't much worried about the way teenagers were breaking the rules by which most parents had lived. She nearly came out with the information that there would be more than one girl of fifteen at the gig, which wouldn't finish until eleven. However, noting the firm attitudes of Emily's parents, she kept quiet.

'I'm sorry about this,' said Matt, 'but the Hammersmith Palais is out, full stop, as far as Emily's concerned. She was a little too ambitious in arranging to go there with you.'

And a little too secretive, thought Rosie.

'Oh, well,' said Maureen brightly, 'we'll go to Emily's usual spot. Brixton, isn't it?' Her agent and photographer, Amos Anderson, would have said she was slumming it, but Maureen wasn't yet the kind of spoiled pussycat other models had become.

'I'll go along with that,' said Matt.

Emily was muttering, fidgeting and generally showing other signs of being totally fed up. Noticing that Giles had a bit of a grin on his face, she regarded him as if he was the epitome of a wet weekend.

'Will you go with the girls, Giles?' asked Rosie.

'He's welcome,' said Maureen. Then, 'Oh, crikey, the taxi, the meter's still running. Come on, Em, come on, Giles, let's go to Brixton in style, shall us? Not half. So long, Aunt Rosie, so long, Uncle Matt. See you again sometime.'

Off they went, the three of them, and almost the first person who ran into Emily when she, Maureen and Giles entered the hall, was Brad, spectacular in his best Teddy boy gear, his waist-coat buttons a gleaming gold.

And he was expansive in his welcome to Emily.

'Well, hello, baby doll, didn't expect to see you here tonight. Talk about the arrival of the Queen of Sheba. Great. Is this gorgeous doll your cousin Maureen? Howdy, Maureen, glad to know you, I'm Brad. OK, Emily, now you are here, let's hit the floor, eh?'

Youthfully resilient, Emily put aside bitter disappointment and fell into line with Brad. Maureen soon found fellers clamouring for the privilege of swinging sweet and high with her, while Giles joined Cindy and her group.

Everything concerning the Hammersmith Palais was forgotten then in the infectious atmosphere engendered by the music, the rhythm and the rapture of being young.

At home, Matt and Rosie discussed the obvious, that Emily had intended to go to Hammersmith without saying so. Very naughty, said Rosie, but neither she nor Matt wanted to make a great family drama of the matter, and so they decided to accept that Emily had let her zest for living it up run away with her.

And certainly, she was back from Brixton by ten thirty, along with Giles.

The Italian restaurant had what the Wolf assumed was a distinctly Bohemian atmosphere. Bohemianism he was not in favour of. In the eyes of the Party, that was one more element of decadence, much despised by the Führer, who had seen too much of it during his struggle for survival in Vienna before the First World War. As the Wolf had lately discovered, in *Mein Kampf* Hitler had emphasized the decadence of the Viennese in those years, and how closely associated the Jews had been with all that was degenerate about Vienna and Austria.

Despite his reservations, the Wolf settled into the restaurant and ordered a meal. He planned to linger and to study the other diners. In keeping with the atmosphere of the place, they all seemed variously decadent, the women sultry-eyed, heavy-lidded and languid, the men raffish in their appearance and in love with their own wit. At least, from the laughter it caused, he presumed wit was present. He knew nothing of wit himself. He was a plain-speaking, plain-thinking man.

The food proved to be eatable, and the Italian waiters, although looking like disreputable artists too hard up to afford a shave more than once a week, offered willing service. The little restaurant filled with the blue haze of cigarette and cigar smoke as diners reached the coffee and liqueur stage, when most seemed to become increasingly in love with themselves and their repartee. He wondered, over his coffee and schnapps, if it could possibly have been people such as these who had, with the Americans, frustrated the Führer and crippled his endeavours to establish a powerful German Empire. It was hardly believable that they had won the war. No, he corrected himself on that point. It had been the swarming millions of primitive Russian peasants who, by their very numbers, had finally defeated Germany.

He also wondered if any of these men present had been British army officers. He should himself have been commissioned as an SS officer, but certain superiors had said he was basically undisciplined. Undisciplined? How could a man who had obeyed every order and applied himself so well to the work of the Final Solution be judged undisciplined? Was that because he used his own initiative at times? Very unfair.

In this way, dawdling, observant and introspective, he passed the evening. The wine he had drunk and the schnapps he had enjoyed combined with a satisfied stomach to give him a sense of well-being. This showed itself in the generous tip he handed over, and was with him when he finally left.

However, as soon as he arrived back at his car a few minutes after eleven, a sudden fever gripped him, his adrenalin rushed and all sense of good humour towards his fellow men vanished. Every nerve was focused on the reason for this visit to London, and on the certainty that within the next two hours he would have avenged Hans. He could then return appeased and satisfied to West Berlin. Yes, on Monday he would speak to Miss Browning for the last time before leaving. He would ask her to give his regards to her young man, a Scotland Yard policeman. Ah, very good, that. Perhaps even witty.

As he opened the car door, with his pulses racing, he asked a silent question of the man he had marked down for death.

'Are you preparing for bed, Colonel Robert Adams, or already there? Well, I am coming for you now. For you and your family.'

'You've another good book there, Polly old girl?' enquired Boots, entering the bedroom from the bathroom after cleaning his teeth.

Polly was abed, her dark brown hair decorating the white pillows, which were banked high, for she intended to do a not unusual spot of reading before settling down. The book in question, *The Diary of Anne Frank*, had succeeded *A Farewell to Arms*.

'It's the one I've been telling you about, old love,' she said. 'Anne Frank's diary. It's astonishing, riveting, and makes me feel a violent hatred of the Nazis. I'm convinced the murderous swines robbed the world of a brilliant and remarkable mind when they sent this young girl to her death in a concentration camp.'

Boots, slipping on his pyjama jacket, said soberly, 'Will the world ever know the extent of the losses it suffered in those camps? Established or potential doctors, scientists, engineers, architects?'

Because of their personal histories, which took in the two world wars, Polly and Boots could slip easily into discussion of one or the other, and without boring each other. It was wise, however, not to indulge in the presence of certain young people who found all wartime subjects very boring indeed, especially in an age when the stars of rock and pop were beginning to make history, of a kind.

Polly sighed, acknowledging the futility of war. 'You won't mind my reading for a while, Boots?'

'Not a bit,' said Boots, slipping in beside her. 'Just make a note that I'd like my turn with the book when you've finished it. Let's see, who bought it?'

'You did, dear man, when we were looking around W.H. Smith,' said Polly. 'I snaffled it as soon as we arrived home.'

'No worries,' murmured Boots, turning on his side, 'what's mine is always all yours.'

'Noted with affection, old soldier,' replied Polly, already absorbed.

The time was eleven twenty. Outside, the night was quiet, except for one house, from which the evening's guests were noisily departing. That lasted for a few minutes before the general peace was re-established.

Boots murmured himself into sleep, and at eleven forty Polly closed her book, switched off the reading light, turned on her side and followed him into slumber. In their respective rooms, James and Gemma were sleeping the deep sleep of the young and active.

The handsome family house was at rest.

Chapter Twenty-Three

In his flat above a hairdressing salon in Bayswater, the proprietor, a Polish immigrant, sat listening to the Sunday morning news as it issued forth from his radio in the calm tones of the announcer. It concerned, first of all, as usual, the current state of the relationship between the democratic West and the totalitarian East. If the West had thought the death of Stalin in 1953 might make that relationship less sour, it had been mistaken. The cold war was as hot as ever.

Towards the end of the bulletin, the announcer touched on an incident that had happened too late last night to make the Sunday morning papers. A car, parked near a hotel in Bloomsbury, had exploded into a fireball a little after eleven o'clock. The vehicle was a burned-out ruin, and the driver had been reduced to ashes.

'Let us call the car your crematorium,' muttered the Polish immigrant, 'and I hope you were aware of that, even if for only the most fleeting second.'

It was already established that the dead driver had been staying at the hotel, that he was a German businessman by the name of Rolf Seidler, and that Scotland Yard was investigating the incident. Fortunately, no-one in the vicinity had been injured.

The weather forecast followed, and it was not very cheerful. That did not upset the Polish immigrant. He was very cheerful himself.

The phone rang. He spoke to the caller.

'Yes, I've heard the news, my son. You were not there yourself, then?'

'No. I spent all day Friday and most of yesterday waiting and watching, and it was all wasted time. He did not use the car, nor had he done so by ten last night, so I left. Then later, boomf! He had switched on the ignition, of course, and up went the car in fire and flame, so I heard. By leaving, I missed it, but I'm not heartbroken, and I'm sure you're not, Papa, not now you know you did your work so well.'

'No, I'm very happy. The pig has been incinerated.'

'I thought you said he was known as the Wolf.'

'Yes, very true,' said Emil Kiernik, a concentration-camp survivor, a secret Communist and an undercover servant for Poland's government. 'But he was also a pig.'

'Well, Papa, as I understand it, the fireball turned him into burnt bacon,' said Andre Kiernik, the executioner's son.

294

*   *   *

'I just don't understand these kind of things,' said Chinese Lady over the leisurely breakfast she and Sir Edwin always enjoyed on Sunday mornings in the kitchen. They now had a new toaster that was simple to use, and not like their first contraption that expelled toast black and smoking, just as if it was at war with them. They had been listening to the radio news. Sir Edwin liked to do this, particularly relishing any political aspect, although Chinese Lady regarded all politics as something invented by bumptious men for the purpose of making a nuisance of themselves.

'I mean, Edwin, could someone have made that car catch fire?'

'Maisie my dear, if the police suspect it was a criminal act,' said Sir Edwin, 'then we have to remind ourselves that in the world of crime there are always men who will use that kind of method to destroy a rival. It doesn't happen in London too much, but it's very common in American cities.'

'Well, we don't want a lot of it over here,' said Chinese Lady, helping herself to marmalade she had made during the season of Seville oranges. 'We've got enough of our own heathen law-breakers. I don't know why some people can't grow up honest and hardworking instead of lazy and work-shy. It's that kind that go in for stealing and thieving. And worse.'

'You're quite right, Maisie,' said Sir Edwin, 'it's the work-shy men who prefer the profits of crime to the wages of an honest job.'

'Yes,' said Chinese Lady, frowning, 'but I still can't think why someone was wicked enough to make that car catch fire and burn the driver alive. The news said he was a German business-man. I might not like Germans, but why should anyone want to give this one such a dreadful death, poor man?'

'There are businessmen from every country who don't play by the rules,' said Sir Edwin. 'We have our own quota of fly merchants.'

'Fly merchants, Edwin?'

'I believe Sammy would refer to them as dubious geezers,' said Sir Edwin with a little smile.

'That Sammy never did use respectable language,' said Chinese Lady, 'and he's still talking common at times. Not like Boots. Mind,' she added hastily, 'I'm not holding one up against the other. I mean, although Boots speaks very nice, you can never trust that what he says is what he means. Nearly all his life I've been telling him that, but he still does it.'

'Boots is always himself,' said Sir Edwin, glad of the warmth of the kitchen, and of the central heating of the house. At eighty-five his bones were beginning to feel the cold. 'Do we have someone coming to tea this afternoon?'

'Why, Tommy and Vi, and Aunt Victoria, if

she's well enough,' said Chinese Lady happily. The ritual of a Sunday family tea always gave her a lift. She was still devoted to its Victorian origins, unaware that up and down the country many teenagers were trying to get it abolished so that they could eat their tea and cake in front of the television. The teenagers of her extensive clan might not kick up a fuss if it were abolished in other families, but never would they suggest it should be done away with in that headed by their much respected and endearing matriarch. During her lifetime, each of them would always go along with it. 'Yes, they'll be here about half past three, Edwin.'

'There's always something to live for,' murmured Sir Edwin.

'Goodness,' said Chinese Lady, looking pleased, 'do you mean for Sunday tea, Edwin?'

'I do,' said Sir Edwin, 'and I'm desperately sorry for that German businessman in more ways than one. If he has never been introduced to English Sunday teas, he has lost all chance now.'

'Poor man,' said Chinese Lady.

As for the one-time all-American girl, Mrs Patsy Adams, she suggested to husband Daniel, apropos the incident in Bloomsbury, that if Chicago mobsters were setting up stall in London, she might as well go back to good old sober Boston, where the only law-breakers were the fighting Irish boyos on St Patrick's night.

'Which is only once a year,' she said.

'Hey, hold up,' said Daniel, who was helping her with the washing up of breakfast dishes in well-trained style, 'if you go back home to Boston, li'l ole honey chile, who's going to do our Monday washing and our Tuesday ironing?'

'Listen, Buffalo Bill,' said Patsy, looking engagingly domestic in a flower-patterned and frilly-edged apron, 'I liked London up to last night. I liked the way it looked, with its blitzed stone, broken marble and smashed chimney pots all cleared up, and Piccadilly all lit up. But I don't like it now, not when it's obvious that old-time gangsters have come to town and are going to celebrate weekends by setting fire to each other.'

'I can see you're against Chicago mobsters, and I can also see why,' said Daniel, 'but I still want to know who's going to do our Monday washing. I can't ask my ma, because she's got her own to do, and I can't do it myself because I'll be at the office, where I happen to be an important cog.'

'Who's kidding who?' asked Patsy. 'All I'm saying in so many words is that whoever roasted some unlucky German last night ought to be grabbed by a posse of twelve good men and true, and roasted himself over a barbecue. Which means slowly.'

'Patsy, you peach,' said Daniel, 'I'm with you all the way on that, and I'm mighty relieved you're staying home.'

'Mum?' Arabella put her head round the kitchen door.

'Yes, honey?' said Patsy.

'Can I put my two sweaters in tomorrow's wash, as well as a lot of my usual stuff?'

'Sure you can,' said Patsy.

'Thanks, Mum, you're tops,' said Arabella. 'Daddy, why're you rolling your eyes?'

'It shows I'm weak with relief,' said Daniel.

'Why?' asked Arabella.

'I was nearly in the way of having to wash your two sweaters and your bagful of other stuff myself,' said Daniel. 'Fortunately, you could say I've just been saved by your mother's loving nature.'

'I don't get it,' said Arabella.

'Some other time, poppet,' said Daniel, who wasn't going to talk to his young daughter about the grisly subject of a man roasted alive in the heart of Bloomsbury.

'It beats me.' That was Sammy's reference to the radio news bulletin. He and Susie were getting ready for a visit to Bow in east London, to the home of their younger son Jimmy and his wife Clare. Jimmy and Clare had invited them to a Sunday roast dinner, Jimmy confident his parents would, as always on their visits, enjoy Clare's talents as a cook.

'You're still talking about someone bombing a car in Bloomsbury?' said Susie, picturesque in a dress of ivy green chenille. At fifty-four, and unlike her bounteous sister-in-law Lizzy, she was still in control of her figure. Sitting at her dressing table, she was applying a modest amount of make-up.

'It wasn't a bomb, was it?' said Sammy, neatly fixing one of his Sunday ties. 'At least, I don't think a bomb was mentioned. But it was still a piece of dirty work, setting a driver and his car on fire. Even the Fat Man wouldn't have gone as far as cooking a competitor.' The Fat Man was a former business rival who used a team of heavies to do nasty crippling jobs on people who got in his way. He'd tried to do one on Sammy, but Sammy's own team had well and truly seen him off. He was now just another overweight, small-time crook. 'I tell you, Susie, if it was a gang killing, Scotland Yard's going to turn London inside out.'

'Well, Sammy love,' said Susie, 'let's get on and make our Sunday visit to Bow while we can.'

'Good point, Susie,' said Sammy, 'I don't want to be turned inside out meself, especially when I'm wearing a Sunday suit. Blimey, that makes me wonder if Mad Marj will turn the offices inside out when she calls tomorrow afternoon.'

'Bear up, Sammy,' said Susie, rising, 'she's only after your fur coat.'

'I don't have a fur coat,' said Sammy, 'they're for bookies.'

'You'll still win,' said Susie, 'Boots will see to that.'

'Well, yes,' said Sammy, slipping on his jacket, 'except I've been thinking lately that his educated head might fall off one day, which means that'll be the day when one of his ideas lands us in the soup. Oh, well, let's get going, Susie. Are we taking anything?'

'Yes, some chrysanthemums for Clare, and a celluloid duck for little Maisie,' said Susie. Maisie, named after Chinese Lady, was the one-year-old daughter of Jimmy and Clare.

'Right,' said Sammy, 'and we'll avoid going by way of Bloomsbury.'

'I should think so,' said Susie, 'who wants to stop and gawp at a burned-out car?'

At her home, Miss Browning, who had told the police all she knew of the man called Rolf Seidler, shuddered from time to time as she thought about the hideousness of his death.

'Here we are, green-fingered lady, what do you think of these?' asked Boots, carrying a trug as he entered the kitchen by way of the back door. He wore an old hat, an old jacket and jersey, and old corduroy trousers. All could have combined to emphasize that he was a bit old hat himself, except that it never seemed to do so. Friends and relatives put it down to the fact that he never allowed a crisis or a setback to worry him overmuch. 'All the produce of your own hand, Polly.' He was referring to what lay in the trug, thick white gleaming leeks touched at their tops with green, bushy roots trimmed.

Polly, aproned, head covered to keep cooking smells out of her hair, took a proud look at the leeks.

'Boots old thing, you may praise me,' she said. She was a first-class gardener, particularly when it came to growing vegetables.

'My compliments,' said Boots, 'and take a bow.'

The twins were present. It was almost coffee time and the kitchen on a Sunday morning was where the family gathered for this, unless the twins had pressing engagements with close friends or a date with the vicar at his church service.

'Crikey, Daddy,' said Gemma, 'they get better every week.'

'That's the beauty of leeks as a winter veg,' said Boots. 'They flourish in the frost. Do homage to your mother for growing them.'

James began, addressing Polly thus.

'Mother Nature, we your—'

'No, you can't call her Mother Nature,' said Gemma, 'that sort of makes her next door to God. She's ever so dear to us, of course, but none of us could live with that.'

'All right,' said James amiably, 'how about Queen of our Onion Bed?'

'Yes, good shot, James,' said Gemma, and

addressed her mother. 'Thank you, Queen of our Onions, for providing us with gorgeous leeks, and could I have mine cooked with a creamy sauce?'

'Ye gods, creamy sauce?' said Polly. 'You all know my talents lie elsewhere, that my cooking is always a hit-and-miss affair. It's true my hot custard isn't lumpy any more, but I couldn't possibly guarantee that my creamy sauce won't be a disaster. What was it like last time?'

'Heavenly,' said Gemma.

'Luscious,' said James.

'A triumph of perseverance,' said Boots.

'I suspect that comment,' said Polly.

'I welcome another triumph today,' said Boots.

'Yes, come on, Mother dear,' said James, 'leeks cooked in creamy sauce.'

Mother dear rolled up her sleeves, as it were.

'Very well, darlings,' she said, 'but I'll need some help. Who's going to peel the potatoes for me, and who's now going to make the coffee?'

Boots volunteered to make the coffee, and the twins volunteered to peel the potatoes, while Mother dear queened it over her preparation of the leg of Welsh lamb.

On the dresser, the kitchen radio stood silent. Polly and her family, whenever gathered together, weren't great radio fans unless something special was being broadcast. They all favoured conversation, and were all great talkers in any event, Polly vivacious, Boots humorous,

Gemma bubbly and James droll, they didn't need radios when they were all present as one.

So they were among many other people who hadn't yet heard the news concerning the fireball in Bloomsbury. Not that Polly or Boots, James or Gemma, would have had any reason to connect it with themselves.

The only person who had known how it would have directly affected them was ex-SS Sergeant Ernst Thurber. Alas for his hopes of vengeance, he had been cremated.

By a concentration-camp survivor, now settled in Bayswater, London.

Chapter Twenty-Four

Monday morning.

'My stepmother,' said Lulu in the precise way
of a would-be MP wishing to be clearly heard and
understood, 'will be here at twelve thirty to join
me for lunch, and will look after Sylvie during
the whole of the time I'm at your offices.'

Sylvie was presently calmly eating her breakfast.

'What a fine woman your stepma is,' said Paul.
'No wonder your dad is always saying what a help
she's been to him in his time as an MP.'

Lulu said she hoped Paul would be just as much
of a help when she herself was an elected Member
of Parliament. It was encouraging to note, she said,
that many modern-minded men were beginning to realize women had a place in industry,
commerce and the governing of the country. Paul
wouldn't deny, would he, that women could be as
important as men in these respects?

Paul said right from his time as a nappy-
wetting baby he'd realized how important one
particular woman was to him personally, and that

was his mum. Certainly, yes, when Lulu took her seat in the House of Commons, he'd help her in every way he could, and that was a promise.

Lulu said she'd grown to rely on him, although she'd always thought to be completely independent of any man. Happily, she'd found it wasn't a humiliation to turn to one's husband for help. In fact, it came naturally. Therefore, she said, she was aware of her obligations whenever Paul asked help of her. So, with regard to the help she'd promised him concerning Marjorie Alsop, she wanted him to know she was going to give that help wholeheartedly, and not lightly.

'After all,' she said, 'being against furs is of small account when compared with the fact that this so-called civilized world is still full of exploited labourers and starving millions. So you can definitely rely on me to do my best this afternoon for you and the firm, Paul.'

'Atta girl,' said Paul. 'I can see myself buying you flowers and Dad giving you a box of chocolates.'

'Your dad's a kind man,' said Lulu, 'so tell him I'd rather have a copy of that Russian novel, *Dr Zhivago*. It wasn't a favourite with Stalin, apparently, so it must be worth reading.' Along with many other people, even including some of the most ardent Socialists, Lulu had gone off Stalin since evidence had come to light of his responsibility for the death or murder of millions of his fellow citizens. 'Oh, and by the way, Paul, ask Uncle Boots if he'd sit in with Marjorie and me this afternoon.'

'Will do,' said Paul. 'I like the thought behind that, and I also like the fact that, as I've said before, you're not just a pretty face, Lulu, you've got a thinking head as well.'

The offices of Adams Enterprises and associated companies were buzzing that afternoon in anticipation of the expected arrival of Marjorie Alsop, stalwart campaigner in the eyes of some people but a pain in the elbow to others, depending, of course, on one's point of view. There was nothing Sammy could have done about keeping her visit unknown to all except himself and Boots. The office grapevine had been operating throughout the building, from the ground to the top floor. George Porter from the top floor did look in on Boots after lunch to wish him good luck in respect of the lady.

'Thanks,' said Boots, 'I hope to survive. Incidentally, how are things now between you and Queenie Richards?'

'Er, well, I used to read a lot of books,' said George. 'I haven't been reading as many lately.'

'My wife likes a good book at bedtime,' smiled Boots. 'I like one on holiday.'

'Ah, er, yes,' said George, who was now less keen on bedtime reading, since his dates with Queenie were fostering the growth of imagination, and imagination, together with Queenie's well-rounded figure, was beginning to build pictures of something more at bedtime than a good book. That imagination had just been stirred by Mr Adams, and George could still blush a bit, and stumble a bit. 'Well, good luck again, sir.' And he disappeared, leaving Boots to his own imagination, which made him smile to himself this time.

Miss Alsop, dressed in an attractive white raincoat and black velvet hat, arrived punctually at three, a cylindrical cardboard container under her arm. Her request was spoken firmly.

'Take me at once to your commanding officer.'

'Beg pardon?' said general-office girl Vanessa.

'What did I say, then?'

'That you wanted to see our commanding officer.'

'No, no, I was mistaken,' said Miss Alsop. 'It so happens I visited the Knightsbridge barracks this morning concerning bearskins, and I suppose I'm still army-minded. I meant, of course, that I'm here as arranged to see your general manager, Mr Adams, Mr Robert Adams.'

'Oh, yes, Miss Alsop,' said Vanessa. 'This way.'

Boots was awaiting the visitor. Sammy, in frank cowardly fashion, was upstairs with his bookkeepers. He meant to avoid Boots's office until the coast was clear. For all his years of allowing no-one to seriously intimidate him, not even the Fat Man and his heavies, he couldn't help feeling, in the presence of Mad Marj, that he was the prime target for her squishy tomatoes and her suspicious mind. And he had to remember that his main responsibility at the moment was to protect the profitable sales in the firm's retail shops of cosy little fur-trimmed numbers that could make any girl look expensive. So he was leaving Boots to take care of Mad Marj, with the help of Lulu.

Boots received the lady at the open door of his office.

'Good afternoon, Miss Alsop,' he said, and shook hands with her.

'Good afternoon, Mr Adams,' said the lady, steeling herself to look him in the eye. He met her challenging gaze with his usual good-humoured smile. She quivered a little, but held herself proud and upright. This time, she told herself, she would definitely find out whether or not his firm really was innocent of selling furs, and if it genuinely did intend to support her campaign.

'Come in, Miss Alsop,' said Boots, 'come in and meet a sister enthusiast.'

Entering his office she saw a young woman standing with her back to the window. She had a wealth of shining black hair, and wore spectacles with horn rims just as black. Through the lenses her eyes looked large, clear and earnest. This, in fact, was a true indication of Lulu's mood. She was earnest indeed in her promise of an

309

attempted conversion, even if only for the peace of mind of Uncle Boots and Uncle Sammy who, although the firm's bosses, were known to be fair to their workers. And besides, she liked them, even while admitting it was a weakness for any staunch Labour Party activist to have a soft spot for capitalists.

She stepped forward.

'Well, hello,' she said. 'I'm Lulu Adams. Mr Adams's niece by marriage. You're Marjorie Alsop, of course.' Lulu had a habit of speaking in staccato fashion when on her soapbox. 'Good-oh, pleasure to meet you.'

'Mr Adams's niece?' said Miss Alsop, who had thought for a moment that she might be looking at his current line in fancy goods. As a woman who had met all sorts, she was pretty sure that men like him and his brother – the one with the electric blue eyes – could attract lady friends on the side.

'How are you?' said Lulu breezily. 'I've heard so much about you. I believe, according to Mr Adams, that you've brought some campaign posters with you. I know a lot about posters. The right kind can work wonders for a cause.'

Miss Alsop, impressed by this reception, glanced at Boots, and he glanced at the cardboard container she was carrying.

'Sit down, Miss Alsop,' he said, 'and show us what you've brought.'

Miss Alsop placed the container on the desk,

and took off her raincoat, revealing her firm body attractively clad in a light brown jersey wool dress, which her mother would have said was a welcome change from a baggy old sweater and skirt. She sat down and drew rolled-up posters from the container. Again she glanced at Boots. Boots smiled in encouragement. Lulu noted both glance and smile.

'There, what d'you think?' asked Miss Alsop, unrolling the first poster. It bore challenging wording in heavy black capitals.

PEOPLE! JOIN WOOF AND FIGHT FOR THE LIVES OF INNOCENT ANIMALS!

'Striking,' said Boots.

'Impactive on the eye,' said Lulu. 'My own local organization uses that kind of poster, often when we're asking the public to join the fight for workers' fair wages. Let's see, remind me, exactly what does WOOF stand for?'

'Simply, "Wool or Fur",' said Miss Alsop, not sure if the presence of a third party was making her less sensitive to the proximity of Mr Adams. 'Yes, it's short for "Wool or Fur". We want to encourage the use of wool in place of fur where suitable. Oh, and here's another poster.' She unrolled it, and its clarion call leapt to the eye in scarlet.

PEOPLE OF THE WORLD! JOIN WOOF AND FIGHT THE FIGHT FOR ANIMAL HUMANITY!

'Trenchant,' said Boots, preparing to slide into

311

a back seat, in a manner of speaking. This, he imagined, was going to be Lulu's hour.

'Yes, trenchant all right,' said Sylvie's Socialist mum, 'but I'm beginning to query WOOF.'

'Pardon?' said Miss Alsop.

'It's doggy,' said Lulu.

'Doggy?' said Miss Alsop.

'Well, don't you think so?' said Lulu. 'It's going to make more than a few people see you as a kind of guardian angel to their tail-waggers.'

'Good grief, that's not what I'm after,' said Miss Alsop.

Someone knocked on the door. Boots opened it and the tea lady from the canteen, bearing a tray containing three cups of tea, a bowl of sugar and a plate of biscuits, smiled up at him.

'Three cups, like you ordered, Mr Adams,' she said.

'Well done, and thanks,' said Boots, and took the tray from her. She essayed a covert glance at the dreaded anti-fur female before departing. Boots placed the tray on the desk. 'Miss Alsop?' He offered her a cup, with saucer.

'Oh, very welcome,' she said, taking it. However, she waved away the proffered sugar bowl. 'No sugar, thanks.'

'Biscuit?'

'Well, yes, I will, thanks,' she said, and took one.

'Lulu, help yourself to tea and biscuits,' said Boots, and Lulu did so.

An amiable atmosphere arrived, into which

Lulu reintroduced the unsuitability of WOOF as a campaign title. She emphasized its 'doggy' nature, and pointed out that some people might even conclude that the organization was against the skinning of dogs, which was a bit off the mark, wasn't it?

'Well, we do explain to interested people that it simply means wool is a more inoffensive material than fur,' said Miss Alsop, and quivered a little as Boots invited her to have another biscuit. He was quite close to her, half-perched against the back of his desk, and seemed, as he had before, a man at ease with life and people. His niece, on the other hand, was all mental energy, and talking with intense conviction.

'Yes, I can see that. I can see explanations might be necessary. People don't always see the light. Not at first. We Labour activists specialize in instantly grabbing the whole attention of the interested. Before they can disappear. Let's see, how many members do you have, Miss Alsop?' enquired Lulu.

'How many?'

'Yes.'

'Well, at the moment I do have a number of helpers.'

'Do you mean you're the only official in your organization?'

'It's all voluntary and I rely on my helpers to post posters, join me in demonstrations and draw in donations.'

'You're a marvel,' said Lulu. 'Running it from the top by yourself alone. But you need paid-up members.'

'Pardon?'

'Now, regarding your cause,' said Lulu. 'Very praiseworthy. Have you considered how it would appeal to our working classes? Take the ordinary man in the street, the everyday worker. He's probably exploited by his bosses. Accordingly, he needs a union to fight for him. Now, he sees all these toffs wearing furs, and what's his first thought? That the furs were indirectly supplied at his expense. That he'd like his union to help change the picture. There's your natural member, Miss Alsop, a starving worker!' Lulu emphasized her point with a figurative exclamation mark. Boots coughed. 'Well, nearly starving,' she said.

'My aim' said Miss Alsop, 'has always been to try to awaken the interest of people who feel for all the fur-bearing animals that are hunted down for the benefit of the furriers and their outlets.'

'Yes, and the rich,' said Lulu. 'Listen, what you need is an organization built around paid-up members. Such as a trade union. Paid-up members give that union strength and funds. Which all unions need in order to fight the bosses. You need it in order to fight the capitalists of the fur trade. They're the people responsible for providing mink and ermine for the filthy rich. D'you get me?'

'Well, yes,' said Miss Alsop, 'I can see that I need—'

The phone rang. Boots murmured an excuse and answered it. It was a business call and he dealt with it informatively and quietly, while Lulu helped herself to one more biscuit and Miss Alsop tried to find firm ground for her feet in place of shifting sand. She asked herself a vital question. How could a woman advance herself and her cause in the presence of these two people, when the proximity of one was so disturbing and the voice of the other so convincing? The answer was to stick it out until, given the opportunity to address herself directly to Mr Adams, she had won for herself and her cause the full support of Adams Enterprises. His niece's arguments were making her wonder, however, if her campaign needed to be reorganized.

Boots, putting the phone down, said, 'Shall we continue this discussion?'

Since he had contributed very little himself, Miss Alsop said, 'I should like to know your own views, Mr Adams.'

'I assure you, my own views coincide with yours and my niece's,' said Boots.

'Oh, really?' said Miss Alsop, not sure exactly what her own views were at the moment, although she did have a feeling of being in agreement with his niece, whose spectacles, when aimed at her, commanded her attention. 'You're sincerely ready to give support, Mr Adams?'

'I'm sincerely ready to interest myself in any good cause,' said Boots, 'so let's carry on, shall we?'

Lulu jumped in at once to point out that Miss Alsop's most immediate needs were a new campaign title and a properly organized membership. She suggested the former should be based on 'Support Animal Welfare', shortened to SAW. That, she said, had a real cutting edge to it.

'SAW?' said Miss Alsop.

'Yes,' said Lulu. 'Sharp and to the point. Like it?'

'Yes, except it doesn't explicitly touch on fur-bearing animals,' said Miss Alsop.

'No problem,' said Lulu. 'Put a sketch of a cuddly bear on the posters. That'll point to the real target. But recruitment of members must also be taken care of. Paid-up members. That kind work towards getting results. Or they feel their subscriptions are wasted. We don't want that. What we do want is a decent Socialist outlook.'

Miss Alsop expressed doubts about whether or not she could take on that label. Her father was a City man and a firm Conservative, who made her a generous allowance so that she could carry on her campaign. He'd have a fit if anything like Socialism crept into it. Lulu said that what she meant was talking to and mingling with the workers of the world. Workers of the world would always do what they could to fight exploitation. In this case, exploitation of alligators to provide handbags for millionaires' wives. And so on.

'Well, I suppose to have workers on our side would be a great advantage,' said Miss Alsop, and went on to say she'd been thinking lately about moving from Twickenham. She'd come to the conclusion that Twickenham wasn't a very good base for an organization like hers.

'Too posh,' said Lulu succinctly.

'I'm thinking, in fact, of getting digs in London,' said Miss Alsop, glancing at Boots once more.

'For action,' said Boots, 'I'd be in favour of London.'

'Oh, I must definitely consider London, then,' said Miss Alsop.

'It's full of workers, your natural supporters,' said Lulu, turning her spectacles on Miss Alsop. The lenses projected the continuing earnestness of a friend and helper.

The phone rang again. Boots answered it.

'A Mr Leslie Parker to speak to you, Mr Adams,' said the switchboard girl.

'I'll take it in Mr Sammy's office,' said Boots.

'I'll hold the line, Mr Adams.'

Boots excused himself again to Lulu and Miss Alsop, then left to allow Lulu to have the lady all to herself. He entered Sammy's office.

Sammy, knowing Miss Alsop was in the building, said, 'No, I'm not here. That's if she wants me.'

'Lend me your phone, old chap,' said Boots, and picked it up.

The switchboard put the caller through then,

and Boots conducted another business conversation, this time with a customer who wanted to know if his next invoice for goods supplied could be paid in advance. Boots, of course, wanted to know if that meant payment before the goods reached the Adams factory.

'Well, it's like this here,' said Mr Parker, a manufacturer of sundries such as buttons and zips. Zips were booming. 'It's Mrs Parker, y'see, Mr Adams, she's put me in overdraft, and the bank's breathing down me neck. She went and bought herself a silver brooch inlaid with rubies to celebrate our silver wedding. Well, we've been married twenty-five years, y'know, and I didn't have the heart to make her take the brooch back, even though the cost took every shirt off me back, including me Sunday ones. Can you help me out, Mr Adams?'

Boots knew his man. Leslie Parker was as sound as any supplier could be.

'Send your invoice, and we'll settle it by return,' he said. 'I'm sure we can rely on delivery of the relevant goods.'

'You've got my word, Mr Adams. Much obliged to yer, and thanks as well.'

'You're welcome,' said Boots, and hung up.

'Well?' said Sammy.

'That was Les Parker,' said Boots. 'He's in a bit of a fix, due to—'

'No, not him,' said Sammy. 'Her.'

'Ah, Miss Alsop, I presume?' said Boots.

Chapter Twenty-Five

Sammy listened while Boots gave him a résumé
of the discussion that had taken place so far
between Lulu and the awkward lady of tomato
fame.

'I'm in the dark,' said Sammy. From his large
and handsome office desk he was usually master
of all he surveyed. He looked a bit uncertain
about things at the moment. 'What's it all
mean?'

'Paul told you, didn't he,' said Boots, 'that Lulu
was going to do her best to get the lady off our
backs?'

'He told me Lulu was going to talk to her
about Socialism,' said Sammy, 'which pained me
considerable. Ever since I started my business
career with that East Street market stall, there's
one thing I've never allowed anywhere near
my operations. Socialism. It's all right for some
people, I ain't disputing that, but it's a danger to
a healthy balance sheet. The fact that it's walking
about in these very offices right now is making

319

me nervous. All right, so it's not actually walking about, but it's still around.'

'And has been since Paul joined the firm,' said Boots.

'Eh?' said Sammy.

'Paul's a Labour Party voter, you know that,' said Boots.

'Well, yes,' said Sammy, 'but he's family, and besides, like he promised me when we gave him the job of assistant to Daniel and Tim, he leaves his Socialism at home while he's working. The point now is will Lulu spread it around unconscious, like? That's without meaning to. What're you doing about it?'

'Listening,' said Boots.

'Just listening?' said Sammy.

'Just that,' said Boots. 'It's a conversion job by Lulu on Marj, not on our staff.'

'Lulu can manage that by herself?' said Sammy.

'Take it from me, Sammy, Lulu doesn't need any help,' said Boots. 'It's the poster lady who's struggling.'

'You sure you're not taking a risk by leaving Lulu alone with her?' said Sammy. 'You sure Mad Marj won't turn the tables while you're here with me?'

'I'm betting on Lulu,' said Boots.

'In that case,' said Sammy, 'consider yourself a relief to my aching head, and stay a bit longer to look over this new contract we're negotiating

320

with Coates. I ain't been able to concentrate on it myself.'

Boots returned to his office twelve minutes later, at the moment when Miss Alsop was promising Lulu to attend the next meeting of Labour Party activists in Brixton. Lulu had convinced her that her most natural supporters would indeed be the workers, because who more than they were genuinely opposed to the fur-wearing filthy rich? Brown bears, black bears, leopards, beavers and suchlike could happily look forward to having the workers of the world as their champions. Well, the Brixton workers to start with. Miss Alsop asked how many that would be.

'All of 'em,' said Lulu in her brisk fashion.

'Oh, yes. Yes, very well,' said Miss Alsop, which provided Boots with the opportunity to give his blessing to the outcome. Miss Alsop regarded him out of slightly glazed but not un-happy eyes.

'Yes?' he said encouragingly.

'You think my change of tactics a wise move?' she said.

'I think you and my niece Lulu will get on extraordinarily well,' said Boots. 'Have you decided on a new title for your campaign?'

'I've decided that your niece's suggestion of SAW will suit the campaign marvellously,' said Miss Alsop. 'She's so right, it has such a sharp edge, the kind manual workers appreciate.'

'I see,' said Boots, 'workers such as carpenters, lumberjacks and so on.'

'Many lumberjacks live close to the wild, you know,' said Miss Alsop.

'Lumberjacks are hairy, and we need that kind as well as the everyday worker,' said Lulu. 'Come on, Marj, I'll walk you to your bus stop. Oh, and by the way, I'll help you find digs somewhere in Brixton. You'll be a lot nearer the action there than in Twickers.'

'Oh, then I'm sure we'll meet again, Mr Adams,' said Miss Alsop fervently. 'Thank you for the use of your office. Goodbye for now.'

'It's been a pleasure,' smiled Boots, which put the lady into a melting mood as she left with Lulu.

Boots reported to Sammy, saying he was pretty sure Lulu had turned Marj off any ideas she had of setting fire to the Adams retail shops. She was now in favour of creating a comradely relationship with the workers of the world, Brixton branch.

'Am I believing of this?' asked Sammy.

'You might as well, Sammy old lad, it's a lot more believable than a flying giraffe,' said Boots.

'I think I'm feeling better,' said Sammy.

'By the way, here's a present from the lady,' said Boots, and placed the item on Sammy's desk.

'Here, what's this?' asked Sammy.

'A container of WOOF posters,' said Boots.

'That's it, make me feel ill again,' said Sammy.

'Not to worry, old lad,' said Boots, 'WOOF is now obsolete, so you can do what you like with the lady's offering.'

'Much obliged, old cock,' said Sammy, 'you're still worth the money we spent on your education.'

Queenie Richards, walking to the bus stop with George Porter at the end of their day's work, asked him if Mr Adams had said anything to him about Marjorie Alsop and what came of her visit.

'Well, no,' said George, 'I haven't seen him since I wished him luck with her just after lunch. But I heard a rumour that she left the offices in company with Lulu Adams, and that they were as thick as thieves.'

'Oh, I spoke to Mr Adams when I took his letters in an hour ago,' said Queenie, 'and d'you know what he told me?'

'Tell me,' said George, advancing protectively with her through the dark wintry evening.

'He told me the firm was now sailing in calm waters, but that he was keeping an eye open for the lady turning up again and rocking the boat.'

'I see,' said George. 'Well, it's often said that some women change their minds a lot, and some can't ever make them up,' he observed.

'Here, d'you mind?' said Queenie. 'Crikey, I could say a few things about men, I could.'

'I meant present company excepted,' said George hastily.

'All right,' said Queenie amicably. 'You can come round tonight, if you want, and you can show me them brochures again about houses that's being built in New Addington.' As the bus queue loomed up, she murmured, 'Did I mention I often think I'd like to live out in the suburbs meself? Yes, I'm sure I did.' Indeed, she had, and it had caused a flutter in George's developing self-confidence.

Now, clearing his throat, he said, 'I'll – er – I'll talk to you about that round at your mum's this evening, then.'

'I'll light the fire in the front room,' said Queenie, 'and you can talk to me there.'

Up came their bus, lights glowing, which seemed to George to promise a very cosy evening.

'You're what?' said Mrs Alsop.

'Yes, I'm joining forces with Lulu Adams, Mr Adams' niece,' said Marjorie, who had arrived home glowing and starry-eyed. 'We're going to recruit Labour Party activists to the cause.'

'Heavens above, if you promise not to mention this to your father, I promise I won't, either,' said Mrs Alsop, who might have fainted at this piece of news from her daughter if she hadn't been the woman she was.

'Oh, Daddy will understand,' said Marjorie. 'I

know he's a true blue Conservative, but he's also a man of the world, like Mr Adams.'

'Mr Adams, is he the one at that fashion firm you visited this afternoon?'

'Yes.' Marjorie went a little dreamy. 'He's worldly in an awfully relaxed way, as if nothing could ever surprise him. When I move into my new digs—'

'You're definitely going to move, then?' said Mrs Alsop.

'I have been saying so, Mother.'

'Well, I'm delighted to know you've made a decision,' said Mrs Alsop. 'Your father and I would find it difficult to live with a Labour Party activist who also goes about sticking posters on the windows of Twickenham's nicest shops. Where are you thinking of moving to?'

'Lulu says—'

'Lulu?'

'Yes, I keep telling you, she's the—'

'Oh, yes, so sorry. Yes, Lulu Adams. You were saying?'

'That she's going to help me find digs in Brixton,' said Marjorie.

'Brixton? Well, my word,' said Mrs Alsop, 'you'll find that a change from here. It bustles, I believe, and has a market, and very solid citizens who throw slightly smelly cabbages at Conservative candidates at election times. Well, my dear, once you are there, your father and I will be wishing you all the luck you deserve in your

325

wild and woolly campaigns for the preservation of our many furry friends.'

'Thank you, Mother,' said Marjorie. 'My mind is quite made up, you know.'

'I repeat, I'm delighted,' said Mrs Alsop. 'We shall miss you, of course, and hope you will come and stay with us some weekends.'

'Happily,' said Marjorie.

'I have to say, my dear, that while you're living in Brixton and aren't creating uproar in Twickenham, your father and I will be able to show ourselves to our friends and neighbours without being looked at.'

'Mother, you are still quite absurd at times,' said Marjorie, 'but there you are, while some women worry about what their neighbours think of them, there are others like me who couldn't care less, not when there are far more important things to concern us than the opinion of a neighbour. Such as the unhappy lot of the world's underpaid workers as well as animal humanity. Well, I think I'll now take a bath.' Drifting out of the room, she was heard to murmur, 'From my digs in Brixton, I'll be able to call on Mr Adams at his office from time to time to make sure his firm really is supporting the cause.'

If Queenie and George had heard that, they might have understood more clearly what was in the mind of their general manager when he'd said he'd keep his eye open for a certain someone turning up and rocking the boat.

'So you don't have to worry any more about Marjorie Alsop?' said Susie to Sammy after his arrival home.

'Well, Boots is pretty sure Lulu's turned her into an active friend of the working classes,' said Sammy. 'I've got to admit it, Susie, I'm not meself when Mad Marj is anywhere near me. She makes me think of flying tomatoes all over me suit, and posters stuck on our shop windows. Very off-putting to customers, her kind of posters.'

'Hurtful to profits, Sammy?' said Susie with a smile.

'Holy Moses,' said Sammy, 'it's just occurred to me, if she gets stuck on Socialism she might start a campaign against profit-making.'

'Buck up, Sammy love,' said Susie, 'Christmas is coming, and our sons and daughters, and our grandchildren, will all be staying with us over the holiday.'

'That's it,' said Sammy, 'that's the point of profit. If there ain't any, we couldn't afford to buy Christmas presents for all of them. Nor a twenty-pound turkey for Christmas dinner. Mind,' he added thoughtfully, 'it does occur to me that my old friend Eli Greenberg could always direct me to one that's fallen off the back of a lorry.'

'No dubious turkeys for a giveaway price, thank you, Sammy,' said Susie. 'Just send Mr Greenberg a Christmas card to let him know we're thinking of him.'

'OK, Susie, you're the boss,' said Sammy.

And how, he asked himself, did that come about?

That evening, Queenie and George enjoyed their cosiest time so far, sitting together hip to hip on the front-room settee, with the fire casting a golden glow. True, they were often hip to hip on their bus rides, which could be fairly cosy, but there was always the close presence of other passengers affecting intimacy. Here, in Queenie's home, they were by themselves, Mrs Richards keeping tactfully out of the way, and so allowing each hip to be very friendly with the other.

They had been looking at brochures detailing and illustrating a housing development in New Addington, Surrey. Queenie had said she couldn't help admiring George's ambition to settle there, that it would be like living in the country, wouldn't it? And George had said the Surrey hills and countryside weren't far away at all.

'Tell you what, Queenie,' he said now, 'how about you and me taking a bus ride there one Sunday, and seeing the new housing, eh?'

'Oh, I'm not doing anything next Sunday,' said Queenie at once.

'Well, if it's a decent day weatherwise,' said George, 'we'll go. After all – ' Cough. 'After all, if we've both got the same idea about getting away from bricks and concrete – ' Cough. 'Well, you never know, we might end up – er – '

'Oh, come on, give us a kiss,' said Queenie, turning in on him.

George blinked and hesitated. But there she was, Queenie, looking as pretty as a picture postcard in a pink sweater that was only an inch away from his shirt. The room was warm and his jacket was off. Thoughts of Humphrey Bogart and strong, confident private eyes suddenly inspired him. He swept Queenie into his arms and began to kiss her. Pink sweater met white shirt, and that did away with all his hesitations. He reached the moment when Queenie found him investigating her sweater, in a manner of speaking, while planting more kisses, firm, positive kisses.

Her breathing became a trifle hoarse, and she felt thrillingly faint.

George swept on.

'George, oh, Lor',' she gasped, a little later and a little fainter, 'I do hope you're going to make an honest woman of me . . .'

Rosie, waking up on Wednesday morning, was immediately conscious that this was the day when her mother would begin her journey to Lyons in the care of a nurse. Rosie felt thankful about the nurse. She frankly acknowledged she would not have cared to take on the escort duty herself.

How wrong am I, she wondered, in disliking so

much about my natural mother? I suppose I've always compared her unfavourably with my adoptive mother. I really must put aside these dislikes and improve the relationship. Perhaps that's already happening. At least I'm now able to conduct a civilized if strained conversation with her, and to accept it's time to forgive and forget, as Matt and I agreed. In any event, I do wish her a trouble-free journey to Lyons, and all the heavenly relief of a successful operation.

Wide awake now, she slipped from the bed to begin her usual daily routine. Matt opened sleepy eyes.

'Time?' he burbled.

'Nearly seven thirty,' said Rosie, 'so out you get, master mechanic.'

Matt sat up, stretched his sinewy arms, yawned, and then came to.

'Isn't this the day of the old lady's departure?' he asked.

'It is,' said Rosie, drawing back the curtains to reveal a morning of misty gloom.

'Well, I hope her train's in better condition than the weather,' said Matt, 'or the wheels will fall off.'

'Brilliant, I don't think,' said Rosie, making for the bathroom.

'I wish her the best of luck,' said Matt.

'That's two of us,' said Rosie.

*　　　*　　　*

The police were hunting for clues that would help them clear up the mystery of the car that had exploded into flame and caused the death of the driver, one Rolf Seidler, a businessman from West Berlin, it seemed. Clues weren't easy to come by when the man's passport had obviously been destroyed with him, and there was nothing to be found in his hotel room except an English-language version of *Mein Kampf*. His briefcase, which the daytime receptionist, Miss Browning, said he often carried with him, was nowhere visible. That too, possibly, had been reduced to ashes.

Fire investigators were probing around the ruins of the car.

Chapter Twenty-Six

'Kids,' said Boots at Saturday lunch, 'a word with
you.'

'Daddy, I protest,' said Gemma.

'And I have to say, Dad, we both do,' said
James.

'You slipped up there, Boots old bean,' said
Polly. 'I think your son and daughter are out of
socks and lollipops.'

'My apologies,' said Boots.

'Granted,' said Gemma.

'Kind of you,' said Boots. 'Where was I?'

'About to have a word with Gemma and me,'
said James.

'So I was,' said Boots. 'Yes, your mother and
I would like to know if the two of you have
anything special in mind for your seventeenth
birthdays which, I believe, will be celebrated in a
couple of weeks.'

'Personally,' said James, 'I'd like an Aston
Martin, but I'd settle for one of those new electric
razors.'

'Ah,' said Boots, and kept his face straight. So did Polly, out of respect for her son's feelings. But Gemma fell about, of course. James regarded her as if she needed a doctor, one in a white coat.

'Listen, funnycuts,' she said, when she was feeling better, 'you're kidding yourself, aren't you? I mean, you don't even have the beginnings of half a moustache.'

'True,' said James, making healthy inroads into a typical Saturday lunch of grilled rashers of bacon, scrambled eggs, fried tomatoes and potato cakes. 'Yes, true.'

'Well, then?' said Gemma.

'I want to be ready,' said James.

'Ready?' said Polly. 'For exactly what, James?'

'For the morning when I wake up with a hairy face,' said James. 'Now what's up with you, Gemma?'

Gemma was falling about again.

While she was having her hysterics, Boots said he'd be happy to fit in with James's need. Polly said she'd go along with that. In about a year, she said. Yes, eighteen's a more probable landmark, except for Latin types, said Boots.

'Oh, you bet,' said Gemma. 'Some Latin types are hairy at fourteen. Still, Daddy, let James have his razor in advance, if he wants. He could practise with it on his toothbrush, as long as he didn't overdo it. Well, I mean, what good's a bald toothbrush?'

'Although I've never been asked that question

before,' said Boots, 'I feel sure there must be an answer.'

'Dad,' said James, 'I'm sorry about Gemma turning out a bit weak in the head, especially as it's not your fault, or Mum's. As for an electric razor, if you and Mum think I should wait a year for one, I'll settle for being treated to an evening out up West, taking in *My Fair Lady*.'

'Oh, whizzo,' said Gemma, 'I'll settle for that too.'

'With dinner at Simpsons thrown in?' smiled Polly.

'Great,' said Gemma.

'I'll see about booking seats,' said Boots, 'and if there's any difficulty I'll ask Eli Greenberg if he can help. We all know, don't we, that our old friend is constantly in touch with items that fall off the backs of lorries.'

'Not theatre tickets, Daddy,' said Gemma. 'They don't see the inside of any lorry.'

'Let's remember,' said Boots, 'that some wonders are always present in the world of Mr Greenberg.'

'Bless the old boy,' said Polly.

Gemma changed the course of the conversation by asking James if there was anyone special among the girlfriends he was inviting to their birthday party. James said no, no-one special. What about Cindy Stevens, asked Polly, isn't she special? Well, yes, she is, said James, to several fellers, but she can't make up her mind if any one

334

of them is special to her. He thought cousin Giles was among the favourites, but as for himself he was remaining free and easy until he could cope with someone special. A feller could cope better when he was eighteen or nineteen instead of sixteen or seventeen.

'Fascinating,' said Polly.

'And consistent with what he's said before,' murmured Boots.

'What he said before and what he's saying now goes for girls too,' declared Gemma. 'At least, it does for one girl, and that one is me. I resolved ages ago not to turn into a hopeless, infantile case of infatuated soppiness. I'm happy to say I can look any of my boyfriends in the eye without twittering.'

'Well, what d'you say to that, Boots old soldier?' asked Polly.

'What can I say?' said Boots. 'Only that our son and daughter are both capable of addressing Parliament.'

'Compliment noted, Dad,' said James. 'Any afters, Mum?'

'Stewed prunes and hot custard?' offered Polly.

'Prunes?' said James, wincing.

'Prunes?' said Gemma, paling.

'Apricots, actually,' smiled Polly.

'Oh, good-oh,' said Gemma. 'By the way, tonight James and I are going to the Brixton dance hall again. Rocky Jingo and his Skifflers are performing.'

'I'm to believe that?' said Polly.

'Myself, I think I'm onto skifflers,' said Boots, 'but Rocky Jingo?'

'Yup, he's great, Dad,' said James.

'Making a name for himself,' said Gemma.

'In my day,' said Boots, 'it would have been something like Bouncing Billy or Fandango Fred.'

Rocky Jingo and his Skifflers were indeed the star turn at Brixton that evening. Emily was present, along with her brother Giles and her plumber's mate, Brad. Giles gravitated towards Cindy and her group, while Brad took Emily deep into the swing of things. In the eyes of Rosie and Matt, Brad was proving a stalwart, for despite his outlandish Teddy boy look, his attitude towards scatterbrained Emily was to see she enjoyed her outings while doing his best to keep her in step with common sense.

Although Emily was sure Rocky Jingo wasn't anywhere near as sexy as the Bopcats' guitarist, she put up with this deficiency on the grounds that he and his Skifflers kept coming up with some terrific numbers.

'Go, baby, go,' said Brad, swinging his hips.

'Don't call me baby,' said Emily.

'How about li'l old lady?' suggested Brad.

'Ugh, you're pathetic,' said Emily.

Cousins Gemma and James were there, as usual, with a group of their friends, but that didn't stop them saying hello to Emily and Brad. And at one point Gemma was swinging with Brad, and James with Emily. It occurred to Emily then that James was extremely attractive in his looks and personality. Tall and free-limbed, he was an echo of his dad, Uncle Boots, and that alone made him exciting to a girl. Brad suddenly seemed ordinary by comparison, even in his very best Teddy boy outfit.

Emily, realizing that here might be an interest that would distract her from her efforts to enter the world of the glamorous and the famous, addressed James when they were catching their breath at the finish of a number.

'D'you go to the flicks much?' she asked.

'Now and again,' said James. 'That is, whenever I want to see a Hitchcock thriller, or how John Wayne won the war.'

Emily smiled and gave him the full light of her starry eyes. 'You could take me sometimes,' she said, as they began to swing to new music.

'Doesn't Brad take you?' asked James.

'Oh, he's only a friend, not my steady date,' said Emily.

James, entirely good-natured, said, 'Fair enough, Em. Phone me when you've got a particular film in mind.'

'Smashing,' said Emily, but didn't mention this to Brad. He and Giles took on their usual responsibility of getting her home on time, and if leaving the dance hall earlier than most of the other young people annoyed her as always, she didn't show it. Her punctual arrival home saved Rosie and Matt from reading the Riot Act again.

Rosie had a frightening dream that night. It took place in a ghostly, misty churchyard, where she was waiting to meet her mother. Why the meeting should be in a churchyard she did not know, only that she had to be there. While waiting, she was aware of the pale figure of a nurse flitting hurriedly in and out of the dream, sometimes casting an accusing look. The waiting lengthened, and it seemed ages before her mother finally appeared. Dressed in shapeless black, she emerged from the white mist with a dreadful, rictus-like smile on her face, which was skeletal, her eyes round black sockets. The smile, full of stained teeth, widened hugely, then suddenly collapsed. The face crumpled and from the sightless eyes tears streamed. Rosie, horrified, ran forward to help, to stay the disintegration of this nightmarish being, only to find herself enveloped by the white mist.

At this point she woke up.

She lay in shock at so vivid and ghastly a dream, and she wondered, of course, if it was a portent of ill tidings. It took her a while to get back to sleep when, mercifully, the horrible images did not recur.

* * *

On Monday morning, Boots called Queenie in to take her daily dictation.

'Oh, good morning, Mr Adams,' she said. Her warm winter sweater of orange glowed, and her face was all smiles. 'What d'you think happened over the weekend?'

'Tell me,' said Boots.

So Queenie told him that George Porter had proposed official to her. Boots, whimsical, wanted to know how official was official.

'Oh, I mean he nearly did it earlier in the week,' said Queenie.

'Nearly did what?' asked Boots, fairly sure the question wouldn't embarrass Queenie, since he was certain that shy old George hadn't become bold enough to actually attempt getting her into bed.

'He nearly proposed after we'd been looking at a housing pamphlet,' said Queenie, 'except he fell over his tongue again like he often does.'

'But he stiffened his sinews over the weekend?' said Boots.

'Crikey, Mr Adams, that don't half sound saucy,' said Queenie, blushing a little, which Boots thought rather nice in this day and age. 'Still, it happened yesterday.'

'Did it?' said Boots. 'Um, what did?'

'He asked me official if I'd marry him.'

'And what did you say?' enquired Boots.

'Oh, I didn't say no, you bet,' said Queenie.

'Well, when you get to know him he's a really nice man, with nice ideas about living where everything's not all bricks and concrete, like what's been done to the Elephant and Castle since the war. Me mum says that before the war it was much more of a friendly place than now, that it had a theatre where Tod Slaughter used to act and the Trocadero Cinema that was the last word in posh flicks. Well, so me mum says.'

'She's right,' said Boots. 'Pre-war, the Elephant and Castle was the hub of Walworth life. Well, I wish you and George luck and a happy future together.'

'Oh, you've been a great help to us, Mr Adams,' said Queenie. 'George would probably still be reading books if you hadn't given him the confidence to see off that 'orrible creep.'

'I think, Queenie, that George's capabilities were always close to the surface,' said Boots. 'Now, before the wedding takes place, shall we do some dictation?'

'Before the— oh, you're a one, you are, Mr Adams.'

As he often did, Boots had lunch at the pub opposite the offices instead of in the firm's canteen. Rosie went with him so that they could talk about what was happening in respect of her mother. The pub, old-fashioned, was little changed, but there was one innovation. Hot soup, creamy and lush with the goodness of its

340

ingredients, had been added to the restricted menu. As ever during these last few years, younger customers who popped in and asked for a quick drink with eggs and bacon were directed to the nearest cafe.

Boots and Rosie each chose a bowl of soup with crusty rolls and butter.

'It's all I shall want,' said Rosie.

'It's all I'll need,' said Boots.

'Any drinks, Mr Adams?' said Joe, the veteran barman, now more of a friend to Boots than the saloon bar's figurehead.

'Rosie?' said Boots.

'Something warming,' said Rosie.

'Rum?' suggested Boots.

'Does it go with soup?' asked Rosie.

'It goes with this kind of day,' said Boots. The weather, indeed, was raw.

'Well, although I'm no sailor, I like the sound of rum, so I'll have a glass, thank you,' said Rosie.

Boots ordered two dark rums, and Joe departed to his bar to prepare the light meal. Boots asked if Rosie had any news of her mother. Rosie said she'd be in the hospital now, since she'd left on Wednesday.

'Wednesday, yes,' said Boots, looking relaxed. He rarely allowed the pressures of business or the responsibilities of family life to disturb him. He could always make a decision and then trust to the favours of the gods. As for Rosie, in her dark grey suit, worn with a thin white roll-neck sweater, she appeared a smart businesswoman whose mood at the moment was thoughtful. Her thoughts were not about business, however, but about her mother. 'Have you heard from her?' asked Boots.

'I'm expecting a letter any moment,' said Rosie. 'She promised to write as soon as she reached the hospital.'

'Allow her time for settling in,' said Boots. 'I don't suppose she felt like writing on the day she arrived.'

'When I do hear, I'll expect to know when the operation is taking place,' said Rosie. 'That's if she's been told.'

'That's very much on your mind, isn't it?' said Boots gently.

'Well, dear man, a tumour on the brain isn't quite like a touch of bronchitis or a sprained wrist,' said Rosie. 'But I have faith in Mr Wainwright and his optimism.'

Joe brought their lunch then, and that halted their conversation for a minute or so. They tried the home-made soup, the product of a rich vegetable recipe, and pronounced it just the job. A sip of rum was the perfect accompaniment. Added to that, as always, they enjoyed each other's company, Boots especially in tune with the moment, mainly due to the deep and abiding affection he had for his adopted daughter.

'Rosie,' he said, 'have you thought about the possibility that after the operation is over, the old

342

lady will need a long period of convalescence? If so, where? In Lyons or here?'

Rosie admitted she hadn't thought about that, only about the return home of her mother after a successful operation. But yes, of course, she couldn't be expected to resume her normal life until she was fully recovered. Well, wherever convalescence took place, the costs would all be met by herself and Matt.

'That, of course, goes without saying,' she added.

Boots's smile reflected much of his affection.

'You really are willing to forgive and forget, aren't you?' he said.

'It's time, don't you think?' said Rosie.

'You've said so before, poppet, and I go along with that.'

Rosie smiled.

'How long have you been calling me poppet?'

'I haven't counted the years, Rosie, I've only been aware that each one has passed too quickly for my liking.'

'Join the club, old soldier,' said Rosie.

Chapter Twenty-Seven

'I still haven't heard,' said Rosie to Matt three evenings later.

'She must have forgotten her promise to write to you,' said Matt.

'Perhaps everything was too much for her when she arrived at the hospital,' said Rosie.

'Well, it's more than possible that she was in a bit of a state,' said Matt, 'what with the strain of the journey and what lay ahead for her, which, let's face it, she must have known was going to be a life-or-death operation.'

'That operation could have taken place by now,' said Rosie. 'It's been more than a week since – oh, my God – Matt – '

'Steady, now, don't think in those terms,' said Matt.

'But we have to consider the worst, the possibility that the outcome was fatal.' Rosie felt sick at the thought. From the beginning this business had caused very mixed emotions. Dislike, revulsion, sympathy and pity had all racked her.

She did not want the death of her natural mother to induce one more unwelcome thought. 'Matt?'

'Her specialist would know of the worst or the best,' said Matt. 'Yes, almost certainly he would, and if the old lady had died under the knife, I'm sure he'd have let you know. Anyway, why not phone Mr Wainwright? I'll do so, if you'd prefer.'

'No, I'll do it,' said Rosie, 'I'll phone him from the office in the morning, when he'll be in his consulting rooms at Tulse Hill.'

'You're really worried, aren't you?' said Matt.

'Not as much,' said Rosie. 'Not now I realize you're right, that we'd have heard from Mr Wainwright if the worst had happened. No, I'm now looking at the best result and the possibility of a long convalescence somewhere. I'm trying not to think unkind thoughts, but I really don't want her convalescing virtually on our doorstep. I hope it will be in France.'

'After the kind of operation she's had or is having,' said Matt, 'I'd bet on the hospital keeping her in for quite some time before sending her to any convalescent home here or there.'

'Yes, I must talk to Mr Wainwright,' said Rosie, silently acknowledging the fact that she and Matt were probably the only people her mother could rely on for all necessary help.

That evening a man by the name of Hubert Williams committed suicide in his parents' house in Walworth. The doctor, called in, found that

death had been caused by a fatal dose of cyanide.
The local newspaper sent a reporter in the morning to cover the tragic incident, but it did not
interest any national daily. To the press it was
simply one more suicide with nothing sensational
about it.

Chapter Twenty-Eight

At ten that morning, Rosie made her phone call to Mr Wainwright from Boots's office. There was no reply, although she hung on for quite a while before she put the phone down.

'He doesn't seem to be there,' she said.

'As a practising consultant, he could be at a hospital,' said Boots. 'Operating, perhaps.'

'Yes, of course,' said Rosie. 'Well, I'll try again later. Now I must dash back to my work. Rachel and I are overwhelmed this morning. All due, old thing, to Sammy's liking for loading Rachel with stuff he considers too unimportant for his own attention.'

'Don't you believe it,' said Boots. 'There's nothing Sammy would ever consider unimportant about business, especially his own business. In the old days, when he was running his glass and china stall in the East Street market, even a slight fault in a cup and saucer was of major importance to him. Why? Because it would mean having to knock a ha'penny or a penny off the price. He'll admit even now that that kind of thing caused him pain.'

'I'll tell Rachel that,' said Rosie, 'and I know what she'll say. That only a true businessman would feel pain at what the sacrifice of a ha'penny can do to a profit and loss account.'

What Rachel actually said was that in those days of old, stallholders battling to make a penny on a bunch of bananas or a cup and saucer was for them like fighting a war, and although Sammy had been wounded many times he had never quit the field and taken himself off to hospital.

Sammy, she said, had always been made of sterner stuff.

So Rosie asked what happened to his sterner stuff when it came up against Marjorie Alsop?

'Sammy,' said Rachel, 'does have one weakness. Warrior women armed with squishy tomatoes alarm him. In his own words, they ain't natural.'

After that comment, Sammy's invaluable lady assistants resumed their busy day's work, not so much with a sigh as with a smile.

At the Southwark mortuary, the body of the suicide had been put into cold storage pending the inquest. His clothes had been divested of his personal belongings, such as keys, a wallet and a pen. Something less humdrum came to light, something that was hidden in his right sock. A suicide note.

It was passed to the coroner's office.

* * *

Rosie, leaving her office at three in the afternoon, her usual finishing time, drove home. Arrived there, she made her second phone call to Mr Wainwright. Again there was no answer. She tried again at four thirty, when Giles and Emily were back from school and doing their homework. Once more there was no answer, and Rosie thought that when he was away from his consulting rooms, Mr Wainwright really ought to have a secretary on hand to attend to phone calls and enquiries.

She hoped his absence from his consulting rooms wasn't due to illness. The winter weather was chilly and filthy, and flu was rearing its unwelcome head.

Sometime after eight, while Giles and Emily were absorbed in a television programme, Matt phoned the number. The ringing tone went on for quite a while, and he was about to hang up when a woman's voice suddenly broke the silence.

'Yes, hello, who's that?'

'Sorry to disturb you,' said Matt, 'but I'd very much like to speak to Mr Wainwright.'

'Oh, you would, would you? Well, so would I.'

'Pardon?' said Matt.

'I'm the houseowner, and he's one of my tenants. Well, he was till he went off some days ago, owing me three weeks' rent.'

'I think we're at cross purposes,' said Matt. 'That is, I don't think your Mr Wainwright is the one I'd like to speak to. My one is Mr Wainwright the surgeon.'

'You'll be lucky. There's no surgeon here, nor has there ever been, just my tenants, including this man Wainwright who took over a first-floor room three months ago. No, he's no surgeon, I tell you that for nothing, he's a crafty fly-by-night, and there's demand notes here from the Post Office warning him they'll cut him off the phone if he doesn't pay his bill. Which I don't suppose he will now that he's done his disappearing trick.'

'Jesus Christ,' breathed Matt.

'What's that?'

'Did you hear this phone go during the day?'

'I'm not here during the day, I'm the manageress of a flower shop.'

'Hoodwinked, by God,' said Matt.

'What?'

'The bugger's a con man.'

'If that means he owes you money too, I'm sorry for you. Look, I'm Mrs Bailey, Nora Bailey, and if I do ever catch sight of Wainwright, I'll let you know. Just now I don't want to stay on this phone any longer than I can help. It's icy cold in this room, and I want to get back to my fireside downstairs. So have you got a phone number? Then I'll ring you if I get to know where Wainwright is.'

Matt, shaken to the core, said, 'Yes, I'd appreciate a phone call any time you have any news.' He gave his name and phone number, Mrs Bailey made a note of them, and they rang off.

Matt silently swore. He was going to have to tell Rosie that Wainwright was no medical man, that he had almost certainly diddled them out of a large sum of money, and paid out a small part of it to send her mother off to France with nothing except blank faces awaiting her at the end of the journey. Could any man so treat a woman suffering from a brain tumour? No, think about it. Wainwright couldn't have done that in any event, not without the connivance of Rosie's mother's GP and a nurse, and that was never going to be possible.

Jesus Christ, that pointed to another blinder.

'Matt?' Rosie entered his study, to see him sitting at his desk looking shell-shocked. 'Matt?'

Matt, coming to, said very soberly, 'Close the door, Rosie.'

'Matt, it isn't bad news, is it?' said Rosie, closing the door.

'Bad news?' said Matt, rising from his chair to put himself eye to eye with his treasured wife. They had their moments, their minor arguments, but he could not recall they'd ever had any kind of real quarrel. Rosie represented life's best gift to him, and no sensible bloke ever quarrelled with that. 'Rosie, I'm not sure what kind of news you'd call it.'

'Try me.' Rosie prepared herself for the unexpected. 'Tell me what Mr Wainwright said.'

'Mr Wainwright? Mr?' Matt made a face. 'Not a word, but his landlady said more than enough. Enough, in fact, to make me think it's just as well you insisted on keeping things dark from the kids. Listen.'

Matt began to give a very detailed résumé of the conversation he had had with Mrs Nora Bailey of Tulse Hill. Rosie's expression, wary at first of what was to come, quickly changed to disbelief of what she was hearing. And disbelief inevitably changed to shock. At the end, she looked as if she doubted whether the day itself was real.

'Matt, I— Matt, did you believe Mrs Bailey?'

'There was no reason not to.'

'It's a bad dream.'

'Dream or no dream, Rosie, we've got to investigate. Look, I'll get home early tomorrow, say about five, and we'll drive to Tulse Hill and talk to Mrs Bailey there. Among other things, I want to find out about the letterheading. It stated clearly the address, phone number and qualifications of Wainwright.'

'So we have reservations, do we, about Mrs Bailey's information?' said Rosie.

'Jesus Christ, Rosie, my reservations take in collusion of some kind between Wainwright and other people,' said Matt.

Very quietly, Rosie said, 'Do other people include my mother?'

'That,' said Matt, 'is the leading question.'

After Giles and Emily had gone to bed, Rosie and Matt sat up late going over and over all the implications and inferences. They wore conjectures down to the bone.

The first person Rosie went straight to see on her arrival at the offices the next morning had to be Boots, of course. He listened intently to all she told him, but did not look shell-shocked. He was too philosophical a man for that. But he did look as if, for once, the quirks and follies of people did not amuse him.

'Sit down, Rosie,' he said, 'while I have a word with Sammy.'

Rosie sat down and waited. In a crisis, she knew she could always rely on maximum support from both her husband and her adoptive father. She had her own strengths, her own ways of coping with the unwelcome or the difficult, but in this particular case she felt herself besieged by the unspeakable, and any offer of help from her adoptive father was never going to be turned down.

He returned after only a few minutes.

'Well, dear old thing?' said Rosie.

'Keep your hat and coat on,' said Boots. Rosie was wearing a fur hat and a coat with a fur collar. 'You and I are going to spend the morning out of the office. We're going to do some investigating.'

'At Tulse Hill? No go,' said Rosie. 'Didn't I mention that Mrs Bailey has a daily job as the manageress of a flower shop?'

'We're not going to investigate Mrs Bailey,' said Boots, 'we're going to talk to your mother's landlady.'

Chapter Twenty-Nine

The house in Effra Road, Brixton, was rented out to Mr and Mrs Barrett, a middle-aged couple who took in lodgers to help augment Mr Barrett's modest wage as a van driver for a laundry. While he kept his eye on his job, Mrs Barrett kept her eye on her lodgers. The first-floor rooms were let to a woman, and the second-floor rooms were the province of two bachelor gents.

She wasn't surprised when a distinguished-looking man in a trench coat and trilby hat, accompanied by an elegant lady in a fur hat and fur-collared coat, knocked on her door to ask about her first-floor tenant.

'Mrs Rainbould, you say? Is she in, you're asking me? Well, no, she ain't, she's gone off and without so much as a by-yer-leave and owing a week's rent.' Mrs Barrett, thin and grey-haired with quick, bright eyes, looked up at Boots in a slightly aggressive way, as if she had a suspicion he was somehow responsible. 'Wait a bit, 'ave you come from some hospital to tell me she's had an accident? I admit I never went much on 'er fancy ways, nor 'er paint and powder, but I wouldn't like to think the reason why she's gone missing is because she's been knocked down by a van or something.'

'No, nothing like that,' said Boots.

'Then it wouldn't surprise me if she's gone off with that bloke that was always coming round and keeping 'er company,' said the aggrieved lady. 'In fact, that's me honest opinion.'

'Um, this bloke,' said Boots, 'do you know if his name was Wainwright?'

'That's 'im all right,' said Mrs Barrett, 'but he ain't been round lately. Well, not since Mrs Rainbould 'opped it.'

'Do you mind us asking a few questions?' enquired Boots.

Mrs Barrett took a new look at him and a fresh look at Rosie, then gave a little birdlike nod.

'Here, come in,' she said, 'I don't like keeping you standing on me doorstep on a day as cold as this. Come into me parlour, I've got me gas fire going a treat, and you can ask all the questions you like.'

So she entertained the visitors in her parlour, where a glowing gas fire welcomed them, and where they were invited to remove their hats and coats and to sit down. Once comfortable, Boots and Rosie began to ask their questions. The answers all pointed to the fact that Rosie's mother and the man Wainwright were as thick as thieves. According to Mrs Barrett, her female lodger had told her that her gentleman friend, Mr Wainwright, was on the stage, and very popular in the parts he played at seaside theatres. That clicked with Boots and Rosie, for they both knew her mother had always hankered after the stage and its players. It also occurred to Boots that Wainwright had enough stage experience, even in bit parts, to pass himself off as a consultant surgeon, especially if this only involved him in phone conversations, and letters written on printed letterheads. The cost of having the letterheads supplied would have been minimal. It all amounted to an adventurous bluff, but it had come off.

Mrs Barrett offered the information that although Mrs Rainbould paid her rent fairly regular, she began to complain about being hard up not long after she'd taken up with Wainwright. Mrs Barrett suspected, from what Mrs Rainbould sometimes said, that whenever she went out with Wainwright to a pub or somewhere up West, she was the one who paid. Mind, about a week or two ago, after admitting she'd just had a nice drop of gin to keep the cold out, she'd said things were going to get a lot better, that she was expecting. Expecting what and from where? asked Mrs Barrett. Her female lodger closed up then, although Mrs Barrett thought something was cooking because she'd had her hair done up and got rid of most of her paint and powder.

'Tell me,' said Rosie, 'has she been seeing her GP lately?'

'Her GP?' queried Mrs Barrett. 'Her doctor, you mean? Gawd knows. Mind, I do remember she sent for 'im last winter, when she put 'erself to bed with the flu. I don't know if she saw 'im after that, but up to the time she done her vanishing trick, it's me honest opinion she'd seen a lot more of Wainwright than any doctor. Is she a friend of yourn, Mr – er – ?'

'Adams,' said Boots, 'and this lady is my adopted daughter.'

'And Mrs Rainbould is my mother,' said Rosie, and beneath that calm and sober declaration there must, thought Boots, be a welter of bitter emotions and feelings.

'Your mother?' said Mrs Barrett, close to incredulity. There had been no occasion when she'd been invited to meet Rosie. Such was her disbelief that she said, 'You sure?'

The enquiry, thought Boots, was born of natural disbelief, since very few people would ever think of relating the striking elegance of Rosie to the raddled appearance of the woman who had given birth to her.

'Yes, Mrs Rainbould is my mother,' said Rosie, 'and I apologize for her. Please allow me to pay you for the rent she owed you when she left.'

'Oh, that's all right, dearie,' said Mrs Barrett, 'I don't see why you should 'ave to do that. Listen, don't you 'ave no idea where she's gone to with that bloke of hers? I mean, if she's yer mum, hasn't she said nothing to you just lately?'

'I was here last Saturday week, in the morning,' said Rosie, 'and I assure you – ' She managed a wry smile. 'I assure you she said plenty.'

Mrs Barrett wanted to know what about. Rosie said it was nothing of consequence. Boots asked the landlady if Mrs Rainbould had left anything in her flat, anything that might give a clue as to where she'd gone. He had in mind something that would point to a high-class resort like Torquay, where a pair of flying pigeons could land and live like royal swans for a year on over fifteen hundred quid at the Palace Hotel. Then, no doubt, they'd cook up some other wheeze. The one minus factor about their deception would be the loss of an automatic monthly allowance from Rosie and Matt. But people of their ilk never looked ahead. A large sum of money would always tempt them into reckless enjoyment of the present.

'Yes, do you know if she left anything in her flat?'

'It's empty,' said Mrs Barrett. 'I been all through it, and so 'as Billy. Billy's me old man. We didn't find even an old envelope or a fishbone. All we did find was a sink full of washing-up, which Billy said was a downright liberty. Meself, I called it a grievous insult, if that's not upsetting you too much.' She directed the last few words at Rosie.

Rosie could have said she had enough on her mind to upset her for a week, but she only smiled, shook her head and glanced at Boots. Boots took the hint.

'It's time we left,' he said to Mrs Barrett. 'We've trespassed too long on your kindness.'

'Oh, don't mention it,' said Mrs Barrett, 'I just 'ope you manage to find out what's 'appened to Mrs Rainbould. Mind,' she added confidentially, 'if you find that man Wainwright, you'll find 'er as well. That's me honest opinion.'

·'And mine,' said Boots. Before he and Rosie left, they tried to get Mrs Barrett to accept what was owing to her by way of the unpaid rent. The landlady was again not in favour. She said on no account did she want anyone to pay the owings except Mrs Rainbould herself. It wasn't anyone else's responsibility, not even Mrs Rainbould's daughter. She hoped everything would sort itself out and wished them luck. Rosie and Boots thanked her for being so helpful, then left.

Boots drove to a Brixton cafe, where he and Rosie found a corner table and sat down to make the most of steaming hot coffee and to exchange opinions on all that Mrs Barrett had told them.

'First and foremost,' said Rosie, 'I have to accept that Matt and I took the bait and swallowed it hook, line and sinker. And I led the way.'

'Only because you were making a gesture of humanity towards a person we all rejected years ago,' said Boots.

'Dear man,' said Rosie, 'I should have remembered that never has she approached you or me except to raid our pockets. I should never have lost sight of that. Instead, because of wanting to forgive and forget, I was too willing, I suppose, to give her the benefit of any doubt. God, she played her part so well. She really looked ill, really sounded ill, but without overdoing it. She's been on the stage herself, of course.'

Boots said he had seen her once, in a Christmas pantomime at the old Camberwell Palace Theatre, when she appeared in spangles and tights as assistant to a second-rate conjuror, one Clarence Rainbould, the man she eventually married.

'It seems now, Rosie, that even as no more than a conjuror's assistant, she acquired the ability to play one part or another. No doubt she met Wainwright by way of a theatre, and together they cooked up this scheme to pluck your feathers, poppet. Well, the day will come all too soon when she'll realize it's cost her the monthly allowance from you and Matt. Let her repent at leisure, she's not worth an ounce of pity from you or me.'

'You never liked her, did you?' said Rosie.

'It's true she was never my favourite person,' said Boots. He could still clearly remember her neglect of five-year-old Rosie, her indifference to the child's need for affection, and how she made her wear glasses, not to help her sight, with which there was nothing wrong, but to make her look plain. To the one-time Milly Pearce, her little daughter was an encumbrance, not a joy. To Boots, she was a joy from the moment when she first brought her shy but eager self to his doorstep. It was on that doorstep that they sat together many times, he telling stories to make her laugh. And how she laughed, as if she had been waiting to do so since birth. 'But there you are, Rosie, I was just as willing as you were to forgive and forget, and to encourage the gesture.'

'You and I, old soldier, are a couple of mugs,' said Rosie.

'If that's the case, poppet, I'm in good company,' said Boots.

Rosie, sipping coffee, looked thoughtful.

'No tumour, no doctor, no surgeon, no nurse, only a wily way of leading Matt and me up the garden path,' she said. 'Looking back, I can see there were all kinds of things I should have checked with her GP, but I never even asked what his name was. However, I managed to do one sensible thing, and that was to obey my instincts and keep her away from Giles and Emily for the time being. Boots, what do I do now? Call on Mrs Bailey this evening with Matt, as he suggested?'

'No need,' said Boots. He pointed out that the information they'd had from Mrs Barrett, coupled with what Mrs Bailey had said so far, was more than enough to paint a full picture of events. He suggested that somewhere in Wainwright's room at Tulse Hill a number of printed letterheads were ready to be found, but was it really necessary to unearth them? 'We've accepted the obvious, Rosie, so let it rest at that, shall we?'

Rosie said that that sounded reasonable, but she rather felt that Matt would insist on doing everything possible to find out where the two tricksters were, and to make them cough up, even if it meant bringing in the police. Where did Boots think they might be?

'France, perhaps?' she prompted.

'Perhaps,' said Boots. 'Or Brighton or Torquay. The money would last longer here than in Paris, say.'

'Somewhere not easy to trace,' said Rosie.

'As to that,' said Boots, 'I wonder myself if your mother had any real worries concerning discovery. One question Wainwright would almost certainly have asked of her was would you report them to the police once you realized you'd been tricked. I think your mother would have said no. She'd have relied on a belief that you aren't the kind of daughter who'd deliver her into the arms of the law.' Boots spoke quietly, but with feeling. 'She would have been right. You don't harbour spite. You are far more the daughter of your natural father than you ever were of Milly Pearce.'

Rosie reached across the table and touched his hand.

'Since the age of five I've never been any man's daughter except yours,' she said. 'You must know that.'

Boots regarded her soberly. She was as striking as she had been in her undergraduate years at Somerville. She looked, as Polly did, born far more for the Ritz than any high street cafe.

'Rosie, you, and other women like you, make the world a better and more civilized place for the rest of us,' he said.

'That's it, now make my day,' said Rosie. 'It's been a lousy one up until now.'

'I suggest you forget this morning, poppet,' said Boots. 'I suggest you let it all slide away. Let the devious duo enjoy their ill-gotten gains, as Victorian characters would say. I know, and Matt will know, that you won't let pity weaken you again. And for your consolation, remember that only Matt, Sammy and I know of what's been going on this last day or so. You're safe from inquisitive family phone calls.'

'That's a relief, as well as a consolation,' said Rosie. 'Thank you, old soldier, for everything.'

'Stay home tonight, don't bother with Tulse Hill,' said Boots. 'Persuade Matt it isn't necessary. Now, let's toddle off back to the office and our desks, shall we?'

'Yes, sir, right away, sir,' smiled Rosie.

*   *   *

Matt was hardly the country's most surprised man when Rosie told him the outcome of her visit with Boots to the house in Effra Road, Brixton.

'Damn all,' he said, ruffling his hair, 'knowing as much as we do about your mother, we might have guessed there was more to it than a promised miracle in France. Well, give the old bird her due, she took the game on and got away with it. How upset are you, Rosie?'

'Mostly, I'm angry with myself, and yet I pity her more than ever,' said Rosie. 'Her life is a sham, a mess, and will never amount to more than that.'

'We'll put a stop on her monthly allowance?' said Matt.

'Yes, Matt, we will,' said Rosie.

'When they've spent what they conned out of us,' said Matt, 'that durned old mother of yours will suddenly wake up to the fact that what she sacrificed for a heap of tarnished silver were reasonable living expenses for the rest of her life.'

'That,' remarked Rosie, 'is almost exactly what Boots said. He also said forget her.'

'Well, damned if I'll find that difficult, Rosie,' said Matt. 'After all, what is she if not a scheming old biddy?'

With the wryest of looks, Rosie said, 'Is there an old Dorset saying for her kind?'

'That there is,' said Matt.

'Speak it, then, man of the land.'
Matt began.

> 'Down by Dorset, so they say,
> There's more to life than oats and hay,
> There's people kind and people good,
> And some as bad as ever could.'

'Which means, I suppose, we aren't the only family linked to a misfit,' said Rosie, then added abstractedly, 'she's lost the only chance she ever had of getting to know our children, Matt.'

'Whatever you say, Rosie.'

Chapter Thirty

No-one in the Adams families expressed any urgent desire to know who was responsible for turning a car into a fireball and burning the German driver to a cinder. It was a news item of an unpleasant kind, yes, but meant very little in a world dominated by the uncomfortable atmosphere of the cold war. The person perhaps most concerned by the event was Patsy. She repeated to Daniel that it might be safer to move to good old Boston, birthplace of American Independence.

'You mentioned that before,' said Daniel. 'Might I point out that I'm staying here, irrespective? For one thing, Grandma Finch would never allow me to emigrate to Boston. Or even to the Isle of Wight.'

'Isn't she a cute old lady?' said Patsy. 'Well, I won't risk upsetting her, so I guess I'll keep right on staying here with you. Right here in our own little homestead.'

'Good on you, cowboy,' said Daniel, and gave her winter woolly a cuddle.

As for Boots and Polly, totally ignorant of the fact that, with their children, they had been selected for elimination by the victim, they gave not the slightest thought to the matter, other than noticing its occasional mentions in the press now and again.

The police, however, were giving it their earnest attention at the request of the West German consulate, but were no nearer solving the mystery surrounding the frightful death of the visitor who had booked into a Bloomsbury hotel under the name of Rolf Seidler of West Berlin. The official verdict given by the fire investigators was that the inferno had been caused by the planting of a lethal incendiary device triggered by the turning of the car's ignition key. The unfortunate man's death, therefore, was judged by the coroner to be murder by a person or persons unknown.

Scotland Yard naturally concluded that Rolf Seidler must have had one or more enemies resident in either the UK or West Berlin. If responsibility lay with the latter, then Seidler must have been followed to London.

Did he ever have any visitors?

None, as far as Miss Browning or any other member of the hotel staff could recall. Nor had he ever named any person he was going to meet, said Miss Browning. Most of his excursions took him either to the City on business or to tourist attractions.

How did she know that?

Because Mr Seidler himself had volunteered the information. Oh, the Saturday night, the night he had died, he had told her he was going to meet some friends and would not be back until very late.

What friends? Did he say?

No, he did not name them or say where he was going to meet them.

The men from Scotland Yard were stuck.

Meanwhile, the Polish immigrant, Emil Kiernik, proprietor of a hairdressing salon in Bayswater, continued his seemingly innocuous way of life by styling ladies' hair in very professional and attractive fashion from nine to six. Outside those hours there were sometimes things to do on behalf of his Communist masters in Warsaw, such as dealing with ex-SS men who had helped with the elimination of concentration-camp inmates and were to be found in England.

After taking Emily to see Elvis Presley in *King Creole*, and receiving several phone calls from her, James came to the inevitable conclusion that she was trying to turn him into her steady boyfriend. James, as he had frequently explained to his sister and his parents, was not ready to develop that kind of relationship with any girl. Further, his instinct was against taking up with Emily on a regular basis. She was far too scatterbrained and irresponsible, and not a bit like her gorgeous mum or her good-natured dad.

So he made a phone call to Teddy boy Brad and informed him he'd got to keep Emily in order, and that if he didn't or couldn't, he'd set a sad example to his kind.

'Gee whiz, James old buddy, what kind d'you mean?' asked Brad.

'The manly kind,' said James.

'Do I know any?' asked Brad.

'Well, you know Emily's dad and your own dad, don't you?' said James. 'And your own dad's master of all he surveys, isn't he?'

'Not much, and not when Ma's around,' said Brad.

'Funny, we've got dads like that in our family,' said James. 'Still, you know what I mean, don't you?'

'Yes, get tough with Emily, and let her know I'm better for her than any other guy,' said Brad.

'Right,' said James.

'Yep, got you,' said Brad.

However, it all went wrong for him at the usual Brixton gig on Saturday evening. No sooner did Emily realize that she was being given a talking-to by Brad, and that James's interest in her was only lukewarm, than she stormed out and went home. Her arrival back as early as eight twenty caused Rosie and Matt to sit up and ask questions.

'I've had a row,' she said, fuming.

'A row? Who with?' asked Matt.

'That back number of a Teddy boy,' said Emily, flouncing about.

'Young Bradley?' said Rosie. 'But I've always thought him rather nice under his fancy waist-coats.'

'He's a jerk,' said Emily, 'and I don't think much of cousin James, either.'

'What's his sin, then?' asked Matt.

'Being born,' said Emily, 'and I'm going up to my room to rethink my life.'

And up she went, more to the amusement than the concern of her parents. A setback emanating from James and Brad might just do her some good.

Emily decided she was going to give up her present mode of life, including boys and dance halls, and concentrate on the possibility of getting a job in public relations as soon as she left school. That is, public relations in the world of the glamorous and the famous.

The suicide of Hubert Williams, which had not aroused much attention so far, became news-worthy after the inquest. The note found in a sock was produced by the coroner and made public. In it, Hubert Williams complained that his parents had run his life for him ever since his birth, allowing him neither friends nor any prospect of marriage. Nor any real freedom. He enlarged on this, and wished everyone to know that for imagined faults, they often kept him confined to his room. He wanted people to know he was confined in such a way on this the last night of his life, for he had managed to obtain just enough cyanide to end it all. There was no-one he wished to say goodbye to. Et cetera.

A local newspaper reporter, attending the proceedings, phoned the news editor of a national daily, giving him the story of the suicide, a man in his thirties who was actually kept locked in his room by his parents from time to time.

Mr and Mrs Williams, the parents, were, of course, an indignant and humiliated couple during the reading of the letter at the inquest, and it wasn't supposed by friends and acquaintances that they liked all that which was printed about themselves and their son in a certain daily newspaper the next morning.

Queenie and George could have added extra details to the story, but did not wish to do so. They were engaged to be married, and wanted no unpleasant publicity.

Queenie was taking care of her figure after being warned by her mother that snacks in between meals might mean walking up the aisle as a fat bride. Horrors.

And George was in touch with the developers of a modern housing estate at New Addington, and thinking about Queenie and a mortgage instead of a fictional private eye name of Mike Finnegan.

Life, even in the changeable Fifties, could still promise happy endings for some people.

The third Friday in December was approaching. It was the day when James and Gemma would be seventeen. A party was being organized for the day itself, the promised theatre and dinner in the West End booked for Saturday. Polly and Boots were busy with arrangements for the party, arrangements that would ensure totally successful celebrations without the risk of the young people bringing the house down. Polly said she didn't want to retire to bed that night if there was no roof on the house, and Boots said that at his age he favoured a cosy bedroom, not a draughty one.

Everyone in all the Adams families had been invited, and Chinese Lady was pleasantly engaged in working out how many that would amount to, while wondering if there were any more on the way. Not, she supposed, that they'd arrive in time for the party.

James and Gemma had also invited friends, and Gemma was buying new rock 'n' roll numbers for her record player. Hence Polly's plea for the new records to be played at modest volume, just in case the noise did blow the roof off, or cause Grandma Finch to be struck deaf.

*　　*　　*

On Thursday evening, Boots answered a knock on the front door, using a switch in the hall to illuminate the doorstep. There, in the light, stood an exquisite-looking young lady in a hat and jacket of glossy fur. She was elegance personified and much, thought Boots, as Polly might have looked in her teens. Her smile was delicious.

'Oh, hello, Mr Adams, long time no see,' she said. 'Do you remember me?'

'How could I forget you? Step in out of the cold, Cathy,' said Boots in hospitable tones.

Miss Cathy Davidson, sixteen, stepped into the warm hall.

'It's really nice to see you again,' she said, and with her smile fluttering a bit, Boots guessed that despite her outward sophistication, she was slightly nervous. So before taking her into the lounge he let her plunge into an account of her life in Paris, where her mother was now the wife of a very rich but awfully strict Frenchman, and everything outside the home was very Latin and lively. She herself had just come back to London to live with an aunt. Boots made another guess, that her move was because she didn't get on with her stepfather. She was shedding her nervousness second by second, Boots waiting until he thought she would be quite ready for a reunion with James. Polly might well not fancy that, she might well see danger there for her son, and do her best to ensure he was saved from acquiring the ex-Mrs Davidson as a mother-in-law. The woman had Russian blood and a taste for the risqué. 'Anyway, Mr Adams, here I am,' said Cathy, ending her discourse.

'Yes, here you are, Cathy, welcome back,' said Boots, then blinked as a blast of music rushed from Gemma's bedroom. She was rehearsing her party music. 'That's Gemma and her record player. Don't let it bite you, come and show yourself to James.'

'Oh, it's his and Gemma's seventeenth tomorrow, isn't it?' said Cathy. 'I remembered that, so I've brought little presents for them from Paris.' Two small packets appeared from inside her fur jacket. 'Mr Adams, could you first ask James to come and see me here in the hall?'

'Of course,' said Boots understandingly. 'Hold on.' He went into the lounge, where Polly and James were discussing some aspect of tomorrow's party. 'James, old chap, you're wanted by a young lady. She's in the hall.'

'A young lady?'

'Yes, and she's waiting.'

James went out to the hall to come face to face with the most striking-looking girl he had ever known, her fur hat a sheer delight to the eye. He stared. Cathy showed a slightly nervous smile. They were each two years older, both were taller, but recognition was instant, although only James was actually bowled over.

'Cathy, is that you?'

'Yes.' Cathy began to gabble. 'And I want to say I'm ever so sorry I haven't written to you for ages, but there was this French boy, you see, and I thought – I thought – well, as it happened he wasn't what I thought, and I've been remembering – James, I've come back to live with an aunt, and would like it ever so much if you'd invite me to your birthday party tomorrow.'

James, mesmerized, stared some more, which turned Cathy a little pink, despite her time among the worldly and cosmopolitan students of Paris. She quivered as another blast of music invaded the house from Gemma's record player, but it helped James to find his tongue.

'Cathy, it's great you're back, you look stunning, and you're invited to the party here and now. But there'll be more of this rock 'n' roll stuff from Gemma's record player, so bring your earmuffs. First of all, of course, bring yourself.' James was wondering if his intention to wait a few years before he took up seriously with any girl was being bombed by the magic emanating from Cathy. 'Oh, um, yes, now come and say hello to my mother.'

When she did appear in front of Polly's eyes, Polly could only ask herself a burning question.

Saints alive, how am I going to save my son now?

Chapter Thirty-one

At mid-morning on Friday, just before the coffee break, Dorothy Calloway, Sammy's present shorthand typist, dashed into his office without knocking, such was her agitation. Boots was there, discussing with Sammy arrangements for an office Christmas party, proposed by Sammy at no charge to any of the staff, unless they wrecked the place.

'Mr Adams! Mr Sammy!' Dorothy was flushed with some kind of crisis. 'She's come back!'

'Who has?' asked Sammy.

'That batty woman,' panted Dorothy, 'the one who tried to ride an elephant out of the London Zoo and messed up the winter fashion show, and she's outside, with some other people, getting them to chuck things like rotten tomatoes at our front office window, and she told Queenie who went out to talk to her, that – well – well – '

'Well what, Dorothy?' asked Boots.

'That we're like a nest of vipers in her bosom – '

'Do what?' said Sammy a little hoarsely. 'No, don't repeat that, it can't be true.'

'Oh, it's true all right, Mr Sammy, she said it twice to Queenie, and she said as well that we're traitors to her cause because she's found out our retail shops sell fur-trimmed garments – oh, help, the front window is all over squashed tomato. Mr Sammy, you'll have to do something, there's a crowd building up.'

Sammy said the first thing that came into his disordered mind.

'Over to you, Boots.'

'Much obliged,' said Boots.

'I told myself, didn't I,' said Sammy, 'that one day one of your brilliant ideas might fall apart and land us in Mother Riley's pea soup. Now see what you've done, getting Lulu to turn Mad Marj into a Socialist. I bet the people out there with her are all near-Commies, all friends of Lulu.'

Dorothy made another plea.

'Mr Sammy, don't sit talking, do something.'

'I ain't here,' said Sammy, 'and nor am I keen to stop a faceful of ancient tomatoes. It's your show, Boots, so come up with something that'll work this time.'

Boots crossed to the window, opened it and glanced down at the pavement fronting the offices. With a gathering crowd looking on, Mad Marj and her activists were besieging the door and the ground-floor office window with cannon-

378

shot. That is, fusillades of tomatoes. In smart gilt lettering the window displayed information.

OFFICES OF ADAMS ENTERPRISES LTD
ADAMS FASHIONS LTD
ADAMS PROPERTY COMPANY LTD

Boots couldn't see the window from where he was, but he could see the demonstrators, and he guessed the gilt lettering was liberally spattered with tomato juice. Banners were being waved aggressively. Amid the noise of the riotous demonstration, Boots heard a yell from Marjorie.

'Down with traitors! Down with Adams Fashions!'

He closed the window and returned to Sammy's desk.

'Lend me your phone, Sammy,' he said, and picked it up. He made a quick and urgent call. Dorothy gaped and Sammy looked disbelieving.

'You've asked for the coppers to call?' said Sammy, when Boots put the phone down. Never before had the family believed in inviting the police to interfere in a crisis.

'Well, just for once we'll get Mr Plod to deal with things,' said Boots. 'I don't think Miss Alsop is in the mood to listen to my life story and how I once saved a mouse from being eaten by Mrs Castle's next-door cat. Not that she overwhelmed me with gratitude to the extent of giving me a

<hr/>

penny. It so happened she liked cats and hated mice. However—'

'Mr Adams!' It was Queenie who burst in then. 'The front office window, they've been and smashed it!'

'Did anyone see it happen?' asked Boots.

'We all did,' gasped Queenie, 'we were all in the front office watching through the window. We didn't have the best kind of view because a good part of it was covered in squashed tomato, but we all saw that loony woman break it with her banner.'

'Good,' said Boots.

'Good?' said Sammy, Dorothy and Queenie.

'Very good,' said Boots. 'It means that when the police arrive they'll have grounds for carting Miss Alsop and her activists off to the station and charging them for obstructing the pavement, causing a disturbance and damaging property.'

'Strike me pink if I don't like the sound of that,' said Sammy, at which point in came Rosie, Rachel and the property company's joint managing directors, Tim and Daniel.

'D'you lot know what's going on?' asked Tim.

'Yes, we know,' said Sammy, 'and it ain't exactly what I bargained for at breakfast this morning. Still, your dad's sorted it out.'

'Yes, he's sent for the police,' said Dorothy.

'The Camberwell bobbies?' said Daniel.

'None other,' said Sammy.

'My life, is that a fact?' said Rachel, and everyone except Boots discussed what everyone knew was highly unusual, calling in the police to help. It was a discussion that went on for long minutes, while outside Mad Marj and her supporters kept calling for the blood of the firm's capitalist directors. 'Capitalist' suggested the influence of Lulu.

Boots eventually pointed out that action by the police would save him and Sammy from having to engage in the fray.

'It'll save us,' he said, 'from having to go down and mop up the lady and her associates ourselves. Which Sammy doesn't fancy and which might end up with both of us wearing ruined suits.'

'That's a fact,' said Sammy, 'and you might all note I speak from personal experience.'

A voice called up from the ground floor.

'Mr Adams! Mr Sammy! The police have come! They're outside arresting all the rioters!'

'Oh, thank goodness,' said Queenie.

'Shall we all relax?' suggested Rosie, her devious mother put out of her mind.

'Well, I can promise you I feel a lot better now,' said Sammy.

'Enjoy the moment,' said Boots. 'I fancy it won't last long.'

'Eh?' said Sammy.

'She'll be back,' said Boots.

'Mad Marj?' said Rosie.

'Yes, the lady herself,' said Boots, 'and probably sometime early in the New Year.'

'Thanks a million,' said Sammy, 'that's made my Christmas, I don't think.'

'Cheer up, Sammy,' smiled Boots, 'next time we'll get Mitch and other old soldiers to defend the premises with defective eggs.' Mitch was ex-Corporal Mitchell, the firm's van driver and one of Boots's Great War comrades.

'I'll take a bet on those kind of eggs beating squishy tomatoes,' said Tim.

'It still won't make my Christmas feel better,' said Sammy, and then he and Boots went down to talk to the Camberwell bobbies, who now had the still-belligerent Marjorie Alsop in handcuffs, much to her disgust.

'Traitors!' she shouted as Sammy and Boots emerged.

'Happy Christmas, Marjorie,' said Boots, watching as she was hustled into a police van, along with her activists, and driven away. He and Sammy then discussed matters with a police sergeant, and everything began to quieten down. The one problem still littering the scene of the siege was the smashed front window. Tim attended to that by phoning the local glaziers and asking them to come round and board up the window prior to having it replaced.

Peace reigned at the offices for the rest of the day, although Sammy kept making dark, muttered comments about what awaited Adams

Enterprises in the New Year, and what he was going to say to Lulu and her upside-down Socialism the next time he saw her.

Scotland Yard called off the hunt for the planter or planters of the death-dealing incendiary bomb in the car of the man known as Rolf Seidler. Clues were simply non-existent, and the West Berlin police had been unable to help. No record existed of a Rolf Seidler.

Just after three thirty, Rosie was home from the office and the phone was ringing.

She answered it.

'Hello?'

'Oh, there you are, Rosie dear, it's your mother 'ere and I've been trying to get you for hours. Rosie, I've suffered an awful time just lately, all through that man Walter Wainwright. It was his idea about me goin' to France – he forced me into it, and now what d'you think's 'appened? We've had all that money stolen from our room in this hotel – it's in Bournemouth – Rosie? Rosie, you there?'

Rosie wasn't. She had hung up. Seconds later she removed the receiver, making a dead thing of the phone and cutting out of her life a woman for whom she had neither liking nor sympathy. Or even pity, for that matter.

She had better things on her mind. Among them was preparing for the big family occasion this evening, the party to celebrate the birthdays of James and Gemma. Everyone would be there, starting with the twins themselves, of course, with their parents Boots and Polly, their half-brother Tim and their half-sister, French-born Eloise. And she herself, long in her own mind the natural daughter of Boots, and the stepdaughter of Polly.

Yes, James and Gemma, Boots and Polly, Tim and Eloise, they were her true family, the people she cherished, and with them her own three. Matt, Giles and Emily.

She needed nothing else, no others.

She belonged, as she always had, to the family of Grandma Finch.

And she belonged especially to Boots, the man who would have defied the law itself to separate her from a devious woman once known as Milly Pearce.

THE END